PROMISE
OF
Passion

PROMISE
OF
Passion

A GREEK ADVENTURE

BARBARA BRADLEY

CROWN
BOOKS NYC

ISBN: 978-1-958869-00-0   (Paperback Edition).
ISBN: 978-1-958869-01-7   (Hardcover Edition)
ISBN: 978-1-956095-75-3   (E-book Edition)

Book Ordering Information

Crown Books NYC
132 West 31st Street, 9th Fl.
New York, NY, 10001 USA

info@crownbooksnyc.com
www.crownbooksnyc.com
1 (347) 537-690

Printed in the United States of America

Jonathon Ehler Photography. Tucson, Arizona

To Demetri and Kari
I will love you both FOREVER

Chapter 1

"**I** love New York!" exclaimed Kristen Davies to her younger sister, Kari Peterson. "I've been away far too long. It's funny how distance and time can separate you from the people and the places you love," she added with a sigh. Bittersweet memories flooded Kristen's brain. In less than a second the wonderful and agonizing times spent here in New York surfaced into her consciousness. She understood quickly that the reason she had not returned for so many years to the city she loved was that it had been too painful. She had heard that time heals all wounds and supposed it was true, because she was finally able to enjoy the city without the constant reminder of *him*, the love of her life.

The two women were exhausted but exhilarated. It was October, 2019 and the first time in years the two sisters had been able to plan a trip together. It was the fifth day of their 10-day sightseeing and theater vacation to the Big Apple. Kristen was actively humming the theme song from Hadestown, the musical they had just attended. She always knew when she loved a musical because she would sing it for weeks afterwards. Tonight was no different. They had decided to have a late after-theater supper at The Acropolis, a Greek restaurant Kristen remembered fondly. It was a Friday night and the place was crowded with the sounds of the patrons happily conversing while the sounds of Bouzouki music played in the background.

Sitting at a booth with her back to the entrance, Kristen had a bird's-eye view of the eatery. She examined the room, observing that it had not changed much over the years. The faded murals depicting a *taverna* on one wall and a ruined Acropolis on the other remained and for a brief moment took Kristen back to her first day in Athens.

Kristen and Kari sipped their wine while waiting for their dinners to be served. The bittersweet feeling swept over Kristen once again as she was reminded of the first time she had dined at the Acropolis. Thirty years had passed since then, when she had spent wonderful evenings eating strange and delicious food, drinking dry red wine, dancing and laughing with Demetri Papas. Those had been giddy days for an unworldly college student—the best of her life.

Kristen's memories were interrupted when Kari asked, "So what did you think of the play?"

"I loved it. What an incredible cast. I loved the rockin' trombone and the New Orleans style music. When I first saw the title I wasn't interested but then I learned that the play is based on the Greek gods Hades and Persephone and the young lovers Orpheus and Eurydice. Of course, anything Greek has always peaked my interest. Too bad it is a tragedy. I always like a happy ending."

Thoughts of Kristen's Greek Tragedy flooded her consciousness. "I know all about Greek tragedies…I have experienced by own," she thought to herself.

"So what should we do tomorrow?" she asked, changing the subject.

"I don't care. You're the tour guide. I'll go wherever you think we'd both like."

Their meals were served by a thin, young waiter dressed in a white shirt, black slacks, and white apron. *Very European,* thought Kristen as she thanked him and let the flavors of the eggplant, the meat, and the spices of the moussaka envelop her senses.

Impressions of the sights they had seen and plans for the next day occupied them while they ate. As they finished their meal, Kristen suddenly felt as if she was being watched. It was nothing tangible, just a sixth sense she had always possessed. She dismissed it, knowing that neither she nor Kari knew anyone in New York. After a few minutes she once again had the same unusual feeling and turned to survey the restaurant. At first she did not notice anything out of the ordinary. Then, in the far reaches of the room, she spotted a dark, well-dressed, handsome, sixty-something man staring at her. Recognition came slowly but inexorably. Kristen could not believe what she saw.

It *was* Demetri. Kristen was so shocked she could barely breathe. Here, walking toward her, was the man who had been the only true passion of her life—the one who had taught her how to love and how to make love. Memories of their wonderful times together swept into her consciousness in an instant—memories she had tried to forget forever. Demetri had also been the one who had torn her life apart and broken her heart so thoroughly that it had taken her years to recover. Memories of the pain, the desperation, and the loss flooded back to her and made her wince from an unexpected tightening in her chest. They had lost each other many years ago, and here they were together in their favorite restaurant.

As Demetri made his way through the restaurant, Kristen saw the stunned expression on his face and understood that he had recognized her.

Kristen noted that Demetri was as handsome as ever. He had always been inescapably attractive to her, and nothing had changed. He still walked with a confident gait; his hair was now a salt-and-pepper color instead of dark brown, but as full and thick as ever; he was slim but not gaunt as he had been in his youth; his face had deep creases from his years in the sun that made him look distinguished; and his eyes were as brown and as sensuous as ever.

She also observed his moods change from incredulity to great happiness to one of great sadness, and then back to happiness. Kristen's expression mirrored Demetri's. Once she realized it was truly him, her glow of happiness was tempered with an undercurrent of grief. Kari noticed her gamut of expressions and turned to see what had occurred. She recognized Demetri immediately, and her shock was only slightly less than Kristen's.

Kristen noticed the change in Kari's face and understood instantly how she must be feeling. Kari had shared those exhilarating days when Kristen and Demetri had first met, and he had become like a much beloved older brother to her. She had lost him too.

Kristen was unable to focus on anything except Demetri. As she looked deeply into his eyes, the years vanished. She was no longer the middle-aged, tired, responsible adult she had become. She was Kristen—young, very much in love, with all the adventures life had to offer ahead of her.

"I cannot believe it!" declared Demetri. "How can this be?" He held out his arms as Kristen slid from the booth to receive a tender embrace.

Demetri, in European fashion, kissed her first on one check and then another. "You haven't changed much. You still have the qualities I always admired."

The sensation of Demetri's lips on her skin sent pulses of electricity through Kristen—a sensation that was all too familiar but one she had not felt in decades. It excited and worried her at the same time. She told herself that everything was all right. Demetri and she would catch up for a few minutes and then go their separate ways, just as most old friends would do.

Kristen was speechless, but Kari found the words: "It's my turn!" Demetri smiled brightly at Kari and held her shoulders in both of his hands as he kissed her on each cheek.

"Hey," exclaimed Kari, "that's not fair. I want a hug too." After a long, warm embrace, Kari pulled away and said, "This is unbelievable. We had no idea you were in the States. Don't you live in Greece now?"

"Yes, I just flew in from Athens this afternoon. I am in town for a few days to resolve a business matter and see old friends."

Kristen could not imagine what kind of business he would still have in New York. He had been away for a very long time, and last she had heard he had cut all ties with his New York business acquaintances. A wave of deep concern swept over her. She remembered the fear she had felt because of those people. It could not be good that Demetri was meeting with them again. *What could they possibly want?* she asked herself with a frown, but she was quickly distracted from her thoughts when she saw Demetri carefully examining her.

"You look just like I remember. Your skin, your eyes, your lips are the same as ever." His obvious admiration made Kristen self-conscious.

Kristen finally found her voice, but it was merely a squeak. "You look wonderful, Demetri. The years have been kind to you," was all she could say. The shock was still too much for her to pull herself together.

Kari took the lead. "If you're alone, would you join us?"

"Even if I wasn't alone, which I am, I would still join you. Nothing could keep me from it."

Demetri helped Kristen back into the booth and slid in next to her. He took her hand in his and whispered, "I have missed you. Words cannot describe how good it is to meet like this. The gods must be watching over us."

"Okay, stranger, what have you been up to for, say, the last fifteen or so years?" asked Kari, who was no longer the shy, introverted girl she once was.

"I still live in Athens part of the year and go to my village near the sea the other. I spend most of each summer on my boat, fishing and swimming. My mother is over eighty years old now, so I help her whenever possible. I still work at a university in Athens, where I am now an administrator most of the time. But I insist on teaching every semester; I still love to teach as much as ever."

"Are you married?" asked Kari bluntly.

"I was, but I am not now," he replied.

Kari gave Kristen a sideways smile and said, "Hmmmm."

Kristen was still in shock and could not respond.

"So what about you, Little One? Does that sound strange at our advanced ages?"

"No, not at all; I always liked it when you called me that, and I still do," said Kari. "To answer your first question, my daughters are now grown. One has graduated, and one is in college. I am married and am too busy with my job, as usual."

"And you?" his question was now directed at Kristen, as was his total attention. His eyes searched hers deeply.

"I can't even begin to explain" was all she managed to say.

"Then let me," Kari piped up. "She works too hard at her medical practice, has a husband named Richard who has been ill for a long time, and needs someone like you to cheer her up."

Kristen gave Kari a sharp look, but Demetri appreciated the candor.

"Is that true, Kristen?" he asked quietly.

"Yes," she managed to say. "It is complicated."

"But are you happy?" Demetri had a way of getting right to the core of things.

"Honestly?" Kristen asked, searching Demetri's expression carefully.

"Of course, you must tell me honestly! When have we ever been anything but totally honest with each other?" he exclaimed.

"There have been happier times in my life, I must admit," said Kristen quietly. Her answer clearly surprised Demetri. He turned to her, saw the sadness in her eyes, embraced her tightly, and did not let go. The communication of that embrace made Kristen uncomfortable; it felt too good, too needed, and very dangerous.

"Can we spend some time together?" whispered Demetri into her ear.

Kristen looked over at Kari for help and assurance. Kari had always been able to see things more rationally than Kristen when it came to Demetri. Kari nodded her head gently as a sign that Kristen should accept. Although Kristen knew the dangers of being with Demetri again, she told herself that she would be able to be sensible about him and that he posed no threat to her relatively stable life. She longed to know more about him. Although he had broken her heart, she had never stopped loving him or wondering whether he was happy and healthy and what had become of his life. Now he was there, next to her, and she knew he was alive and well, but nothing more. "Yes, of course. I would like nothing better," she said after a slight hesitation. "What is your schedule?"

"I have appointments tomorrow morning but am free in the afternoon," he said. "I fly back to Athens in two days. What are your plans?"

"I have nothing else planned tonight. Tomorrow, Kari and I were going to go to the Metropolitan Museum of Art and then play things by ear."

"Good. We have some time to catch up," was all he needed to say. Kristen was aware of his nearness and felt conflicted. There was a time when she had wanted nothing more than to have Demetri next to her. Now, although the chemistry between them had not changed, Kristen's life had. She felt it was wrong for her to feel such a strong attraction. She was married, after all.

Demetri ordered a bottle of ouzo, which they all shared, along with light conversation. They talked of inconsequential things, as old friends do. Kari instinctively knew that Demetri and Kristen needed to be alone, so she made her excuses and let Kristen know everything was okay. "I've got a key. I won't wait up," she said as she kissed Demetri on one cheek. "I hope to see you tomorrow. I have missed you too!"

"*Kalinihta,* Little One. Thank you," he said sincerely.

After Kari disappeared out the restaurant entrance, Demetri turned to Kristen and kissed her lightly. The kiss said, "I am sorry, I have missed you, I worry about you, and I love you," all at once.

Kristen remembered his kisses. They were the best she had ever experienced and could never seem to get enough of them. She longed for more now but pulled away. She did not need to explain the reasons to Demetri. He understood.

"We have a lot of catching up to do. I still can't believe you are here!" she said quietly.

"We are both here, thanks to the gods," he looked up at the sky and pointed.

Kristen was able to examine Demetri closely now. He had aged well and appeared to have mellowed. She did not see the restlessness that had plagued him in his youth, but she still saw the same mischievous expression in his eyes that she had loved so much. She knew that it was dangerous to be alone with him tonight. They had never been able to resist each other, and she knew tonight would be no different.

"*Pame*, let's go. We can walk or have coffee, and you can tell me everything," said Demetri as he pulled her up out of the booth. Kristen noticed that his English was as good as it had ever been, but she loved it when he spoke Greek to her.

They left the restaurant after paying the bill and headed in the direction of Times Square. "Where do you want to go?" Demetri asked.

"I don't care. We can just walk, if you'd like."

They walked in silence for a few minutes, both caught up in their thoughts. The street was unusually quiet, and they found themselves alone. They stopped walking and turned to each other. The lights from a marquee lit their faces. Kristen tilted her head up and looked through his eyes into his heart. Demetri recognized the gaze. No other woman had ever looked at him with such open, unconditional love. It surprised him that things had not changed after the passing of so much time. Kristen became aware of the look that gave her emotions away, but she could not stop herself. She could not change the fact that her face reflected her feelings.

"What brought you here, tonight of all nights?" asked Demetri.

"I guess fate brought me here," replied Kristen, "and a desire to drown myself in as much theater as possible. You see, I still love the theater."

His laugh told her he remembered how she had loved it when he took her to a live performance. It was déjà vu. Here he was, walking with her in the theater district late at night, as if no time had passed at all.

His voice was as she remembered, deep and gravelly, with a soft "t" that was the combination of a "d" and "th." Although his English was excellent, she had always thought that his strongly accented speech was very romantic and sexy. It had changed only in that his accent had become more pronounced. *After all, he's been in Greece for nearly fifteen years. His accent would naturally be thicker,* Kristen thought.

"So, now that we have found each other, what do we do about it?" asked Demetri, as bluntly as always. He had never been one to beat around the bush.

"We spend as much time as possible catching up," she said, with the hope that it would be possible.

"That sounds good to me. We have much to discuss," agreed Demetri. "Look, I believe we need more than just a day. What do you think if I call the airline and change my ticket? We could spend some time together—go out to Long Island and see the old neighborhood," he said spontaneously.

"I'd like that very much," she replied. She had been secretly hoping he was going to suggest something like that. "We need to be careful, Demetri," she added thoughtfully. "I am married. I need you to know that."

"I won't forget it. Nothing will happen unless you agree to it. That goes for words as well as actions."

"I seem to remember you saying something like that in Athens before we set off on our trip to Italy. Look at the trouble we got into there!" Kristen said with a big smile and a sudden knowing expression in her eyes.

"How could I ever forget? Trouble, yes, but such sweet trouble," he replied, with his own knowing expression.

They walked until they found a coffee shop that was still open, and they talked while sipping the drinks they had ordered. "Do you remember the first time we drank coffee together? It was in Athens while we were waiting for the bus to go to Patras."

"Of course! You and Kari had never had Greek coffee," he reminisced. With a sly look, he added, "There were a lot of Greek things you had never experienced."

"Oh, you're terrible!" Kristen laughed. "But correct."

Their time together flew by. Before long it was two in the morning. Although neither wanted to end the evening, it was getting very late.

"Let me escort you to your hotel. Where are you staying?" He hailed a taxi, and held the door open for her to slip into the seat.

"The Waldorf," she replied.

"Fancy. You must be doing well for yourself. I am staying less than two blocks from there. What a coincidence!"

Kristen did not reply. Was it merely a random accident or was it the intentional act of something supernatural? Occasionally, over the years, she had felt "strings" pulling her toward Demetri. Despite their separation, the memories and feelings had never completely left her. Was it the act of something or someone beyond their understanding or something more secular? She had never paid much attention to it until now. This was just too perfect to be a mere chance meeting.

"I'll get out here and then walk to my hotel," Demetri said as the taxi pulled into the underground entrance of the Waldorf.

"Kari is in the room, but I would like it if you would walk me up," said Kristen.

"Of course," he replied.

They walked through the expansive and elegant lobby, now nearly deserted, to the elevators that took them to the twenty-fifth floor. They found the floor plan of the hotel confusing and would have become lost in the maze of hallways had it not been for the signs pointing them in the correct direction. "I have never been able to figure out this hotel, even though I've stayed here many times," she explained as they searched for her room.

Although they walked without holding hands, Kristen was very conscious of Demetri's nearness. Occasionally their arms touched, sending electric sensations through her.

When they arrived at the door, she removed the electronic key from her purse, inserted it into the lock, and then turned to Demetri.

"It was truly wonderful seeing you again," she said sincerely, waiting for him to mention plans for the upcoming day.

"Yes, *poli kala*, it was very good. I will call early in the morning, and we can decide what to do. Does that sound good to you?" he asked.

"It sounds perfect."

"So good night, then," Demetri said softly. He bent forward to give Kristen a gentle kiss. Kristen hesitated a moment and then allowed Demetri's lips to linger on hers for a brief moment.

"Yes, until later," she whispered, and she opened the door quietly. She slipped into bed without waking Kari and fell into an exhausted but restless sleep.

Chapter 2

*D*emetri's brief walk back to his hotel gave him time to begin to absorb the events of the evening. Seeing Kristen again had brought back emotions he had not realized he could still experience: excitement, joy, lust, and deep longing. And shock. Shock that she would have been in New York the day he arrived from Greece. Kristen had lived in Arizona for as long as he could remember and had never, to his knowledge, traveled back to New York.

He had seen an older, but just as beautiful, version of the woman who had changed his life those many years ago. She had been the first woman he had truly and thoroughly loved—possibly the only woman he had loved in that manner. Kristen had been the one for him; he had known it from the first day they had met. His love for her had been so deep that he had been willing to give up everything in his life to be with her. The happy times made him smile, but, like Kristen, Demetri also remembered the betrayal, the breakup, the loss, the devastation, which contorted his face into a deep, furrowed frown. He had never stopped loving her, even though she had made it impossible for them to be together.

He also felt sorrow. Sorrow for all the years he had lived without her and for the children they had never had together. His life, which was full of routine and obligation, had once again been transformed by her, as it had thirty years prior. Perhaps the feelings were exaggerated by being in the United States, a place that was not steeped in traditions and expectations. Or, more likely, it was running into Kristen and seeing her again. He had acted spontaneously for the first time in months. She touched his soul as she always had. Her zest for life shone through her obvious troubles. The wear and tear of life did not seem to have affected her as it had him. "She is as enthusiastic and naturally loving as she ever was. Phenomenal!" he whispered to himself.

He thought of what the next two days might bring. He was painfully aware that her marriage would make anything beyond being just friends impossible. "That is all right," he said to himself. "It will be good to just be in her presence. What happens will happen. Besides, what could happen? She lives in Arizona, I live in Greece. What kind of a relationship is that?"

He knew he needed at least a little sleep before the big day ahead of him, so he forced himself to turn off his overactive brain and sleep. His slumber was interrupted by dreams of his former life in the United States. He awoke to the alarm clock at eight AM, groggy from jet lag and lack of sleep. "I have to be sharp today," he said to himself, and ordered a pot of strong, black coffee to be sent to his room.

Thoughts of Kristen needed to be put aside. "But first I will call her to arrange for this afternoon," he said to himself, dialing the phone. His first call was answered by Kari, who explained that Kristen was still asleep. The second call was successful, and they made plans.

"Now I need to concentrate on the task at hand," he thought. "If I don't, there may be consequences, and I need to finally rid myself of my New York business partners. Things have gone on too long, and I want it to end now and forever," he said as he put on the dark suit he had brought with him specifically for today's meeting. "Then, after I conclude the meeting, I can think about other things. It is vital to stick to my strategy and take charge of the encounter."

The meeting was not something he looked forward to. In fact, he dreaded it. One of the reasons he had left the United States was to get away from the pressure put on him by people he would rather forget. "Why, after more than three decades have they come back to haunt me and disrupt my life? What can they want from me?" Demetri knew it could not be good.

Demetri was determined to say no to whatever it was that they wanted. He had paid his debt and owed nothing to these people. They had tried to possess him before and were unsuccessful. This time would be no different. He had built a life for himself that included unwavering ethics that he refused to compromise.

Most important, he had always kept his loved ones protected from any knowledge of his former life. The only person who had ever been aware of his involvements was Kristen. Telling her the details of his secret life had not only put her in danger, it had caused their breakup. It was something that had devastated both of them and changed their lives forever. He was not going to let that happen again.

He did realize, however, that his business acquaintances' views would not be similar to his own. They would remind him that, once he became a member of the group, he would always be one of them. There was no getting out, no matter how much time passed.

With unfailing determination, Demetri hailed a cab and bravely faced the events ahead of him. "How did I ever get myself into so much trouble?" he asked himself as he rode the short distance to his meeting. The answer to his rhetorical question came to him in a flash.

His mind went back to his early years. He saw himself as a boy growing up in post–World War II Greece. His parents were hardworking but poor and uneducated. He had only one pair of shoes for church on Sundays, lived in a house without electricity or running water, and often went to bed hungry because there was no food.

He lived no differently than any of his friends in the village. Toys were scarce, so the boys often played with the guns left behind by the German army. Some of his friends had been maimed or killed when hand grenades were mistaken for toys. He had been lucky to escape serious injury.

As he grew, he was greatly influenced by the occasional American movie he saw. For the first time he realized there was a better life outside his village—a life where hunger and poverty were nonexistent. Americans drove nice cars, lived in good houses, and wore fine-looking clothes.

At the age of twelve he decided that somehow he would have all those things. The answer for him was to get a good education. That was very difficult for a poor Greek boy without political connections. He decided that the only way to achieve his goals would be to go to America and earn a college degree. From that day on, he never strayed from the path that would ultimately reward him with his dream.

At eighteen, he set out for America. With the help of some cousins who were indebted to his parents for saving them from the Gestapo during the war, Demetri began his American life on Long Island, performing odd jobs for his cousins and driving their limousine. For the first time in his life he experienced the "good life"—riding in Cadillacs and other expensive cars, dining in fine restaurants, wearing tailored suits, and having plenty of pocket money and beautiful women. He was very naive and did not realize that there would be a price to pay for the luxuries he enjoyed.

With hard work and determination, he attended college while continuing to work for his cousins. As time progressed, he was included in more and more of the daily activities of the organization. Eventually he was asked to perform tasks that his strict moral code would not allow. He knew then that he had made a huge mistake and needed to separate himself somehow from the organization. It took him years and proved to be very dangerous. His cousins tried to make him stay by threatening bodily harm, but Demetri did not care what they did to him. It was when they crossed the line and threatened his loved ones, including Kristen, that he had been more determined than ever to free himself. He was eventually able to convince his cousins to leave him alone when he showed them that he would never compromise.

That had been a very long time ago. "Why, after all of these years, are they pressuring me now?" Demetri quietly asked himself. It made no sense. The only way to know would be to meet with them and find out firsthand what they had in mind, which was exactly what he was about to do.

Chapter 3

*K*risten awoke to Kari's vigorous shaking. "Wake up! It's nearly nine. It's the morning after the night before. I've been up since seven, and you've been dead to the world. I've waited long enough to hear what happened last night! So 'fess up."

Kristen opened her eyes and saw that Kari was holding out a white china mug of coffee, and her temporary annoyance vanished. She gratefully accepted the offering and relished her first sip of the morning caffeine she craved. She joined Kari at the small table that overlooked the street and observed the bustling traffic below. She looked up and saw that a little bit of sky was visible and that it was clear and bright and promised a beautiful autumn afternoon.

"Should I order some breakfast?" Kristen asked.

"No, I already ordered it. The food should be here any minute. I ordered fresh fruit and omelets with cranberry muffins."

"I don't care what we eat," Kristen interrupted. "I need a moment to think." Kristen wasn't ready to explain any details of the previous night's events. After a few minutes she answered simply, "It was nice. We walked and had coffee and then came back to the hotel."

"Oh, come on, you need to give me more than that!" exclaimed Kari. "Remember, I'm your sister, not your conscience."

"Okay, I admit I was knocked off my feet last night. But this morning they are planted firmly on the ground."

"Yeah, right!" said Kari with a mildly sarcastic expression. "When have you ever been rational where Demetri is concerned?"

"You know me too well. There's no hiding anything from you, is there?" remarked Kristen as she got up from the table and began pacing the floor. "Let's check to see whether the phone is working. I haven't heard the phone ring, and Demetri said he would call early this morning. It's already after nine."

"Oh, yes, he called, but you were still asleep," said Kari innocently.

Kristen's face turned scarlet with anger. "I can't believe you did not wake me up, you idiot."

"At your age, dear sister, you need all the beauty sleep you can get!" exclaimed Kari with a smirk on her face. She enjoyed teasing her sister.

"Thanks a lot," replied Kristen, her temper barely in check.

"Hey, cool it, sis. Demetri told me specifically not to wake you, and I was only following instructions," said Kari somewhat defensively. "He said he will call again before he leaves for his appointment."

The phone rang. Kari jumped up to answer it, and Kristen gestured to Kari, making it clear that she should go sit down. Kristen then answered after the third ring.

"*Kalimera*," she answered in a brightly musical voice.

"*Kali* what? Is that you, Kristen?"

Kristen was startled. It was Richard's voice, not Demetri's, on the other end of the line.

"Yes, it's me," she replied.

"What did you say? I didn't know you knew another language?"

Kristen was completely caught off guard. Not wanting to lie but not knowing exactly what to say, she stumbled through, "Oh, we went to a Greek restaurant last night and I am trying out some of the words I learned." It sounded a little lame to her, and she held her breath hoping it made sense.

"Oh," was all Richard said. "I'm glad I caught you. I just wanted to say hello and see how you two are doing."

With a great sigh of relief, Kristen was able to switch gears. "How are you?" she asked a little breathlessly.

"About the same, but I don't want to talk about me. I want to hear how you're doing."

"Kari and I are having a great time. We saw Hadestown last night, which I loved. We're going to the Metropolitan Museum of Art today," she said honestly, but felt a small twinge of guilt at telling Richard only a half truth. "And out to dinner tonight."

"Good. You deserve a break. You've worked too hard at your practice and taking care of me. You should have some fun. Well, I'll let you go, because I know you want to begin your day. Say hi to Kari for me. Love you. Bye."

"Same here," Kristen replied. "Call if you need anything," as she hung up the phone.

She had just replaced the receiver when the phone rang again. "Hello?" she said, not quite as brightly as the first time. It was Demetri.

"*Kalimera*. How did you sleep?" were the first words Kristen heard. His voice was cheerful, very sexy, and as natural-sounding as if they had talked every day for the previous twenty years.

"Like a log once I got to sleep, thank you," Kristen replied. "And you?"

"Not so well. You gave me quite a shock last night," he said.

"You did me too!" Kristen responded. "I still can't believe we ran into each other that way."

"It must be fate. So, for our plans," said Demetri, getting directly to the point. "I should finish my business with plenty of time to pick you up at the hotel at two o'clock. I thought we could walk around Central Park and talk. Then I would like to take both you and Kari out for dinner. Is that all right with you?"

"Yes, fine. I know Kari would like to spend some time with you too."

"*Kala*. I will see you this afternoon," he said.

"Until then," replied Kristen as she ended the call.

Kari had been listening intently. "That was short."

"Long enough to turn my world upside down," said Kristen quietly to herself. She turned to Kari and shared the proposed itinerary with her.

"Sounds like a good plan to me. When you go out with Demetri, I'll head over to the Guggenheim. I know how bored you'd be there, and I've been dying to see it. Then we'll get all gussied up to go out on the town with the most handsome man in Manhattan. How could two girls be so lucky?" she said with a smile.

"Yes, so lucky," Kristen mumbled. She had not felt very lucky for quite a while. She hadn't always felt that way. After getting over Demetri she had attended and graduated from medical school and had established her own general medical practice after her residency. She had been a physician for over twenty years. Richard had come into her life relatively late. Although she had dated a number of interesting and successful men, she had never found the same passion for life she had known with Demetri. For years she thought she had been relatively happy with her work and her large extended family surrounding her, but there had always been something missing.

When Richard came into her life, she admired him for his quick smile and humor, his stability, his intellect, and the fact that he loved her thoroughly. She had never felt the passion for him that she had experienced with Demetri, but she figured that was partly a result of age. Kristen loved Richard, although she had never been in love with him. She figured that was as good as anyone could expect. There had been good years together. They could not have children, but she did not fret about it much. Their lives were busy and generally content. Then Richard had fallen ill. Kristen had noticed a nodule on his neck. She knew it was cancer before the biopsy reports were returned. The diagnosis was non-Hodgkin's lymphoma. Although he had been given the most up-to-date treatments, he had not been cured. There had been some short remissions, but every time they thought that he had beaten the odds, the cancer always returned.

Richard's illness had changed everything. Kristen's devotion to her husband had never failed. He depended on her, and she would never have deserted him in his time of need. He deserved better. She had lived for three years in a state of physical and emotional exhaustion. Her days were spent working in her practice; her nights and weekends caring for Richard's physical and mental well-being. Although she had never complained, the stress had taken its toll both on her health and their relationship.

The trip to New York was planned when Richard's cancer was in remission, when he was feeling strong and healthy. It was Kristen's turn for a little respite. Richard had encouraged her to take the trip with Kari to get away for a few days and enjoy some escape in the Big Apple. She was doing just that when her life had been turned upside down the previous evening. Was it a cruel or beneficent coincidence that Demetri had come back into her life at this time? She thought of the relationship that she had had with Demetri. It had always been like a roller coaster ride; the highs were very high, and the lows were unbearable. After they had separated, it had taken a long time for her to recover from the trauma. "But have I ever really recovered?" she had asked herself over the years. She swore that she would never go through something like that again. She would play it safe, and that is exactly what she did. Richard was safe and reliable. Unfortunately, safety had not made Kristen deeply happy. She needed adventure, variety, challenges, excitement, and even romance in her life. Demetri had provided all that.

The thoughts began to overwhelm her. *Stop it!* she screamed silently to herself. *This reunion doesn't need to be anything more than it is: two old lovers becoming reacquainted. Perhaps a friendship will develop. Right, Kristen, and pigs fly too!* she told herself, chuckling. It helped to break her train of thought and allowed her to concentrate on what she had to do in the next few minutes to get ready for the day to come.

Kari brought her back to the present when she said, "How's that for timing? The two most important men in your life calling you at the same time."

"Don't remind me," Kristen retorted.

"So why didn't you tell Richard about running into Demetri, or shouldn't I ask?" nudged Kari.

"Oh, I don't know. There was no point, really. And besides, I've never told Richard anything about Demetri. Why would I say something now?"

There was a knock at the door. "Good, breakfast is here. Let's eat and get going."

Kristen and Kari had a good time together at the Metropolitan Museum of Art. Kari had always been an art enthusiast and spent most of her time at the European exhibit. She had majored in art history in college and had been especially fascinated with Vincent van Gogh's life and work. Today she studied his self-portrait intently. Kari, like van Gogh, suffered from Ménière's disease, a condition that causes deafness and constant ringing in the affected ear. She understood the madness that it could produce and empathized with his plight. She was able to see and understand the pain in his eyes, and attempted to communicate her thoughts to Kristen.

Although Kristen tried to concentrate on the magnificent art, her mind was elsewhere. She went through the motions of examining the paintings Kari described so thoroughly but did not really care about them. She had Demetri on her mind. *What will the day bring?* she asked herself.

With the reawakening of past memories, it was only natural that they would find the Greek and Roman Art gallery. As they examined the marble statues of gods and people long gone, Kristen's mind wandered to the times she had spent at the museums in Athens and the ruins on Delos. She was transported back to Greece, back to the country that was so foreign to her but that had always felt like home. Kari saw the glazed look in Kristen's eyes, understood, and allowed Kristen some uninterrupted time.

The morning seemed to pass slowly for Kristen, although her mind was racing. Each vase, each ancient piece of jewelry, and each statue elicited more memories. It became overwhelming. "Can we go back to the hotel?" she finally asked Kari. "I just can't focus on anything but you know who."

They arrived back at the hotel with plenty of time to prepare for Demetri's arrival. As Kristen examined her meager wardrobe and picked out khaki pants and a striped shirt, Kari blurted out, "You're not going to wear that, are you?"

"This is all I have. There's no time to shop."

"If I had known that, we could have spent the day at Saks. You looking your best is more important than some 150-year-old paintings."

"It's too late now. What do you suggest I do?" Kristen asked.

"I've got the perfect solution," said Kari, after thinking for a moment. "Trust me on this one."

A few minutes later Kristen appeared in the ensemble Kari had lent to her. "How do I look?" she asked.

"It's not fair. You look better in my clothes than I do," Kari said admiringly. Kristen was dressed in a dark-brown pair of dress slacks that fit her perfectly. The matching, form-fitting, long-sleeved jacket accentuated her curves, and the light-blue silk blouse complemented the color of her eyes.

"Yabba dabba," Kari whistled. "The blouse is a little snug, but that's nothing unusual, because you were always more well-endowed than I, and the jacket covers it nicely. Besides, most men enjoy a little cleavage." Kari had always envied Kristen's ample bust line. "Now, for the jewelry and makeup," added Kari. By the time they were finished, Kristen looked stunning and felt fantastic.

"Thank you, Kari. You've worked wonders," said Kristen.

"You're welcome. Now, go out and have a good time. Just be careful. I don't want to see anyone get hurt," Kari said.

Chapter 4

*D*emetri's meeting had not gone well. After the obligatory salutations with his cousin, who was now in his eighties, and his younger partners, they got down to business.

"We understand that you have been away from us for a long time," began his cousin Vassilis, who was sitting behind an expansive mahogany desk, "that you have kept your silence about us, and we appreciate that you have made a life for yourself independent of us."

Demetri had beaten the odds and had successfully broken away from the organization. He had accomplished that by making a solemn oath never to disclose information that could be detrimental to the group. He had kept that promise and had learned early that a promise was never to be broken, without exception.

"I will remind you that even though we allowed you to live your life without interference, you continue to owe us your allegiance and that the bond has not been completely severed," Vassilis lectured as the other six men in the room stood silently, like soldiers protecting their general. "Something needs doing that only you, with your connections in Greece, can accomplish."

Demetri sat directly across from Vassilis and saw the unrelenting power of the man who was speaking to him. Upon hearing his words, the heat of anger began to rise from Demetri's neck into his face, but his expression did not change. Showing anger was similar to showing weakness; it just wasn't done.

"What is it that you want me to do?" he asked calmly.

"Before I tell you of our request, I want to assure you that if you successfully complete this task, we will never ask anything more of you;

your obligation to us will be paid in full forever. You have my word on this," Vassilis continued.

"And if I cannot do what you ask of me?" asked Demetri, trying to keep his fury from showing. He made an effort to control his pounding heart and his clenched fists.

"We do not want to threaten you, you know that. After all, we are family," added Vassilis quietly. His eyes were like steel—hard and cold.

"You have not answered my question," Demetri mirrored in his speech what he saw in Vassilis's eyes.

"We know that threatening you personally with violence will not assure compliance, and I hope that we will not have to use other means of getting your cooperation," Vassilis stated.

The message was vague but perfectly clear to Demetri. Demetri could no longer contain his rage and stood up in a threatening manner, which he instantly realized was a mistake. The men standing guard reacted, reaching for the guns they always carried. With a simple hand gesture, Vassilis signaled them to stand at ease, while Demetri returned to his seat and grasped the arms of the chair to control his anger.

"You see, you have no choice. We have no choice. If we did not need you, we would never have contacted you," continued Vassilis in a low but deadly voice.

"You have a boat in Greece that you use on a regular basis. You go out on week-long voyages every summer and nobody would suspect you of any wrongdoing. The task should not be difficult for someone like you. We need you to take a priceless icon from Greece and deliver it to Korcula, an island off the west coast of Croatia. As you are totally aware, icons have a deep religious significance to the Greek people. This one is particularly important for religious as well as other personal reasons, which we will not describe. That is all you need to do. It would take you less than three days and you would never hear from us again. We would also pay you one hundred thousand dollars."

Demetri sat silently weighing his options. They were asking him to do something illegal, but something that should not involve violence. He would be risking imprisonment and the ruination of his respectable life, but no physical harm should come to anyone. Finally being completely free from his former life was very appealing. He knew they would keep their word.

"May I have some time to think about it?" asked Demetri after a moment of silence.

"There should be nothing to think about; compliance is mandatory. However, I will give you forty-eight hours to agree to our request," Vassilis stated. The meeting was concluded. Demetri was escorted out and offered a ride back to his hotel in the company limousine.

"No thank you. I'll take a taxi," was all Demetri said as the men disappeared back into the building.

Demetri's mood did not improve on the cab ride back to his hotel. It seemed outrageous that he would be threatened so blatantly for something as seemingly trivial as an icon. There were thousands of old icons throughout Greece. What could be so special about this particular one? He would have to decide what to do, but first he wanted to forget about all of it and be with Kristen. She had always been able to lighten his mood, even when it was depressed for good reason.

He had just enough time to stop by Tiffany's on his way to the Waldorf. By the time he arrived at Kristen's room, he was able to disguise his anger and put on a pleasant face. He took a deep breath and knocked on the door.

Chapter 5

*K*ari could not restrain herself from running to the door, flinging it open, and throwing herself into Demitri's arms. They both laughed at her enthusiastic welcome. After a few moments and a heartfelt Euro kiss they happily moved into the room where Kristen was waiting.

"Kari, you are as pretty as ever! You look very well. That is good!"

"You were always full of it, Demetri," she said sweetly.

He did not understand. "Full of what?" he asked.

Kari hesitated. "Charm," she said at the last moment with a smirk.

"And you Kristen, *kalispera*," he greeted her with a Euro kiss and a hug. The mini-makeover that Kari had performed on Kristen paid off. The effect was perfect. Demetri's breath was taken away when he saw her.

"You look *poli orea*, so beautiful!" His face reflected his thoughts. He had not been wrong to love this woman so dearly his whole life. He wanted to take her face in his hands and kiss her tenderly, but he knew it would not be appropriate. A wave of emotion surfaced in him. He looked into her eyes and saw they were misted. His were too. They had never been able to hide their feelings from each other as long as their eyes connected; they said everything. "How was your morning?" he asked.

"It was good. Kari just about walked my feet off in the museum. She was wonderful to have as a guide, because she knows so much about many of the paintings. And," after a hesitation, "how was your meeting?"

"It was very, how do you say, brutal," he said with a frown. "It's just business. It doesn't involve or concern you, so let's forget about it and enjoy the day." But Kristen couldn't forget it. She felt a wave of nausea sweep over her as she remembered what Demetri's cousins were capable of doing.

Demetri had always kept Kristen from knowing anything about the specifics of his New York "friends." She looked deeply into Demetri's eyes, could see past his outward levity, and observed great concern and anger. She had learned the hard way that she should refrain from asking questions, so she stayed silent. He would not share any information with her and she did not really want to know know the details anyway.

Changing the subject, Demetri said, "I have something here for you, Kari," as he presented her with a small, wrapped box.

She opened the package carefully, savoring the moment. She had not expected a gift and was touched to think that he had thought of her. It was a gold locket on a delicate chain with a tiny picture of the three of them together in Athens.

"Where did the picture come from? Surely you haven't kept it in your wallet for all these years!" Kari asked in awe. Demetri nodded his head slightly, indicating that he had.

Kari was excited by the gift and quickly asked Demetri to fasten the chain around her neck. Kristen was deeply touched too, knowing that Demetri had made the effort to include Kari in such a special way. The picture was a symbol of cherished memories never forgotten.

Demetri slowly opened his arms wide, and instantly all three were happily engaged in a group embrace. It was wonderful to have his "two best girls" together with him again. Nothing had changed, not really.

After an appropriate amount of time, Kari said, "You'd better get going. I've got plans, and they can't wait for you two." She did not have any plans, except to go to the Guggenheim Museum, but she wanted Demetri to feel comfortable stealing Kristen away from her.

Kristen gave her a secret smile, thanking her for once again making a possibly awkward moment comfortable. Kari noticed and smiled back, silently mouthing, "Remember to be careful," so Demetri did not see.

"We'll have time to talk tonight, Little One," said Demetri to Kari. "Until then, have a good afternoon. Kristen, are you ready?"

Kristen nodded, and they left.

They spent the afternoon in Central Park walking and talking. It was a very pleasant, sunny day that was warm for that time of year.

The leaves were past their most brilliant foliage, but some still clung to the limbs of the trees. It was a beautiful sight that neither Kristen nor Demetri was able to enjoy very often, as their home environments were primarily desert and without seasonal changes.

"So how are you?" began Demetri, searching her eyes.

"I'm surviving," answered Kristen.

"That is it? Surviving? That is not good enough," he exclaimed.

"It's as good as it can be right now."

"Let's go get something to drink, sit and talk," Demetri suggested. "It is very overdue for us."

Kristen agreed, although her heart was pounding from the anxiety she felt. How could she explain her present life to Demetri and then discuss the feelings she had, and had always had, for him? It could not be done in a limited amount of time. She had always felt somewhat intimidated about telling him what she truly felt. *That's crazy,* she thought to herself. *I'm a successful, respected professional. This man should not make me feel like an insecure coed again. Just be honest with him. What do you have to lose?*

They found an outdoor café, ordered drinks, and settled in for a long chat. When Kristen tried to speak, she found herself choked up with emotion. Demetri came to her rescue by asking, "Where do we begin?"

"Nowhere, everywhere," she replied vaguely and then quickly added, "So tell me about your life, Demetri. I noticed you quit smoking. Good for you!"

"I smoked because I liked to, not because I was addicted. A few years ago I decided it was time to stop, so one day I threw the cigarettes away and have not smoked since." Kristen was impressed but not surprised by Demetri's willpower; it was a part of his character.

"I got off track. Please continue," said Kristen.

"In 1990 I was briefly married, partially to get over you, but we quickly realized it was a huge mistake and amicably divorced. Then in 2000 I moved back to Greece. My parents were getting very old. I was their only child. They had sacrificed much over the years to make sure I went to America and received the education I had craved. It was my time to give back to them."

Kristen wondered how many American sons would do that for their parents.

"At the same time I had become restless in New York. I had been at my university for many years and was going home to an empty apartment every night. I felt that my life needed a change. The timing was right for me to return to Greece. I now live in Athens during the week and most weekends go back to the village where I was born, where I spend as much time as possible on my boat."

Mentioning his boat caused Demetri's mind to wander temporarily to his morning meeting. Kristen noticed the change in him but instinctively knew not to comment. Demetri had a way of solving his own problems without outside intervention. He quickly returned to his original thought.

"After I arrived in Greece, a job at the university became available. First I taught; then I was promoted to my current position. Even though I spend most of my day in administration, I still love to teach. I should be at work now, but this trip was obligatory. I had personal time off saved up and was able to have a colleague cover my classes, so I extended the stay for a few days."

Kristen listened quietly. She was trying to picture what Demetri's life in Greece was like. She envied his students, not only for the opportunity to learn from someone with such knowledge and passion for teaching, but for the time they spent with him—a luxury she had never had. It seemed crazy for her to be jealous of his students, but she was. They had been able to see and be with him nearly every day. She had not; it was that simple. She had longed to know him as a friend as well as a lover but had never had the opportunity.

"I was seriously involved with a woman a number of years ago and thought about marrying her but decided against it. She was from my village. We knew each other when we were small. We met again after I moved back to Greece. We got along well. Although I had strong feelings for her, the cultural differences were too much. You see, I spent most of my life in America and have strong American ties, and she was very traditionally Greek. I did not see it working over the long term, so we went our separate ways. We are friends now, nothing more. She married someone else from the area, has two children, and is content."

"Has it been lonely for you?" asked Kristen.

"Sometimes, but as you know, Greeks are seldom alone. There has been a lot of pressure for me to remarry. It is unnatural for a Greek man of my age to be single. But it has never been right, and, as you know, I will not compromise on certain things," he added. "I have decided to be just friends with the women I meet."

Kristen was reminded of her marriage. She and Richard had become "just friends" before he fell ill. She wondered whether all relationships were doomed to end up like that. Who said, "Familiarity breeds contempt"? Would she and Demetri have ended up as just friends if they had been together all these years? Her thoughts were interrupted by Demetri's question.

"And what about you?" he asked. "I know that you are a doctor in Arizona and are married to Richard. What else?"

"Where do I begin?"

"Begin by telling me what makes you happy," Demetri said quietly, looking deeply into Kristen's eyes and soul.

"I thought I had it all figured out. After finishing my medical education, I built my practice and eventually married Richard, who is a very good man. I thought that was what I wanted in life, since what I really wanted was unavailable to me." She looked at Demetri. He noticed that special look she had always given him and understood exactly what she meant without her having to explain further.

"I am so sorry," said Demetri.

"So am I," she said. Tears came to her eyes. Demetri noticed but said nothing. He did not want to add to her distress.

She continued, "I thought I could handle this but I guess I can't. How is it that thirty years can pass, and the pain can be just as real now as it was then? That is how it feels—like salt is being poured into an open wound. How can that be?"

Both were surprised at her emotional outburst. Kristen was attempting to control her tears without success.

"So what do we do?" asked Demetri.

"Let's be together and not talk too deeply. Let's have fun, laugh, and forget about the pain for now," she pleaded.

"*Entaxi*, okay," he replied.

"You know," said Kristen quietly. "The summer we met was the best time of my life." Kristen's mind drifted into the past.

Chapter 6

It was July 10, 1987. Kristen and Kari Johnston, twenty and eighteen years old respectively, were on an organized student tour of Europe visiting seventeen countries in eight weeks. They were on their summer break from their university studies. It was the first time either had been to Europe and both were eager to experience as much of the culture as possible. They hated being on a tour, especially since the bus was filled with loud, silly girls, and took every opportunity to break away from the organized events to explore on their own.

They felt strongly that only half of Europe could be seen in the daylight; the other half was to be experienced at night when the locals celebrated the end of their day. They especially liked the countries where the natives would promenade in the evenings to get away from the heat of their homes and socialize with friends and family. It gave a festive feeling to an ordinary day.

Kristen and Kari were more likely found away from the crowds, quietly observing. They absorbed the new environments as a dry sponge does warm water. Everything was new and exciting to them. One evening they were invited to join a group of young adults on their way to a party. They happily agreed and had a wonderful time dancing and trying to communicate with facial expressions and hand gestures, since the language was beyond their comprehension. They tried to blend in with their hosts, although it was difficult in the southern countries.

Being of Norwegian descent, Kristen and Kari both had light-blonde hair, light-blue eyes, and very fair complexions. They considered themselves reasonably attractive by American standards but were shocked at the attention they received from the Italian men. In Rome men had jumped out of their cars in the middle of traffic to meet them.

Flattering as it was, Kristen and Kari found it frightening. They became a little more wary of the dark, Italian men after one such incident.

They had traveled through England, France, Switzerland, Italy, and were on the ferry boat from Brindisi, Italy to Patras, Greece, where their tour would continue. They boarded the boat in the early evening and would arrive in Greece the next afternoon. Kristen was looking forward to Greece. She had always been fascinated with its mythology and wondered whether she would be able to feel the presence of the pre-Christian gods. She also wanted to visit as many of the ancient theaters as possible. Her fantasy was to perform one day on a historic Greek stage.

As they were boarding the *Posidonia*, Kristen said to Kari, "I just can't wait to get to Greece. The other countries have been nice, but Greece is so mysterious and exotic."

"Yes, and the men aren't bad to look at, either," replied Kari, laughing. They were soon to find that Kari had never uttered truer words.

"Let's get settled into our cabin and then spend most of our time out on deck," suggested Kristen. "I want to get as much sun as possible. Since I've never been on a ship this size, I want to experience every aspect of it."

They were disappointed when they discovered that their cabin was an open, dorm-style room with approximately twenty cots. They did not mind too much, knowing that they would not be sleeping much anyway.

"Let's sleep up on deck tonight if the weather is good, and it is permitted," suggested Kristen. Kari agreed. She did not like the idea of sleeping in the same room with so many other people.

They threw their overnight bags onto their assigned cots and left the stuffy room for the fresh air and excitement outside. The ferry began departing the harbor just as they arrived on deck. People were waving good-bye to their loved ones as the ship slipped into the sea. Kristen watched, wondering what emotions were being exchanged between the travelers and the people left behind.

Ever since she had been a little girl, it had been difficult for Kristen to say good-bye to anyone. Her mother often reminded Kristen of the huge "alligator tears" she would shed for the most casual parting.

Nothing had changed. Despite her best efforts, she nearly always felt the tears well up in her eyes when she knew she would not be seeing a loved one for a long period of time. Thinking of the strangers leaving for ports unknown, Kristen's eyes became misty; then she smiled, knowing that her sentimentality wasn't a fault—just something she could not control.

"Let's grab a couple of deck chairs and then explore," suggested Kari. Kristen agreed immediately. It took less than a minute for the girls to stake their claim to two chaises and begin their quest.

The *Posidonia* was an old ship that was showing her age. Rust stains were seeping through the many layers of white paint. The lounge areas were filled with travelers from many nations, speaking languages that Kristen and Kari could not understand.

"Isn't it wonderful?" exclaimed Kristen, looking at the people with their possessions spread everywhere.

"I guess so," answered Kari, not entirely convinced. She could not get beyond the thick haze of smoke permeating the room; it seemed like everybody was smoking. Neither Kari nor Kristen had ever taken up the habit. Their parents would have disowned them if they had.

"Oh, come on, Kari, where's your sense of adventure?" replied Kristen. She performed a quick reconnaissance of the area and then turned to continue their exploration. "Let's go back up on deck. It's much nicer up there in the fresh air."

Kristen's exhilaration was balanced by Kari's trepidation. Although Kari had enjoyed Europe, her shy personality had kept her from feeling comfortable with strangers. While Kristen made a point of striking up conversations with just about anyone, Kari was hesitant and careful … and for good reason.

Kari had had quite a scare while she was in Florence. She had joined Kristen and some friends at a local bar and had become lost when she tried to return to the hotel by herself. She could not remember the name of the hotel and panicked when she thought she was being followed. Although everything ended well when a kind shopkeeper called the American embassy, and officers were dispatched to rescue her, she had been slightly traumatized by the event and was "cautious bordering on paranoid" when in a strange environment.

"Kari, look!" exclaimed Kristen. She was pointing to a pod of dolphins swimming and jumping next to the ship. Neither had seen anything like it except on TV.

"Amazing," Kari commented. They watched until the dolphins tired of their game and disappeared. "I hear they are supposed to bring you good luck."

"I sure hope so," added Kristen.

Although it was early evening, the sun blazed and it was very hot. The reflection of the sun on the deck intensified the heat, making it difficult to be comfortable. Only the breeze created by the movement of the ship made the heat bearable. Kari wisely applied sunscreen after remembering how sunburned she had become the previous summer.

Nothing could keep Kristen from soaking in every aspect of the sea ahead of her. She had never spent much time on the water and found that she loved the wind in her face and hair. She went to the bow of the ship and stayed there, too mesmerized by the deep blue color of the water to move. She liked the tranquillity she found there, where she was able to get away from the noise of the giggling American tourists who were her traveling companions. Kari chose to walk around the deck and had arranged to meet Kristen at a later time. They knew that there would be no problem finding each other; the ship wasn't big enough to get lost.

Kristen wanted to stay on the deck longer, but her thirst was driving her inside. She made her way to the crowded bar where she wanted to purchase a drink but was unsure of the currency. She had learned to manage pounds, francs, and, with some difficulty, even lire, but could not quite understand drachmas, the currency that was accepted by the ship's staff. She stood at the bar, ordered a screwdriver, and extended her hand full of change to the bartender. She figured he would take what was fair. From behind her a deep, European-accented voice said in English, "Give him three hundred drachmas and he'll give you fifty back."

She turned to find a tall, very thin, athletic, extremely attractive and exotic Italian-looking man standing behind her. He appeared to be in his late twenties, was about six feet tall (which seemed taller than the Italians Kristen had seen), had very dark-brown, wavy hair that was cut to just above his collar, and was very windblown from spending time out on the deck. He was casually dressed in low-riding jeans, a wide leather belt, and a form-fitting white T-shirt. His eyebrows were dense and black, and his eyes were dark-brown.

"Thank you," said Kristen. "Or should I say *efharisto*?" Kristen was pleased at the kindness of this stranger and had no apprehension about talking with him further. He did not appear to be the typical islander on the prowl for unsuspecting American tourists. She did not know why, but she trusted this man immediately.

"Oh, you speak Greek?" the tall stranger asked.

"No, but I try to learn at least a few words of the language of whatever country I am in," Kristen replied.

"That is very wise. Let me introduce myself. My name is Demetri Papas."

Chapter 7

"And my name is Kristen Johnston," she replied. They shook hands. Kristen looked at him carefully for the first time. He was incredibly handsome in a dark, southern-European way. She noticed his eyes that were very sensual and would have been described as "bedroom eyes." They also seemed to hold the weight of the world in them. He spoke English beautifully, but it was clear from his heavy accent that it was not his first language. She found him extremely sexy, and he intrigued her immediately.

"Tell me, Kristen, what is your destination?" asked Demetri.

"I'm on a tour that is going to Patras, then up to Delphi, and eventually to Athens," she answered, unable to take her eyes off him. "And you?"

She learned that he was traveling back to his native country of Greece because he had been unable to complete the purchase of a car in Italy due to paperwork difficulties. She also learned that his English was excellent because he was an instructor at a university on Long Island, New York, and that he was an American citizen, a possibility that would never have occurred to Kristen. He looked thoroughly European in dress and action.

She sipped her drink while chatting with Demetri. When she finished, he bought her another. Their conversation continued until they were interrupted by Kari, who pulled Kristen away with a look of horror on her face.

"How could you talk to that man?" she asked. "I saw him earlier on the ship. He gives me the creeps. He looks like a Mafia hit man. As a matter of fact, I have been purposely avoiding him, and here I see you with him. How could you?"

"Calm down. We were just talking!" Kristen exclaimed. "Besides, he has been a perfect gentleman. He's the most interesting person I have met on the whole trip. So don't worry."

Kristen's instincts told her that Kari was wrong. This was not someone who would harm her. On the contrary, he appeared to be very protective of her. She did not want to upset Kari any further, so she walked over to Demetri and explained her situation.

"I am sorry, but my sister would like me to spend some time with her. Would it be possible for us to continue this conversation later?"

"Of course. I will look forward to it. Shall we meet at the bow? I will be there later and will wait for you," Demetri responded.

Kristen was blown away. How could this incredibly attractive, intelligent, and worldly man be interested in her? She was flattered beyond belief. She decided that she would not let anything get in the way of meeting him later. For now, though, she would appease Kari and spend time with her. Since it was getting late, they decided to try to go to their cabin.

The ship's accommodations were spartan, to say the least. The American girls were outraged when the male Greek and Italian employees would barge into their quarters without preamble, seeming to enjoy the quick peeks they got of the seminaked American coeds. Privacy was unheard of, and Kristen found sleep impossible. Besides, she had made a date to meet Demetri at the bow of the ship. Although she felt that Demetri would be waiting, she did not want to take any chances that he might tire of being alone.

It was midnight when Kristen made her way to the rendezvous point. Demetri was there with a blanket to protect him from the cool night air.

"I am so glad you decided to join me after all," he said.

"I told you I would, and we had only begun our conversation. I want to learn more about you," she replied. "So where were we?"

They talked for hours without touching. She admired him for his worldliness, his sophistication, and his ability to converse about a multitude of subjects. He admired her for her intelligence, her independent spirit, her positive outlook on life, and her beautiful smile, as well as her gorgeous body. Her smile came easily and traveled from her full, tempting lips into her eyes. It didn't take Demetri long to know that Kristen was special.

Kristen was overwhelmed by Demetri. She could not believe that this older, gorgeous, sophisticated man could possibly be interested in her. She thought of herself as a typical, middle-class college coed without much worldly experience. What could she offer such a man?

Their conversation continued without interruption until just before dawn; she spoke of her life, he of his. They quickly felt very comfortable with each other, almost as if they had known each other for years instead of hours. Each had opened up without restraint about their lives, their opinions, and feelings toward life in general.

It was getting very late. Neither Demetri nor Kristen, however, wished to break the rhythm of their conversation, and both were aware of the time restraints. The ship would dock in Patras, and they would go their separate ways. That was the nature of travel—two ships meeting in the night and passing each other, leaving a memory of their passing, but little more. That was the norm, but Kristen and Demetri were quickly finding that nothing about their relationship would be normal.

"It is getting cold. Come, share my blanket," Demetri beseeched her.

"Thank you, I will," replied Kristen, knowing that the physical closeness they would share would change their casual meeting into something memorable. It seemed natural for them to share the blanket. Demetri opened his left arm wide to receive Kristen into his comforting yet casual embrace. As their bodies touched each other for the first time, they felt the connection, the electricity. It was a shock that both felt in a tangible way. Kristen was a bit frightened by this. She had never experienced such a physical reaction to a man. Was it the sea, the stars, the atmosphere of romance? Or was this man someone who could become important to her?

"Are you comfortable?" asked Demetri as Kristen snuggled into his embrace.

"Yes, oh yes," she whispered, wanting the moment to last forever. She felt completely safe and secure, like an infant in the loving arms of a parent. She had no reason to trust this man, but she did, implicitly. She suspected this would not be just a casual meeting.

Demetri leaned closer to her and kissed her ever so gently. He was in no hurry. His outside world began to fade when he looked at this pretty, delightful young woman. The stresses he had been feeling for weeks suddenly disappeared. He was no longer the angry and frustrated man he had become. He was once again the happy, romantic, carefree youth he had once been. His happiness showed in his eyes. Kristen saw it and kissed him back.

"Your lips are delicious," whispered Demetri as they faced each other. They kissed again, but this time Demetri's tongue gently probed Kristen's mouth. Kristen responded, and the kiss built with intensity that took both by surprise.

This isn't a naive college student, Demetri thought. *She has depth that I did not know she possessed. She could be very special to me. I must be careful with her.*

They watched the morning creep into the sky, happily wrapped in the blanket. The glow of the rising sun was reflected in the glow of Kristen's happiness. The sun rose yellow, and there were no clouds in the sky. The dawn promised that the new day would be clear and hot. It also promised to be a day for the beginning of a new life for both Demetri and Kristen.

"We need to sleep for a while," said Demetri. "Let's meet after we both have had a chance to nap." He was destined to be the practical one.

"Yes, but I was hoping that this would last forever," Kristen admitted, realizing as she said it how it must have sounded. She blushed with embarrassment.

"I feel the same way," said Demetri, dispelling Kristen's noticeable discomfort.

Kristen immediately felt better. She felt like a naive child on her first adventure and that Demetri was the wise leader.

After a few more heartfelt kisses they hesitantly parted and went to their respective cabins. Sleep did not come easily to either. Although they were both fatigued from the lack of sleep, their minds were reeling from this unexpected meeting.

After a restless, two-hour attempt at sleep, Kristen returned to the bow, where she was surprised to see Demetri, concentrating on the horizon in deep thought. She quietly and gently slipped next to him. Finding her there, he opened his arm to welcome her into his life. It felt natural to have her there with him.

"I missed you," admitted Kristen to Demetri.

He looked deeply into her eyes and nodded silently. This seemingly casual statement moved him deeply. He had missed her too. Being away from each other, even for a short time, was unnatural. "You cannot know what a difference you have already made in my life," he whispered.

This shocked Kristen. She could not understand how she could have had the same effect on Demetri that he had had on her. She liked the idea but doubted that she could make a difference in his life. She, after all, was nothing special. She was wrong in that assumption. She had swiftly become very precious to Demetri.

The day was passing too quickly. It was almost noon when they realized they were hungry. Neither had eaten since the previous day. They strolled into the restaurant together but were unable to have lunch together because Kristen was required to eat with the tour group. They sat where they could watch each other, which was nearly as good as being at the same table. Their eyes communicated secret messages that made them both smile.

After lunch Kristen found Kari happily playing pinochle with a group of English students. "When you can take a break, I'd like to talk with you," said Kristen to Kari.

"Sure, no problem. Give me a minute, will you?" replied Kari.

"So what's up?" asked Kari a few minutes later.

"I'm not sure how you're going to take this, but remember that man you warned me about? Well, I spent all last night talking, just talking, with him, and he's wonderful. You are wrong about him. I just wanted you to know," explained Kristen.

"Oh, that. Yes, I saw you together. I figure you know what you're doing, and I shouldn't interfere. Do what you want. You're a big girl. I've seen how he looks at you. He is not a threat. I know that now," replied Kari.

Was this the same nearly hysterical sister she had been with yesterday? It did not appear so.

"Thank you," Kristen said, hugging her sister. "This means a lot to me."

"Just be careful, Kristen," said Kari quietly.

"I will," Kristen replied. She was pleased that she wasn't going to get an argument from Kari. That would have put a damper on what had been the best part of her vacation so far. She returned to Demetri, and they talked and talked about everything and about nothing. Kristen, who was normally a talker, could barely get a word in edgewise. Demetri was animated, talkative, and obviously very happy. Kristen stopped for a moment and just stared at him. He noticed and asked, "What?"

"Oh, nothing. I just wanted to burn your image into my brain and remember this moment forever," Kristen replied.

Kristen heard him say under his breath, "I know exactly what you mean."

Before they knew it, people began to stir, and preparations for landing in Patras were under way. It hadn't occurred to them that the journey would seem so short. Demetri would return to Athens, and Kristen would join the tour group and travel to Delphi and then to Athens in two days.

Demetri could not leave it at this. "May I meet you in Athens when your tour arrives?" he asked.

"I thought you would never ask!" Kristen exclaimed, and they both laughed.

Their relationship would not end there in Patras. They would see each other again. Who knew what they would feel when that happened? Perhaps the feelings were just the result of summer, the heat, and the sea. Chances were good that their feelings would be different—more rational—when they met again.

They solidified their plans to meet at her hotel when she arrived in Athens in two days. They shared one last kiss before the ship docked.

Demetri did not say good-bye. To Kristen's surprise, he ran off the ship and disappeared from sight. This caught her off guard and she did not know how to react. He was still a mystery to her, and she realized she had a lot to learn about him.

A few minutes passed, and to Kristen's delight, Demetri appeared at her side once again. He had purchased some worry beads from a dockside merchant to give to her as a token of their time together. The beads were bright orange and made of plastic. Kristen was unfamiliar with them, so Demetri took a moment to give her a short lesson on the significance of the beads in Greek culture.

"They are a symbol of affection and love when given as a gift," he explained.

Kristen's breath was taken away. Nobody had ever done anything like this for her. The gift wasn't expensive, but it was given with joy and kindness. She knew the beads would remain precious to her for the rest of her life.

One more kiss, and he was gone.

Chapter 8

When the bus pulled up to the Athens hotel two days later, Kristen was delighted beyond belief to see Demetri on the sidewalk, flowers in hand, to welcome her to his home. When the girls on the tour realized that the handsome man was there to meet Kristen, they glared at her. She could not have cared less and was only thinking of Demetri as she left the bus.

Demetri drew her up in his arms and kissed her European style, a kiss on each cheek. Kristen wanted a real kiss, but that would happen at a more appropriate time. Within moments his arms encircled her again, this time in a less friendly and more intimate way. Kristen approved. She felt that they fit together perfectly.

"*Kalispera*," Demetri said to Kristen. "I have missed you." Kristen's heart rate quickened with delight.

Demetri had not forgotten Kristen's sister. Only a portion of the flowers he had brought were for Kristen. The others were offered to Kari as she stepped off the bus. The act of kindness was rewarded by a visible warming of Kari's attitude toward him.

"*Yia sou*, Kari," said Demetri. "I have heard so much about you and am happy now to begin to know you."

"Thank you. And *yia sou* to you too, whatever that means," Kari said. It was the first time she had been able to assess this stranger who had stolen her sister's heart. She looked deeply into his eyes, turned to her sister, and said, "I think he'll do."

All three laughed as Kari was folded into Demetri's arms along with Kristen.

"Give us a few minutes to get settled into our room, and then we'll be ready to roll," Kristen said to Demetri.

"That's okay. Take your time," Demetri replied happily. "I will wait for you here."

"See, I told you," said Kristen to Kari as they walked up the stairs to their assigned room.

"Okay, I'll admit he's gorgeous and charming. But I want to make sure he is good enough for you. And that he'll be good to you. You are my favorite sister, after all."

"You'll find out he's something very special. I am sure of it," Kristen replied. "Come on, let's get a move on. I don't want to waste one minute of the time we can spend with him."

Kristen and Kari threw their satchels on the bed, freshened up by splashing some water on their faces and washing their hands, and were ready to go. Neither one used much makeup. First, they did not really need it. Secondly, Athens was hot and their makeup was bound to run. It was definitely not worth the bother for either of them.

"Let me go down first, will you?" asked Kristen of Kari. "I want a few minutes alone with him before you arrive."

"Sure, that's only fair," replied Kari, but she felt a little like a fifth wheel. She considered begging off going and letting the other two explore Athens alone, but she did not want to be left alone in the hotel and was hesitant to venture out on her own. Athens was hot, busy, noisy, and a bit intimidating. Besides, she wasn't sure where to begin.

"Hello," Kristen whispered to Demetri as she quietly came up behind him. He was startled at first and then relaxed visibly when he realized that it was Kristen who had snuck up on him.

Kristen noticed the tension Demetri displayed and wondered what would make him so skittish. "It's probably nothing," she said to herself and immediately forgot the incident.

As he turned to look at her, his eyes smiled along with his mouth. "You look beautiful," he said as he drew her close to him and gave her a gentle kiss. "I have missed you."

"And I you," Kristen replied. "It's crazy to feel this way after knowing you such a short amount of time. I wasn't sure I would ever see you again. You seemed too good to be true."

"Me! You," said Demetri excitedly. "When I watched you board your tour bus in Patras, I suddenly felt very alone. That is unusual for a Greek, because we are seldom alone, with our large families constantly being together. I was in a very bad mood when I boarded the ferry in Brindisi. My spirits were lifted by your warmth and your laughter. I did not know how I was going to manage it, but I was determined to meet you today. It wasn't easy, but I was able to rearrange commitments and be here. It was something I wanted to do. I wouldn't have missed it for the world. Besides, I promised to meet you here today. I always keep my promises. A promise is sacred to me."

Kristen was touched by his sincerity and openness and that this incredible man was here to see her.

Demetri broke her train of thought by asking, "So where do you want to go, and what do you want to see? My time is all yours now."

"Is it okay for Kari to join us?" Kristen asked hesitantly. "She would like to get the guided tour too."

"Of course it is okay!" exclaimed Demetri. "She is important to you. You are important to me. That makes Kari also important to me. She is welcome like a sister to me."

That wasn't the response she had expected. It warmed her heart to know that Demetri would accept Kari into his life too. She did not think that an American man would have been quite so willing to have a chaperone.

"Go get Kari, and let's leave. I have much to show you, and it is already late afternoon. It is a good thing that Athens is at its best in the night time."

"Thanks. I'll do that and will be right back."

Demetri watched Kristen as she left the room. Everything about her was appealing to him—her physical beauty, of course, but also her kindness toward Kari, and her enthusiasm about life. Merely thinking about Kristen lightened his heart.

What has this woman done to me? Demetri asked himself. *Has she cast a spell? It feels that way. I have never felt such a connection to anyone before, even after knowing that person for a very long time. It makes me feel so happy just to be with her. I must be careful, though. Can this be real? And if so, is it fair for me to involve her in my life?*

He decided to treat Kristen like any other visitor; he would show her around to the best of his ability, and he would let her decide what she wanted. If she was comfortable and wanted to be with him, it would please him very much. He knew he was trustworthy. They would be together for the next two days and would see how things went—nothing more, nothing less.

Kari and Kristen appeared with large hats to protect them from the sun. Kari saw Demetri's amused expression and said, "Yes, I know we look like tourists. It's better to look like tourists than cooked lobsters." They all laughed and happily left the hotel lobby.

Kristen and Kari were struck by how busy Athens was. People drove at high rates of speed and then jammed on their brakes while honking their horns incessantly. Neither Kristen nor Kari could figure out the traffic regulations, if any existed. They saw cars driving on the sidewalks to bypass stalled traffic.

"Did you see that?" Kristen pointed to a car that had just missed a pedestrian on the sidewalk. "Is everyone crazy here or just the drivers? And why do they blow their horns so much?"

"It is Greece. What can I say?" replied Demetri. He shrugged his shoulders as if to say, "Who knows?"

"Here in Athens we have a saying that one one-hundredth of a second is the time it takes a person to blow his horn at the car in front of him after the light turns green," Demetri added.

Both Kristen and Kari believed it. They were glad that Demetri was there to help them cross the busy streets. He would always position them away from the traffic pattern, so they would feel safe. Kristen noticed his thoughtfulness.

Demetri stopped. "Turn around and look up," he said, pointing.

"Look up there!" Kari exclaimed. "It's the Acropolis!"

Kristen looked up above the buildings of the city and saw for the first time the white stone pillars of the Parthenon on the hill known as the Acropolis. "It's beautiful!! Can we go there?"

"Of course we can. I only hope you have good walking shoes on, because it is quite a hike," answered Demetri. "And I would like to show you something first."

They crossed Syntagma (Constitution) Square. "This is considered the heart of Athens," Demetri explained. Hundreds of people were sitting at café tables, sipping coffees, sodas, or beers, while casually watching others walk by. Kristen liked that and hoped that they could stop for a while later on. But for now she was too anxious to see what Athens had to offer to consider sitting.

They crossed the street in front of the Parliament building. The guards standing watch fascinated Kristen and Kari. They had seen the Queen's guards in London, with their scarlet uniforms, and thought the Greek guards looked very unusual, with their ruffled skirts and the pom-poms on their shoes. One close look showed the girls that there was nothing feminine about the guards. They were all male and meant business.

"Demetri, will you take a picture of Kari and me next to the guards?" Kristen asked.

"Okay, but then let's get someone to take a picture of the three of us together." Which they did. Demetri wrapped Kristen in his right arm and held Kari under his left, and they all smiled happily into the camera.

Demetri showed the sisters the places that were special to him. They walked the dusty, irregular sidewalk until they arrived at the Royal Gardens, which were open to the public. As they strolled down one of the bush-lined paths, Demetri stopped and pointed to a vine-covered building.

"Do you see this?" Demetri asked, pointing to some letters that had been carved into a column of the building.

"Yes, is it ancient Greek?" asked Kari.

"No," he replied. "It is my name. I carved it there fifteen years ago when I was a high school student studying here in Athens."

She had to believe him, because the letters could have said anything. She and Kristen could not read it because it was in Greek, and they had not learned how to decipher the strange-looking letters.

"Shame on you!" teased Kristen. "Defacing an historic monument is terrible."

"It's not graffiti. If it stays there long enough, it too will be historic," retorted Demetri. He made a good point, and all three laughed at the joke.

Kristen appreciated Demetri's quick wit and sense of humor. She was touched to know that Demetri was sharing a bit of his childhood with her. She wanted to know all about his life in Greece but knew that that would have to wait for another time.

They saw the ruins of Hadrian's Arch close to the Royal Gardens.

"Can you believe this?" asked Kari. "The columns were made of separately carved pieces of sandstone that were piled on top of one another. I don't know how they could have done this."

Since Demetri was serving as their guide, they hadn't purchased a book to help in their quest. The dates and other specific information weren't important to Kristen. What was important was that she was discovering Athens with Demetri. It was all very exciting and very romantic.

They had been walking for more than an hour and were hot and thirsty. Although it was almost five p.m., the temperature was 38 degrees Centigrade. They walked to an outdoor café on Syntagma Square, where they ordered a Coke and watched the throngs of people pass by. Kristen loved listening to Demetri give the order to the waiter in Greek. She admired him for his ability to speak more than one language.

"How do you switch from Greek to English so easily?" she asked.

"Oh, it just happens. It is interesting, but when I first went to the United States, I had to learn English. I knew I was doing well when I began to think in English. And I knew I was doing *very* well when I began to dream in English. That took many years, but it is second nature to me now."

Both Kari and Kristen could not get enough of his accented English. It sounded very sophisticated to them. They asked him more questions, just so he would talk more.

"There is something else that you might find amusing. When I am in the States, I swear in Greek, but when I am in Greece, I swear in English. I guess it is safer that way," Demetri added.

They all laughed. Kristen did not think she had heard him swear. But then again, he easily could have, and she would not have understood. Kristen was enthralled and did not want to forget a moment of their time together.

"Can we go up to the Acropolis now?" asked Kari.

Demetri shrugged his shoulders as if to say, "Perhaps." Instead he said, "Why don't I take you back to your hotel?" Both girls showed their disappointment. "Wait, before I have a revolt on my hands, listen to what I have to say. It is very hot. Athenians don't do anything in this heat except rest. Why don't I take you back to the hotel where you can rest and have a shower? I will pick you up in a couple of hours and then we can go to the Acropolis and have dinner in Plaka, which is the area below the Acropolis and is now filled with shops and *tavernas*. You will like it very much. It will be cooler then, and we will enjoy our time much more."

Kristen could not imagine enjoying her time more, although she had to admit that she was feeling very sweaty and dirty from their walk. She would have preferred to stay with Demetri, even if she was uncomfortable, but she knew his suggestion was practical. She was finding that Demetri liked being in charge—an attribute that she appreciated now, though she wondered how it would be in a long-term relationship, since she had always been very independent and self-sufficient.

"That sounds fine, thank you," she conceded.

"Then tomorrow, you can either go with your tour group, or I will take you in my car to Cape Sunion and the beach," Demetri added.

Both girls beamed with delight and practically yelled out that they would love to go with him to Cape Sunion, whatever that was. They would have been happy to go anywhere with him as long as they could spend time together.

"So, my friends, I will be back in two hours," Demetri said as he dropped them at the hotel. He took Kristen's hand in his, gave it a squeeze, and kissed her lightly on the lips before he turned and walked around the corner.

Kristen saw his expression change from smiling and jovial to one of concern as he turned away from her and performed a complete reconnaissance of the area. She wondered why he would be examining the place as if he expected to see someone he knew, and why that someone would not be a friend. *That's strange*, she thought.

"Oh, my gosh," said Kari. "Now I know what you mean about him. He's amazing. I guess I was wrong, and am happy to admit it to you."

Kristen turned to Kari and gave her a big hug. "I knew you'd like him when you got to know him."

They went up to their room, which was barely adequate, but they did not mind. They found the lukewarm shower a little disturbing, but they figured that it was an inexpensive tour, and they weren't going to complain.

Kristen lay on the rock-hard mattress and tried to get comfortable. The pillow reminded her of some of the stones she had seen at Hadrian's Arch. Thoughts of Demetri swirled around her mind until she drifted off to sleep.

She awoke to the blare of the telephone. "Hello," she said groggily.

"*Kalispera*, sleepyhead. Get up. It is time to go out and discover Athens by night," Demetri teased.

Kristen looked and saw that it was already eight o'clock. They had slept longer than they had expected.

"We'll be right down. I'm sorry you have to wait," said Kristen, now wide awake.

"*Tipota*, it is nothing. You come down when you are ready. I will wait for you."

Since they had already showered, it only took Kristen and Kari ten minutes to prepare for their night out.

"Let me go first. I want a few minutes alone with him if you don't mind," said Kristen to Kari as she had earlier in the day. She was happy to have Kari along, but she had not had an opportunity to be alone with Demetri, and she wanted a few moments of private time before their evening out.

"Sure, and after dinner I'll make myself scarce, so you two can be alone," Kari said, without any suggestion of hurt or resentment.

"Thanks, I appreciate that!" said Kristen.

Kristen bounded down the stairs, anxious to see Demetri.

"*Sega, sega*," Demetri cried as he saw her skipping down the stairs. "Slow down, there is plenty of time."

Demetri looked wonderful to Kristen. His clothes enhanced his slim, athletic body. He was dressed in a lightweight, short-sleeved shirt, lightweight beige slacks, and moccasin-styled shoes. Kristen could hardly keep herself from staring at this Adonis. How could she have been so lucky to find such a wonderful, attractive man? She gave a silent word of thanks to the heavens for bringing him into her life.

"Where is Kari?" asked Demetri.

"She'll be down in a minute. I wanted some time alone with you before she came."

Demetri looked into Kristen's face and smiled. "So you want to be alone with me? Come outside for a second."

He took her hand and led her outside to the edge of the building, where they could have a private moment. He took her face in his strong but gentle hands and kissed her, gently at first and then with more feeling.

Something stirred in Kristen. Tingling coursed through her body. It startled her a bit.

Demetri ended the kiss but kept his face close to Kristen's. She could smell a faint aroma of cigarettes mingled with his natural body scent.

He wore no cologne, and Kristen liked that. The scent was irresistible. She wanted more. She pulled him to her for another longer, and more intimate, kiss.

It was Demetri's turn to be surprised. This woman had a streak of passion in her that he had not expected. This was no innocent coed who needed to be handled gently, but a full-blown woman who knew what she wanted and was willing to express her needs.

Demetri's tongue probed Kristen's willing mouth. She tasted delicious. Her lips were full and expressive, her teeth even and smooth. He wanted to learn more, but the time was not right. It was not appropriate to be acting like this in a public place.

Reluctantly, Demetri backed out of the kiss. They looked into each other's eyes. For a moment their expressions showed the emotions they were feeling. Then the moment passed, and they smiled warmly at each other. They both knew that during that last kiss things had changed. This was no longer a casual summer fling, but something with possibilities and a future.

Kari arrived at that moment. She saw that there was something very hot going on and decided to break things up.

"Okay, you two lovebirds, let's get going. I'm hungry!" It was the perfect thing to say, setting the mood for a light and carefree evening.

Since the hotel was located on the edge of Plaka, they had only a few blocks to walk before passing *tavernas* and the many shops located under the shadow of the Acropolis. As the sun moved closer to the horizon, the air cooled. A welcome breeze caressed their skin and made their walk very comfortable.

"Let's go to the Acropolis first and then we can shop and eat," Demetri recommended. "It is still too early for dinner. In Greece only the tourists eat before nine p.m. Tonight, you are Greek."

The enjoyment of the stroll was heightened by plenty of friendly banter among the three companions. After what seemed an endless climb, Kristen was glad that they had not tried to visit the top of the hill earlier in the day. She hadn't realized it would be such a strenuous hike up the dusty, rocky trail. She wished she had worn sturdier shoes and eventually took her sandals off and walked barefoot. There was less possibility of slipping without her shoes, although she was a bit of a tenderfoot and had to be careful where she walked. It also gave her an excuse to hold Demetri's arm, which she did at every opportunity.

Eventually they reached the top. The Parthenon was on their right, the smaller building, the Erechtheum, on their left. The city was below and made an awe inspiringly beautiful landscape, with thousands of lights twinkling in all directions. It took Kristen's breath away.

There were no ropes to keep tourists out, so they were able to walk inside the buildings. The feeling of history overwhelmed Kristen. She was temporarily transported back in time and imagined she was walking in the very place that Aristotle had walked. She wondered what it must have been like all those years ago, before the buildings had been left in ruins by wars and neglect.

Demetri came up beside her and whispered, "You feel it, don't you?"

She knew what he spoke of. "Yes, it's magical."

"Not many do. You must have an old soul to be affected this way. Perhaps you were Greek at one time, eh?" Demetri observed.

"Perhaps I was. Although I have never been here before, I feel as if I am coming home. It's strange."

"Not strange. You have a rare gift of perception. You are blessed."

Kristen did not really understand what he meant, but she appreciated the sentiment.

Kristen seemed to feel some supernatural presence that was not necessarily Christian, as one might expect in Greece. No, it felt older to her. It was as if the ancient gods were surrounding her. She shivered, even though she was not cold. She closed her eyes to concentrate on her other senses. Although she heard nothing unusual, she could feel warmth and peace traveling through her body. Again, this was a sensation she had never experienced. Was it Athens? Was it Demetri? Or a combination of both? Whatever it was, she liked it.

She was moved to say a prayer. "Please bless Demetri and me. Bless this new love and help us to keep it forever." It was a simple prayer, but Kristen felt that it had been heard.

She opened her eyes and saw that Demetri was playing hide-and-seek with Kari and had hidden behind the ancient stone blocks. Kristen imagined Demetri frolicking here as a boy. *His playground was very different from mine as a child. How different we are. Would I ever truly fit into his life?* she asked herself.

She went over to Demetri and Kari, who were breathless from their game. It was as though they were a family, even though they were just beginning to know each other.

"You two are going to get us all in trouble," Kristen chastised them.

"Yes, Kari, act your age," Demetri added, laughing heartily. He was already feeling toward Kari as he would toward a sister. Perhaps someday Kari would actually be his sister.

"*Pame*, let's go," Demetri waved. "It's time to eat."

"Gladly! I'm starving," answered Kari.

"I'll race you to the entrance," Demetri challenged her.

"You're on," she said, and began running. She did not have a chance of catching Demetri. He was a born athlete and swift on his feet.

Kristen stared at Demetri as he effortlessly maneuvered around the uneven floor. He was her Adonis, her Greek god. Was a mere mortal like herself worthy of such a man? She hoped so with all her heart.

The walk back down the hill was much easier. Demetri had gathered up Kristen and Kari, one on each side, and they walked into Plaka looking like a six-legged giant.

The Greeks stared at the threesome as they passed by. It was unusual for a Greek man to be so familiar with young women in public, even in Plaka, where merriment was the norm. The contrast of Demetri's dark skin, hair, and eyes with Kristen's and Kari's light-blonde hair, blue eyes, and very fair skin was striking. They looked like the reverse version of an Oreo cookie. All three of them noticed the stares and tried to ignore them.

"Why are people staring?" asked Kristen.

"They are not used to seeing true blondes. And especially not with someone who looks like me. They are jealous!" said Demetri emphatically. Kristen noticed that a dark shadow had swept over Demetri's face, and his eyes darted from left to right.

"Is there something wrong?" Kristen asked him quietly.

"Nothing for you to concern yourself with," he replied and quickly changed the subject. "Where would you like to eat? It is your choice."

"Let's find a place with authentic Greek music," Kristen suggested.

They were in luck. After five minutes of searching, they found the perfect *taverna*. It was surrounded by flower-covered vines, had a view of the fully lit Acropolis, and the bouzouki band was just beginning to play their first song.

"I don't think I would ever tire of seeing the Acropolis," Kristen said to Demetri. "It is so beautiful and majestic, especially at night."

"Let's sit where we can have a view," Demetri said as he led the way to the perfect table. Kristen and Demetri sat on one side of the table and Kari on the other. Kristen reached under the table and squeezed Demetri's hand. The pleasure he felt was obvious by the expression on his face.

A freshly laundered white tablecloth was spread over the table. The waiter brought over a basket with bread and butter, silverware and napkins and dinner began.

"Demetri, please order for us," Kristen requested. "We have no idea of what anything is. We have never had Greek food before." Kari nodded in agreement.

"What do you like?"

"We really don't know. No octopus, please. I don't think I could enjoy it as my first meal," added Kari.

"Okay. I will order us a feast, and everyone will have something they like." Demetri signaled the waiter and ordered for them. Of course, Kristen and Kari had no idea what to expect. They hadn't understood a word that was said, but they enjoyed the sound of it.

"I have ordered some local wine that I hope you will enjoy," said Demetri.

"Please don't order much for either of us," said Kristen, somewhat apologetically. Kari and Kristen weren't very experienced drinkers. "We had too much wine during our gondola ride in Venice, and we're still trying to recover." The memory of the hangover less than a week before wasn't pleasant, and the thought of wine was not enticing to either Kari or Kristen.

"I'll have just a little," Kari said. "Could you please order me a Coke?"

"Yes, okay," Demetri said. "I have also ordered some bottled water, since we are all thirsty from our walk."

The drinks were brought to the table. Kristen and Kari eagerly drank two glasses of water each. They had not realized how thirsty they had become.

"Hmmm, the wine is good," Kristen asserted, trying to believe her words. "It's very dry, isn't it? What's that funny flavor?"

Demetri chuckled. "That is retsina you are drinking. It is a very ancient variety of wine that dates back almost two thousand years before Christ. What you taste is the pine resin added to preserve the wine."

"You mean they put turpentine in it? It tastes a lot like it," said Kristen.

"Don't you like it?" asked Demetri, who knew that retsina would be a stretch of anyone's palate.

"Well, it is unusual," said Kristen, trying to be diplomatic.

"Don't worry, the more you drink the better it tastes. By the fourth glass it is delicious," he said to both women and added, "Just like your lips," quietly, so only Kristen would hear.

Demetri knew just the right things to say, Kristen thought, and it did not sound stilted in any way. She did not believe that these were lines he used on numerous women to get their attention and felt that he was being sincere with her.

The meal was served family-style, with a different kind of food on each platter. Little was recognizable, either to Kristen or Kari, but they were willing to try anything once.

"Okay, this is feta cheese on top of the salad. Try it," Demetri encouraged them.

Both Kari and Kristen took a taste. They both smiled, even though Kari thought that the feta tasted a little like vomit. She figured it was an acquired taste. Next, they tasted the fried eggplant and zucchini, which they loved.

Demetri had ordered some moussaka, stuffed peppers, and a lamb dish that they all shared. Although the flavors were foreign to their palates, the women enjoyed the dinner very much. The music enhanced their dining experience. Kristen had never heard Greek music before, but she liked it from the first note. She liked the minor chords, the soulful sound of the lyrics, as well as the syncopated rhythm of the songs.

Performers appeared and began to dance. "It is the syrtaki, a dance that is made up as the dancer is moved by the music," Demetri explained. As the performance continued, men from the audience joined in to add their version to the song.

"Why don't you go up, Demetri?" asked Kristen.

"No, disco is more my style, I'm afraid," he replied.

Dinner lasted over two hours. Kristen and Kari learned that in Greece one does not merely eat; one dines. Dinner is a time for animated conversation and leisurely eating. Time does not matter much. What is, is. This concept of time was strange to Kristen, but attractive, at least while on vacation. She thought it might become a little frustrating while trying to live on a daily basis.

Demetri paid the bill, and the three began their leisurely stroll through the narrow shop-lined streets of Plaka and Monastaraki. Kristen and Kari were astonished at the tiny shops that were crammed with merchandise.

"We will have to come back here and shop," said Kari to Kristen.

"You bet, if we find the time. Perhaps we should buy now if we see something we like. We might not have a chance to come back," added Kristen. "Demetri, is it okay if we browse a little?"

"We have no time restraints. Do what pleases you," was his reply.

That wasn't the reply she would have received from most of the men she had ever known. Most would have made Kristen feel bad so that she would give in to what they wanted to do. This endeared Demetri to her even more.

Kristen and Kari spent the next hour flitting from one store to another. They bought leather sandals from Stavros Melissinos, better known as the poet sandal maker of Athens; postcards to send to family and friends at home; and a pair of earrings each. One thing Kristen made a point of not buying for others were sets of worry beads. She did not want to dilute the meaning of the beads that Demetri had bought for her.

They eventually made their way all the way down the hill to within two blocks of the hotel.

"You know what? I'm really tired. I'd like to go back to the hotel now. I can find it myself this time. Don't worry. Give me the packages, and I'll take them back," Kari said.

"Are you sure?" Demetri asked. "We should walk you there."

"No thanks. I can see the entrance of the hotel from here. You two go and have some time together. Thank you so much for the beautiful evening, Demetri!" Kari said.

"See you tomorrow, Little One." Kari was flattered that he thought enough of her to give her such a sweet nickname.

Kari disappeared around the corner, and Kristen and Demetri were alone at last.

"Why don't we get a coffee?" suggested Demetri.

"That sounds great," said Kristen as she moved slightly closer into Demetri's arm. He noticed the change of position and squeezed her shoulder for a moment. They were perfectly comfortable together.

They settled into their table at the café and sat quietly as they watched the couples parading by their table. For the first time in her life, Kristin did not feel the slightest bit of jealousy for the seemingly happy couples. She was as happy tonight as she had ever been in her life.

"It's late," Demetri said eventually, after they had drunk their coffee. It was after one AM "I had better get you back to your hotel."

"I guess so, even though I hate to have this perfect evening end," conceded Kristen.

"We have tomorrow," Demetri added.

"Yes, tomorrow. What time would you like us to be ready?" asked Kristen.

"Can you be ready about ten? That will give you time to have a good sleep and breakfast without hurrying. Be sure to bring a bathing suit with you. I hope we'll be able to swim in the sea."

"It sounds wonderful. Thank you, Demetri. The evening was perfect," Kristen said as they arrived at the hotel's front entrance.

There was no awkwardness as they kissed good night. Kissing each other felt like the most natural thing for them to do. When Demetri pulled away, Kristen begged for another and another.

He laughed, kissed her again, and said, "*kalinichta*, Kristen. I will see you soon," as he waved good-bye.

Kristen was suddenly alone but incredibly happy. The evening had been everything she had hoped for and more. They would be seeing each other again tomorrow, or was it today? Whatever—all was right with the world.

She climbed the stairs to the room and tried to get ready for bed as quietly as she could. Kari was still awake, however, and startled Kristen by surprising her with, "Well, that was some evening."

"Yes, it was. Isn't he incredible?" Kristen exclaimed.

"I must admit I really like him, and I am not too proud to admit when I'm wrong."

"We better not talk tonight. We are to meet him at ten and need our beauty sleep. Good night," said Kristen as she turned out the light. Sleep came quickly after the excitement of the last few days.

Chapter 9

Kari and Kristen arose as brightly as the Athens sun at eight. They had looked forward to the first cup of coffee and were bitterly disappointed to find that the restaurant was only serving tea, instead of the brewed coffee they were accustomed to drinking.

"Hey, caffeine is caffeine. Beggars can't be choosers," Kari reminded Kristen.

An idea had come to Kristen in the night, and she could not wait to talk to Kari about it, but she did not know how to broach the subject.

"You're right. This is definitely not the top-of-the-line tour," Kristen agreed. This was the perfect segue into the subject she wanted to discuss with Kari. "As a matter of fact, we don't have much time in Athens on the tour. I want some more time to get to know Demetri, and if we stay on the tour, it won't happen. I've got an idea that you are going to think is absolutely crazy, but hear me out. What do you think of us staying in Athens for a few more days and then catching up with the tour in Austria in a week or so? The tour is going to be driving through Yugoslavia, and I'm not terribly interested in it, and I really want to spend some time with Demetri, so … what do you think? Please say yes, please, please, please!" Kristen pleaded.

Kari thought for a minute, and, with a frown on her face, slowly said, "I think it's a brilliant idea."

From the expression on Kari's face, Kristen had thought she was going to nix the plan. It was Kari's way of "pulling her sister's chain." It worked. Kristen was so relieved by Kari's agreement that she gave her sister a big hug and knocked over the water jug on the table.

"Hey, steady on, old girl, as the British like to say," laughed Kari. "There are plans to be made. Have you discussed this with 'you know who' yet?"

"No, I just thought of it. I'm sure he'd be happy to spend some more time with us. Things are wonderful between him and me. I just don't know what kind of schedule he has. Demetri did say he had some family obligations while he is here in Greece. I'm not sure what he meant by that, but we can discuss it with him when we go out to Sunion."

"Well, then, we'd better get a move on. There is a lot to do before he arrives in less than an hour," said Kari.

"Oh, I love you, little sister!" exclaimed Kristen, giving Kari a proper hug without incident.

Demetri, prompt as always, was ringing their room at exactly 10:00 AM. "Rise and shine, the day awaits," he said cheerfully when Kari answered the phone.

"Good morning, or is it '*Kalimera*'?" asked Kari cheerfully.

"You are learning to speak Greek. Bravo. Perhaps today I will teach you some new words. Are you ready?" asked Demetri.

"Yes, we'll be right down."

It took less than two minutes before Kristen and Kari were in the lobby.

"*Kalimerasas*, my beautiful ladies. How did you sleep?" asked Demetri after seeing their bright smiles.

"Just great, thanks to last night's wine," Kari replied.

Demetri kissed Kari Euro-style and then kissed Kristen Euro-style, and finished with a light kiss, American-style. Kristen thought that it was the perfect way to begin the day.

"*Pame*, the day awaits, and my car is double-parked out front," said Demetri.

Demetri had borrowed a cousin's car, which was just big enough for the three of them and all the provisions needed for their outing.

"Maybe I should have bought a new car to accommodate all your gear," Demetri teased.

"Well, you said we are going to the beach. We don't want to burn, so we need extra stuff. And we brought towels and extra shoes and a change of clothes."

"As I said, a new car may be in order. Perhaps a tank," Demetri continued to tease.

Kristen liked that Demetri felt comfortable enough to kid around with them.

"So where are we going?" she asked as Kari climbed into the back seat of the car and she rode shotgun.

"I will take you out to the beaches of Voulagmeni and Varkiza. They are very nice. We will swim, have some lunch, swim some more, and then later we will drive to Cape Sunion."

"It sounds great. Isn't Cape Sunion famous?" asked Kristen.

"Oh yes, it is the place where the Temple of Poseidon is located. It was built to appease the famous sea god after the goddess Athena was chosen as the patron of Athens," lectured Demetri. "Thousands of people go there every year for some of the world's most beautiful sunsets."

"Oh, how picturesque. I'll have to remember to get extra film," exclaimed Kristen. She was desperate to capture as many of the magical moments as possible, especially pictures with Demetri in them. Her camera was seldom idle as they drove to the beach.

"I believe this is also the place where Theseus's father, King Aegeus of Athens, killed himself after mistakenly believing that his son was dead," continued Demetri.

"Oh, how awful!" exclaimed Kristen.

"Yes. Well, if you study Greek mythology, you will find that there are many tragedies and conflicts in the stories," said Demetri.

"I never thought of it that way," added Kristen.

"Greece has had a history, both ancient and modern, of war, occupation, starvation, and poverty," said Demetri. "Greece went through terrible times during the German occupation in World War II and then during the time of the Communist invasion. My family and I barely survived those times."

"It's nearly impossible to believe, seeing you today," Kristen replied.

"Oh yes, we are all a result of our childhood. With the help of my parents, I was able to go to America and get a good education. That is the only reason I look as successful as I do today. They made great sacrifices for me, and I have had to make compromises in my life to achieve my goals."

"I would like to hear all about your life," Kristen said with conviction.

"You will when the time is right. But now, let's have some fun and be together, the three of us, on this beautiful day," Demetri added.

Kari had been silently riding and listening from the back seat. She thought she heard more to Demetri's words than he was actually saying. Was there something dark in his life that he wasn't telling them? But the moment passed when a car swerved in front of theirs, cutting them off. Demetri had to slam on the brakes to avoid an accident.

"Those Greek drivers!" Demetri exclaimed.

"But you are a Greek driver," Kari pointed out from the back.

"Oh no, I am a bastardized Greek now, Half-Greek half-American. It's different. I had forgotten how crazy the drivers are here because I have been in America too long."

They continued out of central Athens to the coast, where traffic was still heavy but manageable. Kristen wanted to take Demetri's hand, but the car had standard transmission, requiring him to use that hand continuously. She brushed her hand against his whenever possible. If Demetri noticed, he did not show it.

"It has been many years since I have been out here. Things have changed," Demetri said as he observed all the new high-rise buildings along the shoreline. "This area has become very prestigious and expensive."

"It's very nice," Kristen observed. The buildings were across the road from the water and most had unobstructed views of the calm, inviting sea. "There are beaches everywhere and hardly any people!"

"It is early yet. The beaches will become very crowded by midday." Demetri added.

Demetri turned on the radio. A Mikis Theodorakis song was playing. The syncopated rhythms and the soulful lyrics appealed to Kristen immediately. The only Greek music she had heard before coming to Europe was the theme song from *Zorba the Greek*.

"Much of his music was written to protest the dictatorial government in the early 1970s," said Demetri.

"We know nothing about the politics in Greece. It is difficult enough for us to know what's going on in the United States. Conflicts in the Middle East are always on the news. I am ashamed to admit it, but I don't pay much attention to politics. I'm too busy with studying and having a good time, I guess."

"Everyone in Greece is interested in politics. Just walk by any coffee house or outdoor *taverna*, and you will hear men arguing about some local or national politician or policy. Everyone is an expert. Voting is mandatory, which is the way it should be in the United States," Demetri said. "I teach government and history in New York, remember?"

"Oh yes, of course. No wonder you are so interested in it," said Kristen. She had seen Demetri get visibly disturbed when he talked about politics. *Everyone has their pet peeves*, Kristen told herself and then settled in to listen to the music.

"Are we there yet?" called Kari from the back. They had been driving for over an hour, and she was getting stiff from being crammed in the back seat.

"Almost, Little One," answered Demetri. "It will be just a few more minutes."

"Little One. I like that," commented Kari. It made her smile to think that Demetri thought of her that way.

"This is my favorite spot," said Demetri as he pulled the car over and parked. "Last one in the water is a rotten egg."

All three had their swimsuits under their clothes. Kari and Demetri jumped out of the car and began tearing their outer clothes off as they ran toward the water. Kristen observed quietly and tenderly. She watched Demetri's physical grace and dexterity, as well as his childlike playfulness, with wonder.

His skin was dark-brown and tanned. His chest was hairless, with the musculature of a soccer player. His abdomen was flat, his legs lean and strong, and his long, thick, dark-brown hair flowed out behind him as he ran and dove into the sea without the slightest hesitation. She watched him with awe as he swam with full, strong strokes through the calm water. Only after he had swum one hundred yards did he look back to see what the others were doing.

"*Ella*, Kristen. Come here. The water is beautiful and waiting for you," Demetri called. "As am I," he added.

Kristen was pulled out of her trance by his words. She had to shake her head to clear the thoughts that were swimming in her mind. She removed her shirt and shorts and ran into the water, which was just cool enough to refresh her already sweating body.

Demetri had also been watching Kristen as she shed her clothes and gingerly made her way across the already hot sand into the water. Her hair was light-blonde and reflected the sun. Her skin had not yet been touched by the sun and was pale. He admired her firm thighs and perfect, statuesque figure. This was no girl, but a woman ripe as a sweet, succulent peach. Her unassuming and natural beauty tugged at his heart and his loins. He smiled and thought that it was good that the water was so deep. He did not want his excitement to be revealed.

Kristen swam out to Demetri without effort. The calm, warm seawater felt like heaven to her. She had never been in water like this. It felt as if it was a part of her, not something separate. She dived down and swam under the water until her lungs could take no more. She broke the surface, gulped the clear, clean air and thanked heaven for such a glorious experience. She swam back to Demetri underwater and surfaced directly in front of him, startling him a little.

"Kiss me, you fool," Kristen demanded.

Demetri obeyed. There was nothing friendly about this kiss. It brought out all the pent up passion that both had been feeling for the last days but were afraid to display. Their bodies seemed to become one as they brought their lips together.

Kari saw them and smiled indulgently. After a while, she broke it up by yelling, "Hey, you guys. Get a room! You're going to drown over there."

Her comment interrupted the moment. Demetri and Kristen swam over to Kari and dunked her head under the water and splashed her. They were not angry. They were relieved. They had been trying to keep their cool, and their embrace had been a little more intimate than either of them had expected. Kari had intervened at exactly the right moment.

They spent the next two hours swimming and sunbathing. Demetri had brought a sleeping bag that he spread out on the beach and that the three of them shared. Demetri and Kristen touched discreetly whenever possible. The sensation of his hand in hers or on her bare skin thrilled Kristen. She especially liked it when Demetri volunteered to spread suntan lotion over her back and shoulders. His hands were strong and yet gentle. It was an irresistible combination.

Kari seemed to be perfectly at ease with Demetri and Kristen. They talked, laughed, swam and relaxed together without any self-consciousness or hesitation.

"Let's go to the *taverna* across the road and have some lunch," Demetri finally suggested.

"Great," said Kari and Kristen simultaneously. They put on their shirts before walking across to a table at the edge of the open-air restaurant, just under the awning, which kept the sun off their overheated bodies. There was a gentle breeze that cooled them and felt wonderful. Kristen noticed that all her senses were heightened in Greece. Was it the country or Demetri's nearness? Everything in life seemed larger and brighter now. She did not ponder the reason but relished the sensation.

Kristen loved eating outside. Except for the occasional picnic, she seldom ate al fresco. The tradition of dining in the fresh air had never caught on in the States, and Kristen did not understand why. It was truly an enjoyable experience.

"What would you like?" asked Demetri.

"Let's try something different. How about seafood? Why don't you order for us?

You did a great job last night, so I think we can trust you," answered Kristen. "Is that okay with you, Kari?"

"Sure, we can always eat bread, if nothing else. Let's be adventurous," Kari replied.

Demetri ordered lunch. Within minutes a carafe of rose wine appeared at the table with six small glasses and a large bottle of mineral water. Everyone was very thirsty after their morning in the sun and sea, and they drank the water immediately. The wine was a local dry variety. Kari and Kristen liked it better than the retsina they had tried the previous night, and they sipped it with delight.

Kristen was anxious to talk with Demetri about the plans that she and Kari had discussed, but she waited until the food was served. She was nervous about what he might say. Perhaps it would come across as too assertive or aggressive. But, on the other hand, she thought that Demetri would enjoy spending more time with them. Their time had been too short, and they had not had a chance to get to know each other as well as she had hoped.

The meal was served. There was the requisite Greek salad, filled with plump, juicy red tomatoes, cucumbers, onions, black Kalamata olives, and a thick slice of feta cheese. There were also plates of stuffed grape leaves, grilled meatballs, fried potatoes, and a plate of something that looked like fried onion rings.

Kari pointed to the plate with the "onion rings." "What's that?" she inquired.

"That is calamari. Try it. It is delicious," replied Demetri.

Both Kari and Kristen wrinkled their noses at the idea, but they obeyed Demetri's instructions and carefully tried one piece each.

"It's very interesting," said Kristen politely.

"Yuk. It tastes like fried rubber!" exclaimed Kari. She was being honest.

"You at least tried it. I commend you for that. I am afraid it is an acquired taste, and you obviously have not acquired it yet," said Demetri.

"No kidding. It's really gross," said Kari as she made another face, indicating her dislike of the squid.

They continued their lunch with more success when they tried the other dishes, which they thought were delicious.

It was time for Kristen to tell Demetri of their plans to stay longer in Greece. She suddenly felt extremely nervous about what Demetri's reaction might be. Her heart pounded, her palms were suddenly moist, and she began to shake with anxiety before she took a deep breath and began. Kari noticed this and realized that Kristen was about to suggest their idea. She believed that Kristen and Demetri should be alone, so she excused herself and walked across the road and made herself comfortable on the sleeping bag. She was dying to hear the conversation but knew Kristen would tell her everything when the right time came; she always did. They had no secrets from each other.

"Demetri, Kari and I have been talking. We thought we'd leave the tour for a few days and stay in Athens. We would then either fly or take the train to Austria and catch up with the tour there. That would give us more time to spend and get to know each other better." She held her breath when she saw the frown on his face. "What do you think?"

Demetri looked Kristen straight in the eye and said, "I don't think it's a very good idea."

Kristen was devastated when she heard Demetri say those words. Her romantic image of the two of them spending time together evaporated in an instant. She could not understand why he felt that way. Had she read the signs incorrectly? Was this just a casual matter to Demetri? She would have sworn that his feelings were genuine, but from his reaction she was suddenly unsure. She could not keep her hurt from showing on her face.

Demetri saw the expression and quickly assured her, saying, "I am sorry. I am too blunt sometimes. That is one of my faults. People misunderstand my meanings because my words come out of my mouth too quickly."

He took Kristen's hands in his. She tried to pull them away, but he held them fast and looked her deeply in the eyes. "Let me explain. It would be very nice for you to stay in Athens if I was going to be here. I haven't told you, but I have been called back to Italy. My car is ready to be picked up. I leave to go back to Brindisi tomorrow," Demetri explained.

"Oh, I had no idea," she said in a disappointed voice. "I guess we hadn't talked about anything beyond today. I just thought it would be a good idea." Kristen tried to be reasonable, but on the inside she was so disappointed that she wanted to cry. Against her efforts to the contrary, her eyes misted up. Kristen had never had a poker face. What she felt showed on her face. She could not help it.

Demetri saw her tears and understood. He pulled her to him and said, "I have made you sad. I am sorry. I had no idea." He had never had anyone care for him this way. How could he let this beautiful, sensitive woman slip from his life simply because of technicalities?

He had always admired spontaneity in others because he liked it in himself. Kristen had shown her affection for him by being willing to change her plans for him. Why should he be any different? An idea came to him. Without hesitating, he turned to Kristen and asked, "Would you come to Italy with me? I could drive you up to Rome, where you could catch a train to Austria and meet your tour group there."

Upon hearing his words, her tears changed to laughter. This would be a wonderful adventure and would give her and Demetri a chance to discover what they really meant to each other. She would not leave Kari alone, however. Having Kari along would not bother her, and she hoped that Demetri would feel the same way. She loved her sister and knew she would have a good time on the trip too.

Before giving Demetri an answer, Kristen excused herself to go and talk with Kari.

"He's asked if I would go to Italy with him," said Kristen to Kari. "I won't go without you, because I know how much you would hate to be on the tour alone. I would not do that to you. I want to go so much. Will you go too?"

To Kristen's surprise, Kari immediately said, "Yes, I'll go, and thank you for thinking about me." It was not like Kari to be so adventurous. She had always been the painfully shy, quiet one of the family who followed the rules without question.

Kristen's eyes welled up with tears again—this time with happiness. Demetri and she would have some time to get to know each other and to find out whether this was just a summer fling or something real.

She returned to where Demetri was sitting and finishing off the last of the wine. "I talked things over with Kari, and if it's okay with you, I would like to take her along with us."

"You mean you will go with me?" asked Demetri with more than a little amazement in his voice.

"Of course I will. Just don't tell my parents. They would have a fit if they found out," said Kristen, thinking of the consequences if somehow they found out about her trip. The thought of having not one, but two daughters, driving around Italy with a near total stranger would have put them over the edge of concern into panic. Kristen tried not to think about it. She was an adult now and could make her own decisions, good or bad. Besides, what they did not know would not hurt them. They were thousands of miles away and had been out of touch for over three weeks. She naturally trusted that Demetri would care for them as he would for relatives, with respect and consideration.

"You are crazy!" he exclaimed. "You are totally crazy. *I* know I am trustworthy, but how can *you* know?"

"Oh, I know," said Kristen as she took his hand and squeezed it. "I know."

"Well, in that case we'd better get back to Athens and make the necessary arrangements," suggested Demetri. "Cape Sunion will have to wait until next time."

Kristen thought to herself, *So he's thinking there will be a next time.*

"Well, I guess we'd better!" said Kristen, laughing at the look of utter incredulity on Demetri's face.

"*Ella*, Kari," called Kristen. "Bring the sleeping bag. We have to get packed. We're going back to Italy."

Demetri was surprised but did not think that Kristen's reaction was that of a crazy American tourist, although the next day he kept telling her that he thought she was one. He had lived in America during the sixties and was not shocked easily. It was quite natural to him that she had said yes. He would have four days to be with Kristen in Italy—time that was needed to know her better, even though he felt that he knew all he needed to know about her already. Kari's joining them was no problem. He would have two beautiful women with him, and they made a nice-looking trio, as many inquisitive eyes would prove for most of their trip together.

Demetri's smile was broad and spontaneous. He stood holding his arms wide to encircle both of his "two best girls." Kari knew then that Demetri would become an important part of her life too. Her sister was falling in love with this man. So was she, but as a sister.

They drove to a travel agency where they bought tickets for the next day's ship back to Brindisi. They were all excited at the prospect of being away from the pressures of the outside world. They made their way back to the hotel, where Kristen and Kari packed a small bag each and arranged for their suitcases to be taken on the bus until they were able to meet the tour in Austria.

Demetri had arrangements to make too and would need the rest of the day to prepare.

"I will pick you up tomorrow at 7:30 AM," he said simply. He dropped Kristen and Kari off at the hotel, but not before giving Kristen a good, old-fashioned passionate kiss to keep her warm for the night.

With light hearts and secretive smiles, Kristen and Kari joined the tour group for an evening of dinner, wine, and music at a restaurant in Plaka. The glow of the Acropolis above them seemed dim compared to the glow in their hearts.

Chapter 10

The next day began early for Kristen and Kari. Their excitement over the impending adventure had kept them from sleeping soundly. Any fatigue they felt was overcome by the adrenaline their bodies were producing in anticipation of the adventure ahead of them.

"Okay, do we have everything we need? Passports, tickets, money?" asked Kristen.

"How about some mace, just in case Demetri turns out to be a serial rapist?" added Kari. Both laughed. Although Kari had liked Demetri once she got to know him, she could not completely shake off her first impression of him. The thought was quickly dismissed.

"I'm so nervous!" exclaimed Kristen.

"You should be. So have you decided if you're going to have sex with him?"

"Kari! How can you ask me that?" cried Kristen with an expression of artificial shock. "Actually, I told Demetri I wouldn't, in order to give him a chance to back out of his offer in case he was expecting 'favors.' He said that no matter what, he wanted to spend time with me, sex or no sex. How about that!"

"And you believed him? Gee, I thought I was the naive one," exclaimed Kari.

"Okay, okay, let's get going before we're late," Kristen said, changing the subject. She had thought about the sex issue. Demetri was extremely attractive and seemingly wonderful, but she wasn't sure she was ready to jump into bed with him. His kisses were incredible, as she imagined sex with Demetri would be, but she wasn't in the habit of having promiscuous relations. They were both physically and emotionally dangerous.

Just as they were entering the lobby, Demetri appeared through the front door.

"Perfect timing!" observed Kari.

"*Kalimerasas* to you both," Demetri greeted them, taking them into an embrace, one in each arm. Kari got a Euro kiss. Kristen got a light kiss on the lips. "Are you ready? Where is your luggage?"

"It's here," said Kristen, pointing to two small bags.

"Is that all? That is very good, because the car I am picking up in Bari is very small," said Demetri.

Kari and Kristen hadn't bothered to ask about the car. "What kind is it?" asked Kari.

"It's a Alfa Romeo Spider," answered Demetri. Neither Kari nor Kristen knew what that was. "It's a convertible sports car," explained Demetri.

"Like a Mustang?" asked Kristen.

"Not really," said Demetri, but his thoughts were interrupted and he did not explain further. "*Pame*, we must be on time!"

It turned out that they had plenty of time and hadn't needed to rush. The bus to Patras was almost an hour late, and they had time to get coffee.

"*Tria cafe para kalo*," Demetri said to the waiter.

When the coffee arrived, Kristen and Kari were surprised at the tiny cups that had been placed in front of them, along with a glass of plain water. They had become used to big mugs at home. "Oh well," they thought, and, without hesitation, tipped the cups up to drain the contents.

Both girls ended up with coffee grounds as well as looks of disgust on their faces.

"This is so gross!" exclaimed Kari. "Why do they leave the grounds in the drink? And yuck, it's so strong!"

Demetri laughed so hard that tears rolled down his face, and his sides hurt. It took a few moments for him to compose himself. He had forgotten how amusing it was to see tourists adjusting to the Greek way of life.

Kari and Kristen had seen Demetri's reaction and had laughed along with him while they cleaned off their faces. There was no need to take things too seriously.

"Okay, what's the scoop?" asked Kristen.

"This is like Turkish coffee. You are not supposed to gulp it. You should sip it. And you only drink the liquid, not the grounds. It is very good when you drink it properly," replied Demetri.

"Okay, if you say so," said Kari, unconvinced. "Will you excuse me? I have to go to the bathroom. Do you know where it is?"

"No, but if you ask for directions, ask for the toilet and not the bathroom," Demetri advised.

The word *toilet* sounded a bit crass to Kari, but she decided it would be best. It wasn't more than a minute later that Kari arrived with a look of total disgust on her face. "Someone stole the toilet!" she exclaimed. "And it stank."

Demetri felt the laughter build up in him despite his attempt to control himself. "No, Little One, that is the way public toilets are in Greece. There are two footprints where you stand and the hole in the ground is where you 'go.' You will notice a chain hanging from the ceiling. When you are done, pull the chain, but be careful not to get your shoes wet."

"Are you kidding? I'm not going anywhere near there again!" declared Kari.

"It will be a long trip to Patras, and there is no facility on the bus," explained Demetri patiently, as if talking to a small child.

"Come on, Kari, I'll go with you," said Kristen. "We'll be right back."

"Well, that was quite an experience!" declared Kristen when they returned to the table. "One I hope I won't have to repeat often. I'm trying to keep an open mind, but I agree with Kari. That was gross."

"Yes, we men have certain advantages," Demetri commented and said nothing more.

"Well, all I know is that I am not drinking any more water until we get on the boat, so I don't have to go again!" said Kari. Everyone agreed that she had a very good idea.

The bus arrived, and they boarded, Kari in front of the seat that Demetri and Kristen shared. They sat on the right-hand side so Demetri could point out his village as they rode by it. Kristen wished that they could stop there so she could see it firsthand, but she knew that would have to wait until another time. They had a boat to catch.

The coach was rustic and not much better than a school bus without air conditioning. It was still early morning, so the heat had not become oppressive with the windows open. Kristen looked around and noticed that the other passengers appeared to use the bus not only as transportation but as their only means of shipping. Many people were carrying large, wrapped boxes and bicycle tires, and one woman was tightly clinging to a thrashing chicken. *Interesting*, Kristen thought.

She spent her time staring at two things—the scenery and Demetri's face. Her expression would change when she looked at him. He noticed the change in her color and expression and knew that she was falling in love with him. He did not mind, because he was feeling a similar emotion, although he hid it better. *I need to be careful*, he thought to himself. *She is too precious to hurt in any way. I have a responsibility for both Kristen and Kari.*

The bus trip to Patras passed over the Corinth Canal. Demetri, always the teacher, explained a bit about its purpose and the feat of its construction. He also pointed out the place he was born and where he had spent the first years of his life. Kristen was awed by the barren beauty she saw around her. She was especially interested, since she was seeing Demetri's birthplace. It helped her to understand him just a tiny bit more.

The bus stopped for a short break halfway through the journey. "Let's get out for a minute and stretch," Demetri suggested. "I want you to try something I think you will like." Demetri purchased some souvlaki for each of them, similar to American shish kebob made of lamb. Kristen and Kari had never tasted anything like it and decided it was surprisingly delicious.

"Now this is more like it!" exclaimed Kari as she took her second bite.

After reboarding the bus and once again getting under way, Kristen felt sleepy. She tried to stay awake but could not and used Demetri's shoulder for a pillow. Demetri watched her sleep and thought she looked like an angel. He felt her closeness, the comfort of having her near him, and knew that saying good-bye to her, when the time came, would be one of the most difficult things he would ever have to do. But for now, he would enjoy the moment. He let himself slip into unconsciousness.

They awakened as the bus slowed and turned into the Patras terminal.

"Okay, sleepyheads, up and at 'em," said Kari cheerfully. She had secretly snapped a picture of them sleeping on the bus and was sure she could use the photo as blackmail for years to come. Kristen had not realized she had been asleep so long. She pulled out a small mirror to check to see whether she had been drooling, which she hadn't. *Good*, she thought.

They walked the short distance to the ship and presented their tickets and passports. A border guard stopped Demetri, inquiring whether he had served in the Greek army.

"No," replied Demetri, who showed his anger and frustration with the man, but was able to give a good explanation without totally losing his temper. The guard let him pass.

"What was that all about?" inquired Kristen.

"All Greek males must serve in the army for one year. I told him I am an American citizen, but he said I was also Greek and would not be able to leave the country."

"How did you get him to change his mind?"

"I told him I was escorting two beautiful American girls to Italy and would be returning to Greece in less than a week. When he saw you and Kari, he must have figured I was telling the truth and let me go."

The explanation seemed pretty lame, but Kristen accepted it without question. It had been the first time she had seen an angry Demetri. She wasn't bothered by his anger as much as the possibility of their adventure being ruined by his detention. She was greatly relieved knowing that they all had been permitted to board the ship.

"Isn't this the same ship we came over on?" asked Kari.

"Yes, I think so," said Kristen. Demetri had booked a single cabin, and the two girls had deck tickets, figuring they would share the cabin among the three of them.

"Oh my goodness! I thought our accommodations were bad on the way over. This cabin is so tiny you would have to go outside of it to change your mind!" Kari exclaimed. "And I think it's about 120 degrees in here. I don't know how anyone can be expected to sleep in this sauna."

Kristen was a little annoyed with her sister. "Well, it's a good thing we only have tickets that allow us to sleep out on deck, then, isn't it?"

Kari got the message and quit complaining.

They took no time at all to stow their gear and head up to the deck to see the ship launch. Demetri loved the sea. He had spent most of his youth around boats and never seemed to tire of it. Even in New York he had a small boat that he used nearly every weekend.

Kari went in search of a place to take a nap. She was tired from the trip and the lack of sleep caused by anticipation of their early departure. She ended up choosing the cabin in spite of its stifling heat.

Kristen enjoyed spending some time alone with Demetri.

"Alone at last," she said to him.

"Yes, what shall we talk about?" Demetri teased.

"Anything and everything," replied Kristen. "I want to know about your whole life up to this point."

Demetri laughed. "That will probably take a little longer than we have right now. I will give you a condensed version, but if you ask me a question, I will answer it."

He began his story by saying, "I was born in a very poor and tiny village in 1960. This wasn't the worst time to be born in Greece but the country was still recovering from World War II where the Germans had occupied Greece and later the communists invaded ..."

His story continued for two hours and ended with his description of his high school days in Athens and his undying determination to emigrate to the United States and get a college education.

"I had no idea," she said, flabbergasted. She had hardly said a word for over two hours. Once Demetri began telling his story, she had not wanted to interrupt. "Your parents, especially your mother, were very brave and clever to survive and to bring up such a fine son."

"I love them very much," he said. Kristen felt even closer to Demetri for his candor. An American man would not have openly admitted so close a connection to his parents. She also began to realize that there were depths to Demetri that she had not suspected. He had lived through poverty and war and had overcome both to become a success. She admired him all the more for it. Was love far behind?

Kari appeared seemingly out of nowhere. "Hi, what's going on?"

"I am a bit tired from the trip. Would you mind if I take a nap in the cabin?" Demetri asked Kristen.

"Of course not! If you tell me how long you want to sleep, I'll wake you up at that time," said Kristen.

"About two hours should be enough."

"Okay, then. I'll be looking forward to seeing you in two hours," replied Kristen as Demetri kissed her gently and disappeared from the deck.

Kari saw the expression of rapture on Kristen's face. "Okay, what's been going on?" she demanded.

"We spent the last couple of hours talking about Demetri's early life. You just would not believe what he and his parents went through!"

"So tell me all about it," Kari prompted, and Kristen gave her an even more abridged version.

"Amazing," said Kari when the story was finished. "I knew there was something different about him. I just did not know what. He certainly had a different childhood than we did!"

"No kidding! Instead of thinking less of him for his poverty, I admire him for overcoming it," said Kristen. "Not many people would have been dedicated and stubborn enough to do what he did."

"You're right about that," Kari added, with new respect for Demetri.

"Will you be okay by yourself for a while? I want to go spend some time with him alone," inquired Kristen.

"Sure, I can't get very lost on the ship. Besides, I can always scream if I get into trouble, and someone will come to my rescue," she laughed. "Go, but be good. And if you can't be good, be careful!" She smiled knowingly.

Kristen smiled back but said nothing. She was being drawn to Demetri. *What will happen next?* she asked herself as she walked down the stairs in the direction of the cabin.

Chapter 11

*K*risten was being pulled to Demetri as if he was calling her. Her desire was mounting as she approached the cabin. She felt more excited than she remembered ever being—and a bit nervous when she anticipated what might occur. She had had boyfriends in high school and college, but no relationship had touched her as this had. She was ready to take things to the next level.

As she silently opened the cabin door, she knew that Demetri would be overheated from having been in the stifling cabin. She took a clean towel to the lavatory, soaked it with cool water, and wrung it out. She then slipped silently into the cabin, not wanting to wake Demetri. She paused a moment, knowing that this would be the first time they were totally alone. He was sleeping on top of the sheet, clothed only in a pair of blue boxer shorts. His skin glistened with perspiration, and his face was peaceful with sleep. Kristen could barely control her emotions. He was so beautiful. He reminded her of a Michelangelo statue she had seen in Florence. His body was perfect, and she loved his soul. She knew she wanted him in a way that she had never before wanted anyone or probably ever would in the future. Demetri was destined to be the love of her life.

She gently placed the cool cloth on his forehead. He stirred and then opened his eyes in response to her touch. His pleasure was apparent when his eyes focused on Kristen's. Her eyes showed love, lust and trust all rolled into one. Who could resist that?

He beckoned her with his arms outstretched, and she joined him on the tiny berth. The cabin was sweltering, but neither noticed. It was too hot for clothes. Kristen removed her shirt and bra before sliding onto him. The feeling of her bare breasts on his chest excited her as nothing ever had. She wanted to be one with this miraculous man.

Demetri lay still while Kristen moved her body up his, caressing his abdomen and chest with her bare breasts. As she moved toward his face, Demetri rose to meet her. Their lips touched, and then their tongues slowly explored every inch of each other's mouths. Demetri took Kristen's lower lip into his and nipped it gently. She was surprised with delight at how her body responded.

Kristen's pleasure was immeasurable. She could not get enough as she kissed him over and over. Demetri flipped Kristen onto her back, gently pinning her shoulders to the thin mattress. He kissed her face, her neck, and her breasts as Kristen's hips rose to bring her body closer to his.

Kristen breathed in Demetri's scent, which was enhanced by his sweat. The scent was only him. There was no cologne or deodorant, and it was indescribably appealing to her.

Their bodies molded together and they began to lose themselves. She could no longer control herself. The moist warmth she felt in her loins needed to be satiated. She writhed with ecstasy at Demetri's touch. She wanted to make love to him at that very moment!

Suddenly she felt Demetri pull away and became confused. "What's wrong?" she whispered.

"There is nothing wrong," Demetri replied. "But this is not the time nor the place for the first time we make love. It needs to be special, something we will remember all our lives. I want you more right this second than you can ever know. This is not just a physical attraction but something so much more. Our souls are beginning to melt into each other. Perhaps it is the heat, but I doubt it. This is something deep and very real."

Kristen was moved by Demetri's words. He was strong where she was weak. This was obviously as important to him as it was to her. With great discipline on both their parts, they let their bodies cool down. They could hardly breathe, not only from the heat but also from the emotional and physical turmoil they were experiencing.

They lay quietly, without talking, languishing in their closeness, each with his or her private thoughts. Eventually the heat overcame them. They found it difficult to breathe and decided it was time to leave the cabin. They dressed each other carefully and slowly, exploring the other's body with admiration and tenderness. Hesitantly they left the cabin and went to look for Kari, whom they had forgotten. How long had it been? Where could she be? They found her on deck where Kristen had left her.

The rest of the crossing was spent in pleasant conversation, eating dinner in the miserable little onboard café, and promenading the decks. Neither Kristen nor Demetri could sit for long. They walked, hand in hand, watching the sea pass by, wondering what lay ahead. They avoided the cabin, since it was too airless to sustain any modicum of comfortable existence. They found two unoccupied deck chairs where they slept, holding hands. Kristen's dreams were full of the happiness she was feeling while conscious. What a wonderfully romantic adventure!

Chapter 12

*T*he boat docked early the next morning and Demetri, Kristen, and Kari were met at the pier and driven to the Alfa Romeo dealership where Demetri's car was waiting. After a few details were completed, Demetri introduced his new possession to the girls.

"Where's the rest of your car?" asked Kari sarcastically. "And where am I supposed to sit?" She was dismayed when she saw that the back seat didn't look big enough to hold a briefcase, much less an adult woman.

"Ah," Demetri responded. "The cars here are much smaller than you are used to back in the States. And this is what you would call a roadster. I am sorry there is not much room, but this is the best I can do."

Kari knew that she was going to have to make the best of an uncomfortable situation and gingerly climbed into the back seat and folded her legs into the tiny space as best as she could.

"Thank goodness I'm short!" she added. "And that the car's a convertible with the top down. There's no way I would fit otherwise."

Kristen slipped into the passenger seat as Demetri acquainted himself with the dashboard and instruments.

"Here we go," he added as he stepped on the clutch and put the car into first gear.

"Yahoo," cried Kari. "Italy, watch out! You may never be the same again."

Yes, yahoo indeed, Kristen thought. *Italy may always be the same, but after today I doubt I will be.*

With some effort and a few wrong turns, Demetri found the Autostrada bound for Rome. He kept the car at a very conservative speed in order to break in the engine. Everyone enjoyed the relaxed atmosphere and the scenery, regardless of the speed or lack thereof.

As they drove, a car pulled up next to the Spider. The male driver, alone in the car, called to Demetri and spoke to him in Italian for a few moments. Demetri replied in a belligerent tone of voice. The other driver raised his fist in what looked to Kristen like a very rude gesture and drove away.

"What was that all about?" asked Kristen.

"He wanted to know how I was lucky enough to have two beautiful, blonde young women with me, and would I want to share one with him," he explained. "I think you can guess what my response was."

Both Kari and Kristen were flattered and happy that they had a "knight in shining armor" to protect their virtue. *Kari's, at least*, Kristen thought to herself.

After getting tangled in the traffic of Naples, they traveled north. It was time to find a place to have dinner and stay for the night.

"Can we get off the Autostrada and see if there is a coastal route?" Kristen asked.

"*Entaxi*, okay, but I'm not sure about the road," said Demetri, and turned off the highway at the next exit.

They soon found out that, Robert Frost notwithstanding, it was a mistake to take the road less traveled. It had become very dark, without any evidence of civilization. All three were tired and hungry, and they were anxious to find a place to stop. Demetri wanted to show the two girls a great time and looked for a respectable restaurant or *taverna*. At long last they spotted something. It looked run-down, but all three travelers were so weary they decided to give it a try. At that point they were ready for a meal, no matter how bad it might be.

They were not surprised when the *taverna* was unsavory. "We wanted authentic, and it looks like we got it," said Kari. "I'm going to be more careful what I ask for from now on."

"I am sorry it is not nicer," said Demetri.

"Don't be. You wanted to stay on the main road, and I convinced you to be adventurous. It's my fault," replied Kristen. "I'm the one who should be apologizing."

"It doesn't matter. Let's get something to eat and get out of here," added Kari. "This place gives me the creeps."

"This doesn't look too bad," said Kristen hopefully as they were led to an open patio for dinner.

They all ordered shrimp scampi, thinking that it would be a safe choice because they were so close to the sea. Demetri smiled when the dinners were served, and Kristen exclaimed loudly, "Oh no, they fried the shrimp and left the head and shells on. Yuck!" Both Kristen and Kari filled up on bread and wine and ate little else.

The combination of the wine and the long day left Demetri not wanting to drive farther. He was suspicious of the men leering at Kristen and Kari. Although his instincts told him to go elsewhere, he inquired about sleeping accommodations. After a brief discussion, he informed the girls that there was one triple room available and, despite the disgusting environment, they agreed to stay.

"It's only for one night," said Kristen. "It's okay." Kari agreed. Demetri was thankful for their positive attitudes in the face of mild hardship.

They were led down a set of stairs into a large room that reminded Kari of Miss Haversham's wedding reception in the Charles Dickens novel *Great Expectations*. The room was decorated, but it appeared that the party had taken place months or years previously to their arrival. The crepe paper streamers were faded, and dust covered the tables and miscellaneous decorations.

The bedroom they were shown was large, with one twin and one king-size bed and an adjoining bath. Upon seeing the configuration, Kari threw herself onto the twin bed and exclaimed to the others, "This is where I'm sleeping. You're going to have to figure the rest out for yourselves." Kristen could have kissed her for making a very awkward situation comfortable.

The room was a nightmare and would lend itself to funny anecdotes for years to come. Kari, who always seemed to have to use the toilet, walked into the bathroom and yelled to the others, "You have got to see this!"

Kristen and Demetri joined Kari for the official tour. The "shower" was merely a pipe sticking out of the wall. The toilet had no seat and Kari was appalled when her "tinkling" could be heard in the bedroom, which was extremely embarrassing for her. Demetri just chuckled at her modesty.

Kristen and Demetri wanted some privacy. Kari assured them that she would be fine in the room by herself. After locking the door securely, they ventured out to the car, where they could be alone for a short time. They found a deserted beach, spread the sleeping bag out on the sand, and positioned themselves comfortably on it. Although the original intention was to talk, little conversation followed. They quickly became consumed with the desire that they had been suppressing. Both Demetri and Kristen found the other irresistible. It wasn't long before each of their bodies ached for the other's. Knowing that a passerby could discover them increased their desire; it gave an aura of danger to their intimacy. There was no moon, and the beach was very dark. Looking into each other's eyes with knowing expressions, they decided to take a chance.

Slowly, carefully, and very tenderly, Demetri removed Kristen's clothes. Although she knew Demetri could hardly see her, she began to move her hands to cover her nakedness. Demetri stopped her. "No, don't hide yourself. You are the most beautiful creature I have ever seen, and I want to know all of you." His fingers explored her thoroughly—first her hair, then her face and neck, and then her arms and hands. She could hardly control her excitement when he touched her breasts and hesitated momentarily on his journey. Her body rose slightly to meet his hands. He said, "No, don't move, I want to finish," before continuing on to her flat abdomen into her pubic area and down her legs to her feet. She had never experienced anything like it. It aroused her in a way that nothing ever had. This wasn't just sex; it was the beginning of lovemaking.

Taking Demetri's lead, Kristen reciprocated, gently removing his shirt and the rest of his clothes. Her hands stoked his hair, his face, his chest, his manhood, his legs and feet. He was the most perfect specimen of a man she had ever seen. She could no longer control herself. Her commitment not to have sex with this man vanished completely. She wanted him badly and wanted him immediately.

He was lying on his back. She slid up his body until hers was on his, their faces millimeters apart. She sucked on his bottom lip and then kissed his eyes and chest. Knowing that they would always remember this as the first time, they continued to restrain their passion just a while longer. They wanted this moment to last as long as possible. The wave of desire that swept over them could no longer be controlled. The kisses became stronger and more desperate. Their bodies responded by uniting in a blissful state of ecstasy.

Demetri was a passionate and considerate lover. He brought Kristen to a quick orgasm and cried out when he climaxed. The emotional, as well as the physical release, verged on pain for both. They lay joined, neither wishing to break the spell cast over them. As close as they were, they wanted to be closer, without knowing how. They wanted to be joined eternally.

Overcome with emotion, Demetri knew that this wasn't just a summer fling to be forgotten as soon as they went their separate ways. On the contrary, he believed he was falling in love with this woman, so he did something spontaneous. He reached up to the back of his neck, unfastened the chain that held the medal he had worn around his neck continuously for ten years and held it in the air. It had the likeness of the Madonna and the Christ Child on the front, and the words "I am a Greek Orthodox" on the back. This medal had great meaning to him; his mother had given it to him just before he left Greece to emigrate to America. He placed it in Kristen's palm and closed her hand around it.

When Kristen realized its significance, she was touched more deeply than she could express; the simple silver medallion was more valuable to her than diamonds could ever be. She started to put it around her neck when Demetri stopped her. "No, don't put it on. Just keep it close to you." She did not know why he hadn't wanted her to wear it; she never really would.

Suddenly, they became aware of a noise about one hundred yards away and realized it was a voice. They did not want to be discovered, so they silently and quickly dressed and tiptoed back to the car. There they kissed and caressed each other with the hood of the car as their support. Their delight with each other was immeasurable. They continued to touch each other on their short drive back to the inn, which was challenging, with the manual gearshift separating them. They laughed at themselves and knew their happiness was complete.

When they arrived back to their room, Kari was asleep and snoring quietly. They did not disturb her as they slipped under the sheets and quietly made love again. Sleep did not come easily, although they were both exhausted. They knew their time together was extremely limited and did not want sleep to deprive them of anything, unless absolutely necessary. They finally slept, with Kristen snuggled into Demetri and one leg draped over his.

Chapter 13

Demetri, Kristen and Kari awoke the next morning and could not get out of the dreadful inn fast enough for any of their likings. They drove away without having breakfast, knowing that even hunger would be an improvement over the accommodations they had endured the night before. At least they had been left alone by the leering men in the tavern. Demetri was thankful for that.

Their next goal was to find someplace nice for the next two days and nights. They came upon the little town of Terracina on the west coast of Italy between Naples and Rome, and fell in love with it immediately. It was perfect. The beach was impeccable, the water warm and clear, and the mountains surrounding the village made the perfect backdrop. They found a beautiful hotel that only had one room available. They all looked at each other and agreed to take it, since they were used to being together. Even under awful conditions, they had done very nicely the previous night.

They checked into the room, which was lovely. Again, it had one king-size bed and one twin. There was no question of the sleeping arrangements this time. The room had marble floors, a large bath, and a spectacular view of the calm sea from a private balcony.

"Now, this is more like it!" exclaimed Kari. "I could stay here forever." The others nodded their agreement. "Okay, where's the restaurant? I'm starving!"

Brunch was being served on the patio, so the three decided to have lunch and then go to the beach afterward. They dined on salad and pasta, with fruit and cheese for dessert.

"That was delicious," said Kristen. "I had no idea how hungry I was until I began eating."

"Let's go to the beach and swim for a while, then take a siesta," suggested Demetri. "None of us got much sleep last night." He looked at Kristen, who smiled back, knowing why their sleep had been shortened.

"No kidding," added Kari. "What time did you get back last night, or shouldn't I ask?"

The sea was warm and inviting. It soothed their muscles, fatigued from the long drive. Afterward, all three ended up on the big bed with Kristen in Demetri's arms and Kari close by. There was never any feeling of impropriety. Kari's presence was one of a close family member, nothing more or less.

The midday nap revived the tired travelers and they were able to do a little sightseeing around the small, popular coastal town with enthusiasm. They stopped and bought some plates with "Terracina" painted on them; they knew they were extremely touristy but loved them anyway. They made a perfect threesome, with an easily found comfort level and plenty of animated banter. Only Demetri noticed the villagers staring at the two girls who walked on each of Demetri's arms.

After dinner, Kristen and Demetri once again wanted to spend some time alone. It was good having Kari around to "chaperone." It helped to keep them balanced. When night fell, however, they felt it was their time to be together in whatever way they saw fit.

They went down to the seaside and found a remote area, away from the commercial portion of the beach. Again, the night was dark and very quiet, except for the gentle crashing of the waves in front of them. They talked for hours about their beliefs and values, their mounting feelings for each other, and plans for the upcoming two days. Knowing their time was very limited, they attempted to make every minute count.

Kristen was beginning to dread the passage of time. She knew this dream encounter would end before long, and it made her sad. She was afraid she would awake to find that none of it had been real.

Demetri had his own dreads. The realities of his life were beginning to nag at his conscience. He could see Kristen falling deeper and deeper in love with him, and he needed to be straight with her before she became too involved. It wasn't fair to involve her in his entanglements in New York without telling her about them. She had the right to know and make her own educated decisions, even if it meant that she would choose to leave. He decided to tell her the next night. But tonight he would have her in the purest form. He knew she adored him and he, her. That was enough. He would face the rest tomorrow.

They once again made perfect love. Kristen could not have been happier as they made their way back to the hotel for a well-deserved night's sleep.

The next morning they awoke to another bright sunny day. They had slept well in the clean, comfortable room and were glad that the comparison with the first night's stay was like night and day. One thing was similar, however. When the three breakfasted in the hotel's small restaurant, many eyes stared at them with disapproval. Terracina was a small beach town whose residents who were aware of everything that went on, and gossip was the main pastime. Word had spread quickly about the man sharing one room with two foreign women. Surely not his sisters, but what else could they be? Tradition and values there were still very different from the ones that Demetri, Kristen, and Kari found to be natural and acceptable in the United States.

Demetri did not wish to challenge that, nor did he want to attract more attention than they already had. He made a conscious effort to appear in public as if they were three friends who were visitors to the area enjoying the scenery and the wine. He shared his concerns with Kristen and Kari. They all agreed to keep any public display of affection to a minimum.

After a pleasant morning spent strolling through the town and having lunch, Demetri became very quiet and tense. He excused himself and went to the room, asking the girls to meet him on the beach. After an hour he joined them. His mood was dark, and he seemed upset. Kristen did not know why. She had no way of knowing the secrets he held inside him; and Demetri had no way of knowing what her reaction would be when she heard the truth. He did not want to lose her, but knew he had to be honest if they were to have any future together.

Kari knew it was time to allow them some privacy, so she went to swim and play in the waves. The water was warm and clear, and the bottom was sandy and clean. What a magnificent beach! The only thing that would have made it better for her was to have her own boyfriend with whom to share this.

"Kristen," Demetri began, "in the very short time we have known each other you have become very dear to me. I have seen the way you look at me. Do you love me?"

Kristen was startled by his direct manner. She did not know how to be coy and answered honestly, "Yes, I do, very much."

"That is good, because I love you, too." Kristen's heart nearly exploded when she heard the words. She knew that they were sincere. "I do not know how we have been able to know each other so well in such a short amount of time. It usually takes years for people to be so open and to develop these kinds of feelings."

Kristen almost replied, but she did not want to interrupt Demetri's thoughts.

"This was so unexpected and not something forgotten easily. I was not looking for a summer romance. We need to know if this is real or if it is just the sun, the sea, and the heat. I have never felt this way before. You have become my world, and I want you in it."

Kristen could see the sincerity in his face but was concerned when she also saw heaviness in his eyes and mouth. She knew Demetri was trying to tell her something but could not. Tremendous anxiety overcame her, and she suddenly felt very insecure. What could he be trying to tell her?

"What is it, Demetri? I feel that there is something terrible you want to tell me. Is it something I have done wrong?" asked Kristen in dismay. The words that Demetri had uttered not more than five minutes before were replayed in her mind. *I love you too.* She could not begin to know what could be wrong at a time when two people had expressed the love they felt for each other for the first time.

Demetri became so upset, he could not continue. "Kristen, please, will you join Kari for a while? It is not you. You are wonderful. You have become the center of my universe. Please believe that. It is just that there are things I haven't told you. I am afraid they may change everything between us."

Kristen was on the brink of panic. She instinctively understood that when Demetri asked to be alone, he meant it. He had told her that he had been a loner most of his life, even when he was among groups of friends or relatives. He needed to be by himself in times of suffering. He was suffering. Kristen could see it on his face.

What could be so terrible that would make him this upset? Kristen wondered. *Is he married with six children? Does he have a terminal illness and only have a few months to live?* Kristen could not think of anything else that would affect someone so drastically.

She quietly left him, but not without first caressing his shoulder and back. She also kissed him softly on the cheek, hoping to soothe whatever was bothering him so badly.

She joined Kari, and after waiting what seemed like an eternity for Demetri to join them, Kristen and Kari began playing the childhood game they remembered. They tried having a "tea party" where each sank to the sandy bottom, where she sat with her legs crossed and mimed drinking out of a teacup. Their game wasn't very successful, because the water was very salty, and they floated to the surface in spite of their efforts. The girls smiled and laughed, although Kristen's heart was pounding.

Eventually, Kristen allowed herself to be washed up onto the sand by the waves. Kari went to Demetri and asked, "Can we keep her?" hoping to lighten the mood. She was as confused as Kristen about what was happening.

Demetri wasn't amused. "Please Kari, give me more time. Don't worry, everything will be all right," he said, but Kari wasn't convinced. She could see that Demetri needed time to control his raging emotions.

To try to control her increasing feelings of frustration and dread, Kristen went back into the water for a while. She swam vigorously, and the exertion helped to release some of the tension she was feeling, but not all of it.

She then got out of the water, and began a long, slow walk down the beach away from Demetri. She had gone nearly five hundred yards before looking behind her, only to find Demetri forty yards away. She turned and continued her walk away from him as he tried to catch up with her. She turned once more, saw him, and ran into his arms. He held her tightly for nearly five minutes before releasing her.

Kristen looked into his face and saw that his eyes were more bloodshot than usual. "I haven't cried for ten years, and that was from the pain of my appendix bursting. But today, I have cried twice. The pain today is just as real, but emotional, not physical."

Kristen was now beyond panic. Her heart was pounding so that she could feel it in her throat. Words did not come easily, but she was able to squeak out, "Whatever you say can't be as bad as what is in my head right now. Not knowing what is causing you this pain is worse than anything you could tell me."

Demetri was in turmoil. He knew he had to be frank with her. It wasn't fair to her to put her through this uncertainty.

"I just can't right now. Let us try to enjoy the afternoon together. We will talk tonight."

Kristen bowed to Demetri's wish. She took his hand in hers and refused to let go, despite the villagers' curious stares. She wanted him to know that whatever it was he had to tell her, things would be all right. The only thing he could tell her that would break her heart would be that he did not really love her and that he had only been playing with her. She knew that wasn't what Demetri was worried about. She tried to put it out of her mind, since there was nothing she could do.

They walked back to the hotel. Kristen was covered in salt and wished to bathe. Kari was tired and wanted to nap. Demetri wanted the tension to be over.

Although Kristen preferred a shower, there was none, so a bath would have to suffice. Demetri joined Kristen as she was about to undress. He asked if he should stay or leave. She wanted him to stay. He very slowly and carefully undressed her, marveling at her body, the body he had come to know and love.

The marble tub was large, claw-footed, and deep. The water was cold. Demetri saw the goose bumps on Kristen's skin and smiled. He added more hot water to make the temperature comfortable. He surprised her when he asked whether he could wash her hair. She agreed.

Demetri knelt, poured the shampoo into the palm of his hand, and gently spread it over Kristen's hair. The strokes were firm but gentle and oh, so erotic. She marveled at how this aroused and delighted her. She felt a bit guilty because he was doing all the work. He continued to clean her hair with deliberately slow massages. She closed her eyes and wished the sensation would last forever.

As he was rinsing her hair, she could control herself no longer. Although he was fully dressed, she reached for him with arms outstretched. He moved into her arms, and their kiss was wet and warm.

It wasn't long until Demetri was in the bath with her. Their soapy bodies slid over each other, giving them a new sensation of closeness. Neither was self-conscious; they both knew that they were mesmerized by the beauty of the other's body. Neither had ever felt so natural with another person, clothed or unclothed. They lingered in the joy of discovering each other over and over again. Although it was daylight, there was no hiding, no covering. They loved each other completely.

They made passionate love in the bath and then on the cool, hard marble floor. They simply could not get enough of each other. The physical need was heightened by knowing that the dark cloud of separation was looming over them.

With towels wrapped around them, they crept into the room and slipped under the sheets naked. Kari was asleep, and they wanted to be sure not to disturb her in any way. They slept for three hours, comfortable and very close.

They all awoke at eight and wanted to walk in the sand, but the restaurant was about to close, so they dined first.

After a very pleasant dinner, they all went to the beach. Spirits were high, and all three romped like children. Kari ran ahead of the others and wrote phrases like "true love" and "Demetri loves Kristen" in the sand for them to find. Demetri and Kari had a broad jumping contest, which nobody won. Demetri ran down the beach and karate chopped the umbrella poles with his feet. Everyone laughed with delight.

Demetri could not bring himself to end this magic. He had one more day to explain himself. He would do it tomorrow.

The three spent the evening together on the beach, until the sun set, and it became dark. They then went to the bar and had a drink before returning to their room.

"Tomorrow is tomorrow. We have all day. Let's not talk about anything tonight except good things," Demetri whispered to Kristen. "Know that I love you and always will, no matter what. That is my promise to you, and I always keep my promises—always!"

Kristen forced herself not to think about anything except how she loved this man. She would not think about tomorrow or next week or next year. Tonight was all that mattered. *I am with the man I will love all my life. That is what matters*, she told herself.

The next morning, they decided to spend their last full day together in Terracina. They could have driven to Rome but did not want the hassle of dealing with the busy, crowded city when they could enjoy the slow, easy pace of the beach resort. They weren't bored; they wanted the magic to last as long as possible.

The day passed easily, with the three spending most of it together. Although Kristen could see Demetri's face cloud over occasionally, he did not display the anguish he had shown the previous day. She ignored it, wishing it to go away. Of course she knew it would not. She dreaded the coming of night, knowing that whatever it was Demetri had to tell her would have to be said then.

Finally, after dinner, Demetri could procrastinate no longer. Kristen's heart was pounding. Her skin seemed to crawl with anxiety. They left Kari in the room, and found a secluded spot on the dark beach where they could talk. And talk they did.

Demetri began by saying, "Let me tell you first what I feel for you. I believe with all my heart that I love you, and that I am destined to love you always. We need to be apart for a while, to know if this love is real or a fantasy. I believe it is real. I have never felt this way before."

"What I am about to tell you I have never told anybody—not my parents, nobody. I need you to promise that you will not tell anybody, even Kari, what I tell you."

"I promise," she said, puzzled. She had no way of knowing that he considered a promise sacred and something that must never be broken.

"Before I can explain what has been bothering me so much, you need to know about my life after high school," Demetri began.

Kristen had wanted to know everything about Demetri's life. "I want to hear everything, no matter how long it takes."

"Where should I begin?" Demetri thought a minute, took a deep cleansing breath, and then began a long and detailed history of his early life. Kristen listened intently without comment as Demetri told his story of growing up poor, his ambitions of obtaining a better life in the United States, working for his cousins and becoming more and more deeply involved with their illegal operations until a time came when he could no longer agree to their demands because of his strict moral code, the struggle to free himself, and his concern for his loved ones, now including her.

She was both mesmerized and shocked by Demetri's story. "What did they ask you to do?" she asked.

"Details of that time are not important. You would not know me better to hear the particulars, because that wasn't me. I wanted out, but they were not people to take no for an answer. It has taken me many years to distance myself from them, but they still hound me," he answered. "I am afraid what they might do if they find out about you," he continued. "When I am alone what can they do to me? Hurt me, kill me? What good would that do them? But when there is a third party involved, someone I love and want no harm to come to, they have leverage and would not be afraid to use it. I don't care what they do to me; it doesn't matter. But if they did anything to you, I could not bear it.

"I haven't lied to you. You deserve the truth. Nobody else—not my mother, not anyone—knows about this. To them, I am a devoted son, teacher, and an average American who works hard to be the best person I can be. That is what I truly am. Can you see that? Do you understand now why I have been so moody and preoccupied?"

Kristen was stunned. She had expected something terrible, but not anything like this! She sat there, unmoving. She could not breathe. How could this be true? She knew she hadn't been wrong about this man.

Suddenly, Kristen could not deal with it any longer. Great sobs rose from deep inside of her and poured out without restraint. The night was still, except for the sound of her life crashing in around her. Demetri watched but did not touch. His heart was breaking, knowing that he had brought such pain to the woman he was now sure he loved.

Then Kristen did something that so totally surprised Demetri, he would never forget it. She stopped crying, looked deeply into his tear-filled eyes, and told him she loved him so much that it did not matter, that they would somehow find a way to make things right. As foolish as it might have seemed to an outsider, and perhaps to her too, she would do whatever it took to stay with him. She would have gladly taken a bullet for him that night, if it could have stopped his pain.

They clung to each other, while Kristen allowed all that Demetri had told her to sink in. She felt safe in his embrace, knowing that he would not let any harm come to her. Slowly, she relaxed into his arms. Demetri felt the change in Kristen, and began stroking her soft, luxuriant hair. Kristen responded by raising her lips to his, kissing him gently. Lust surged through Demetri's body. He took Kristen's face in his hands and kissed her eyes, her cheeks, her forehead, her ears and then, with slight hesitation, her full, longing lips. This was too much for Kristen to resist. She found Demetri's lower lip and sucked on it until his tongue found hers. Passion overtook each of them. Their lovemaking was hungry, uninhibited and rough. Neither Demetri nor Kristen minded; they wanted to enter each other's souls as well as bodies without thought of comfort or pain. They could not contain their cries as they reached simultaneous orgasms. Afterward, they did not move for several minutes as their conscious awareness of their environment returned.

"Whew, what was that!" whispered Kristen to Demetri after awhile.

"Heaven and Hell mixed together," Demetri replied. "The Hell I have just put us both through was cleansed by the Heaven we just experienced."

"Amen to that," Kristen exclaimed, and they both laughed at her comment, made without thought, which helped to release the tension of the previous hours.

Suddenly Demetri tensed. He had heard something about fifty feet from where they were on the beach. His street sense kicked into high gear. He had developed a keen awareness of when danger was close, and he felt it now. Someone was out there in the dark with the intention of harming them. Could it be one of the villagers who had merely stumbled upon them, or someone who planned to rob them, or the worst possible thing: a cousin who had followed them throughout their trip who intended to do bodily harm to one or both of them? He whispered quietly, but very firmly, for Kristen get to dressed as quickly as possible, get up without making any noise, and run to the car as fast as she could. Although terrified, Kristen was able to do as Demetri had instructed. After taking a quick look around him and seeing no one, Demetri followed her to the car. They made it back to the hotel without any incident, but she was badly shaken.

"Who or what was that?" Kristen asked shakily.

"I do not know. All I know is that whoever it was, he wasn't there by accident. We were lucky to get away so easily. Are you okay?" Demetri asked, searching her eyes deeply.

"Yes, although I haven't felt so much adrenaline ever before, or want to ever again," she said bravely.

"I promise that I will not let any harm come to you; and, as I have said, I always keep my promises. That is sacred to me."

"Yes, you told me," replied Kristen as she nuzzled into Demetri's arms.

Sleep did not come easily to either Kristen or Demetri. They clung to each other, knowing that their lives had changed forever—and also knowing that this would be their last night together for an indeterminate period of time. Despite their efforts to stay awake, they eventually fell into an exhausted sleep, comfortably entwined together.

Chapter 14

"What are we going to do?" Kristen asked Demetri. She was distraught at the thought of having to leave him at Brindisi. "We only have a few more hours."

"This separation is nothing," said Demetri, trying to be positive. "You need to finish your tour; I need to go back to Greece and make arrangements."

"Couldn't I go with you?"

"No, we need to do what we need to do. It won't harm us; it will be good. It will give you a chance to let your head think instead of your heart," Demetri said firmly.

"I don't need my head to think. I know what I want. It is you, forever," Kristen cried.

"I feel the same way, but we must be sure. Do you know I love you? I will always love you, no matter what. I promised you that," he said soothingly, almost as if he were speaking to a child.

Kristen could say nothing else. The ecstasy of his words and the grief of parting later in the day overwhelmed her. She knew it had to be. Their time together was limited, at least now.

"I will write to you," said Demetri. "I have the addresses for your tour. You will hear from me."

"How will I write back?" asked Kristen.

"Write to me in care of the American Express office in Athens. Send the letters there, and I will receive them." Demetri saw Kristen's expression. "Oh, my dear; it won't be long. Try not to be sad."

Against her will, she began crying and could not stop until Demetri kissed the tears from her face and eyelids.

"You mustn't cry, my love. You will break my heart if you do," said Demetri through the tears that were welling up in his own eyes.

They clung to each other with the desperation of two lovers about to be torn apart; neither wanted to be the first to break the connection. Kari once again saved the day by entering the room and saying, "Okay, you two. Break it up; the boat isn't going to wait for us." Although her words were harsh, her heart was breaking too. She had grown to love Demetri and would miss him. Their time together had been the best of her life. It had been filled with laughter, love, and adventure, and had brought her closer to her sister. She knew that Demetri would be good to and for Kristen and was convinced that he loved her deeply.

Kari had privately teased her about the "perfect" wedding for Kristen and Demetri. It would be on the *Posidonia*, the ship on which they had met. There would be flowers everywhere on the upper deck, but especially the bow, where they would exchange their vows. Of course, it was just a fantasy, but a lovely one.

Demetri and Kristen had talked about marriage in abstract terms, mostly by fantasizing. They had talked of the children they would have. Demetri wanted at least six. They talked about what the children would look like. They would have his dark hair, her blue eyes, his slim build, her teeth (she had a great smile), and a combination of both of their personalities and skin.

"I am tempted to put us both on a plane to Tucson today, and talk to your parents," said Demetri. "That is how serious I am about you. You are *it*! You are the one I have been looking for. And, most important, I know I will make you very happy!"

Kristen could barely breathe, much less move. She was speechless. How could this wonderful man love her so deeply? She was an ordinary girl; he was extraordinary in every way.

The memory of those words spoken, so sincerely, gave Kristen the courage to get into the car. Instead of losing Demetri today, she now understood that it was a necessary step to take to travel toward the future they would have together.

It was another beautiful summer's morning in Terracina—sunny, cloudless, and hot. Demetri pointed the car toward Brindisi, still driving slowly, since the car had not been driven the five hundred miles required to condition the engine.

It was a difficult day for all, and there was little laughter among them. This was the day that Demetri would go back to Greece; Kari and Kristen would catch a train to Austria. As hard as they tried, they could not force themselves to be cheerful.

Kristen thought of the previous night. It had been a time of great despair and exaltation. In spite of the barriers they would face, Kristen was convinced that she and Demetri would spend the rest of their lives together. She loved him desperately and was willing to do whatever it took to make things work between them.

Their lovemaking had demonstrated the desperation they both felt. The impending separation heightened their emotions and sensations to a level that neither one had previously experienced. They hoped that by fitting together perfectly they would somehow avoid the inevitable separation. They had tried to become one, but mere mortals are unable to achieve such permanent perfection. Theirs was perfect, but temporary.

As they got closer to Brindisi, Kristen tried desperately but unsuccessfully not to cry. She watched Demetri's profile, ignoring the surrounding scenery, for miles. Demetri was aware of her stares and was flattered. He was going through much of the same emotional turmoil that Kristen was feeling and was barely able to control his emotions by concentrating on the challenges of driving.

He was heading back to the reality of family, obligation, and routine. He knew that he needed to be away from Kristen to find out whether their relationship had been a summer fling or was real. The separation would clear his head. He had promised Kristen that he would see her again. No matter what the circumstances in New York, he would find a way to rid himself of his cousins and make a safe and positive environment for Kristen's and his future together.

As they arrived at the harbor, Demetri observed that the ferry was boarding. He had thought that he would have at least two hours to say good-bye and arrange the train tickets for the girls. Demetri realized that, instead of the prolonged agony of a lengthy parting, he had to move quickly, or the ferry would leave without him. The car was unpacked in less than two minutes, Demetri pointed to the train station, knowing that Kristen and Kari would be fine, gave Kari a big hug and a tender kiss on the lips as a way of saying, "Thanks, little sister," and turned to Kristen, who was crying without restraint. He looked into her face with tear-filled eyes and said, "This is not good-bye; this is only the beginning of many hellos," kissed her deeply and tenderly, got back into the car, and drove onto the boat. He had made it just in time. Immediately the ferry began moving and was almost out of sight when Demetri appeared on deck, waving kisses to Kristen and Kari. All three were crying now, Kari and Kristen openly, and Demetri to himself.

Demetri had never felt so alone. *I should have missed the boat!* he said to himself over and over. As he sat on deck watching the water slip by, he noticed a school of dolphins escorting the boat on its way to Greece. He reached in his left breast pocket for the pack of cigarettes he kept there, and discovered the pearl ring that Kristen had worn, with a tiny note saying, "This is my token of us to you. Keep it safe, as you would keep our love safe. Return it to me when the time is right. With undying love, Kristen."

Seeing Demetri get smaller and smaller as the ferry left the harbor broke Kristen's heart. "What am I going to do now?" she asked rhetorically.

"We're going to figure out how to get to Vienna, that's what," Kari said firmly. "Let's go! There's no use in moping around when we have a train to catch." Kari was sad to see Demetri go, but knew that she had to get Kristen thinking about other things.

Their Italian was nonexistent, and the ticket seller's English was not much better. They finally learned there was an overnight train that would take them to Vienna. Before leaving the window, Kristen examined the second-class tickets carefully. It appeared that they were, indeed, going to Vienna.

It was only after they were settled into the compartment of the train that the emotions and events of the day overwhelmed Kristen. It had been one of the best and worst days of her life. The best, because she was sure of Demetri's love and devotion, the worst because she had had to say good-bye to the man she was sure was the love of her life.

"Well, that was quite an adventure," Kari said to cut the tension of the moment.

"The world's biggest understatement!" exclaimed Kristen, and gave Kari a goofy look, which cracked them up. Both Kristen and Kari began laughing, softly at first, growing to a state of hysteria until total exhaustion and the gentle swaying of the moving train eased them into deep, dreamless sleep.

They arrived in Vienna the next morning and were able to locate the hotel and rejoin the tour group. Although the other tour members asked numerous questions about their absence, Kristen and Kari said nothing. They did not want to share their adventure with anyone.

Kristen looked forward to receiving Demetri's first letter, which arrived in Heidelberg. It was a postcard mailed in an envelope for privacy. *"I was looking forward to this trip to Greece; however it has been bad. Your face follows me every place I am. I miss you so much. My trip back was empty and my mind full of crazy thoughts. You have my love and devotion. Say hello to "my honey." S'agapo (I love you), Demetri.*

She read the words at least one hundred times and tucked Demetri's postcard in a special pocket of her suitcase where she also kept the worry beads he had given her. That pocket would have many more letters before she flew back to the States. She treasured every one of them.

The tour continued through Austria, Berlin, Denmark, Germany, and Brussels before ending in Paris. A postcard awaited her arrival at every hotel, each one with a heartfelt greeting. Demetri had chosen postcards that depicted parts of Greece that Kristen has missed visiting because she had chosen to go to Italy with him. There were two postcards of Cape Sunion at sunset, one of the sun setting over the sea, which reminded Kristen of Terracina, and others from historic parts of Greece. Each talked of his deep unhappiness at being away from her, his frustration over not being able to give her promises for the future, and that although he could not give her everything he wanted to, she had all his being and love, and that he lived in hopes of hearing from her soon.

Kristen was deeply touched by the short but heartfelt notes. Demetri had lived up to his promise to write her. She wrote to him daily and hoped the letters would reach him.

Kari and Kristen went home to Arizona after the tour finished. She described Demetri to her parents, who, to her surprise, seemed genuinely happy for her, since they could see the glow in her face and eyes when she talked about him.

Chapter 15

*D*emetri had gone back to his village after leaving Kristen and Kari in Brindisi. His world, which had been so joy-filled for a week, was once again lonely, although he was always surrounded by family and friends. He wished that he had missed the boat! His thoughts were of Kristen and how he would manage to make his life worthy of her love and devotion. There was much to be done, and most of it had to be accomplished once he returned to New York. He was willing to do whatever it took to make a life for them.

He looked forward to his trips to the American Express office, where he would find a small stack of letters from Kristen waiting for him. He would open them slowly and read every word as he sat at an outdoor café on Syntagma Square. They were like a great cup of coffee and needed to be savored.

Demetri also looked forward to writing letters to Kristen. It gave him the opportunity to be perfectly open with his thoughts and feelings. It was a way to release some of the frustration he was feeling now that they were physically separated.

Kristen, yia sou.

I send you greetings from Greece, which has been hectic. Why? Because of things. These greetings of course are followed by much love, the only thing that I can give you knowing that it is also pure and not influenced by anything. You see, I happen to adore you in my own way and my dedication to you is only followed by the love I have for you, without any reservations.

Maybe I sound weird in my letter, but if I was with you now things would be simpler. Furthermore, this is nothing but a piece of paper staring at me with its cold eyes ... something quite different than your eyes that are so warm and so blue. When you read this, think that I am there across from you, talking to you like we did the short time we were together.

Your letters have been a drop of beauty in the ugly, bitter time that I have been having. Our love has been the most beautiful secret I have ever had. Please, let it be a secret, for both our sakes.

You never know what the future is. You never know what the rest of the "building" is going to be like. You do know that the foundations are solid; these foundations could be outlined by one word, our love. Remember what I told you ... no matter what happens, I will love you, no matter what!

I received your letters all at once. As I read them I closed my eyes and relived our being together. I can still feel your fingers in my hair while I was driving. I dreamed that we were making love and I was careful not to hurt your lips for they were sunburned.

The other day I found myself down at the seashore calling your name loudly while trying to top the sounds of the waves. It may sound corny, but there is nothing corny in what I tell you, for it is real and since it is real it is important. You did something to me. I was never gentle with women before. With you I felt like I was handling the most precious thing I have. I love and miss you very much.

This is the first letter of its kind I have ever written. Do take care and love me, oh please love me, I need you. OH GOD WHEN, WHERE AND HOW IN THE NAME OF HELL. HOW! With all of me there. S'agapo. Demetri

That was the last letter he wrote until he returned to the States. Then he stopped writing because he was unsure of Kristen's location and did not want the letters to be read by anyone but her.

At the end of August he arranged to ship the car to New York and traveled back to Italy on a ship called *Eleana*. It was a miserable trip. The ship caught fire while in the middle of the journey, causing two deaths and much damage. Luckily, Demetri and his car were untouched. He hoped that Kristen had not heard of the tragedy on the news and was worrying.

Although the phone lines were undependable at best, he decided to call Kristen as soon as he arrived in Italy.

"Hello" she answered the phone.

"*Yia sou,* Kristen," he said.

Kristen's heart jumped into her throat. "Demetri, I can't believe it's you. I have missed you desperately!"

"And I, you. I just needed to hear your voice to make sure you were not a dream."

"How are you?" asked Kristen.

"That is why I call you now. There was an accident on the boat, but I am fine. I did not want you to worry."

"Oh my gosh. I hadn't heard. I did not know where you were. You stopped writing. I was so worried."

"Don't worry about anything, my love, I will take care of everything. I can't talk long. I just want you to know that I love you and that I am making arrangements so we can be together."

"And I love you, desperately. I miss your voice, your touch, your kisses and ..." she smiled.

"Yes, I miss all of that too. I hope it won't be long. I must go. I love you." And he was gone.

Kristen's heart soared. He was well, and he loved her. She had not been imagining all of this. He would be back in the States soon, and everything would be fine. All was well with her world.

Kristen's and Demetri's days were filled with thoughts of each other. Kristen had returned to Northern Arizona University. Demetri returned to New York in early September and began his teaching schedule. They wrote each other long letters daily. Both lived for the mail delivery so they could continue their love affair, if not physically, then at least by mail. The letters were filled with words of love and plans, and accounts of the everyday activities of life. Demetri wrote to Kristen from his office. Kristen would write between classes. It kept them close.

Kristen lived in a dorm without private telephone access, so phone calls needed prior arrangement. Kristen would wait by the public phone at the appointed time. When she heard his voice, her whole body would shiver with delight. They could talk about the most serious issues or about nothing at all. It did not matter, as long as they talked.

Kristen would have given up school to be with Demetri, but he would have none of that. Education was extremely important to him, and he would not interfere with her finishing school. Besides, he had not been able to complete arrangements in New York to ensure her safety, but things were moving forward.

"Will you come to New York for Thanksgiving?" asked Demetri.

"I would love to," she replied. She would need to get permission from her parents, but she thought they would agree. This gave her something specific to look forward to. She and Demetri would be together. Her life was good!

Kristen arranged her school schedule so she could spend ten days in New York instead of the normal four-day Thanksgiving break. She wanted the maximum amount of time for them to be together. It would give them a chance to be "normal" and really get to know each other.

She knew that Demetri was sharing a house with two other men to save money, which had been in short supply. There had been a wage freeze at the school system, and he had debts from the summer. He would have wanted to have Kristen totally to himself during her visit, but it was not possible. His roommates understood how important Kristen was to him and agreed without hesitation to her visit.

Kristen arranged to fly to New York one day earlier than Demetri had expected her to arrive. She wanted to surprise him and arranged for Christos, his roommate, to pick her up at JFK airport.

Her excitement mounted as they approached the house. Demetri was having a drink at a local bar when she arrived, and she was able to clean up a bit while she waited for him to return home. She was so excited she could barely control herself.

Christos went to Demetri at the bar. "Hey, I have a message for you from Kristen. It's something about her having to postpone the trip, and she was very upset. I told her to call back in twenty minutes. You better get back to the house right away."

"Did she say anything else?" he asked desperately.

"No, just get home."

Demetri paid his bill, walked quickly to the exit, and drove home as quickly as he could. As he walked into the living room, the expression on his face was one of concern and sadness. He started pacing while he waited for the phone to ring. Kristen was waiting for him in his little bedroom directly off the living room.

He noticed that his bedroom door was closed, which was unusual. He never closed it when he was away from home. He opened it to hang up his coat, and saw Kristen sitting on the bed waiting for him.

Demetri's expression quickly changed to surprise and then delight. He went to Kristen with his arms extended and pulled her up off the bed. He kissed her over and over again. "Holy shit," he kept saying, after the initial shock had worn off.

"That was the exact response I was hoping for. If you had reacted in any other way I would have been very embarrassed," said Kristen, her face glowing with happiness and love as she looked at Demetri.

"Christos, I'm going to kill you, you devil," Demetri said, smiling appreciatively.

"My pleasure," he replied.

Kristen and Demetri needed to be alone. Kristen wanted to devour him, but Demetri was still in a state of shock and wanted some time to let everything set in. "Let's go for a ride," he said and grabbed his coat.

"I thought you'd never ask," said Kristen.

"You look wonderful, Kristen! I am so happy to see you. How did you manage this?"

"I wanted to surprise you."

"Well, you certainly did. I am glad I am healthy; otherwise I could have had a heart attack."

Kristen laughed and held Demetri's arm. His right hand was busy with the gear shift. "I am too. If I'm going to give you a heart attack, it shouldn't be from surprise. It should be from making love to you."

"What a way to go!"

"The best. Where are we going, by the way?"

"I thought I would show you where I work and then we can get something to eat. Are you hungry?"

"Just for your kisses and your body," she said with a grin.

Demetri smiled. She was in a hurry. He wanted to savor this time. This was one of the best moments of his life, and he wanted to remember every second of it. There would be time for lovemaking later. The anticipation would make it that much more enjoyable.

He wanted to show Kristen his world. They stopped by the college where he taught and looked at the classroom where he normally held his classes as well as his office. It thrilled Kristen to know that she was being invited into his world.

After the tour of the facility, they stopped at a diner nearby and had some coffee. Neither Demetri nor Kristen was hungry—not for food, anyway. They snuggled into a booth where their bodies touched as they talked.

"You really got me. I had no idea anything was going on. I wanted to make sure everything was perfect for your arrival tomorrow and hadn't finished. I'm a bit embarrassed," said Demetri.

"It *is* perfect. The expression on your face said it all. It could not have been better! And you look wonderful to me," replied Kristen.

"You are just as I remember you. It only took me a minute after I got on the boat back to Greece to know that I was miserable without you. I have had no other goal for the last three months than for us to be together."

Kristen had been hoping and praying for the exact words that Demetri was now saying. Her heart soared. It appeared that all would be well after all.

When they returned to the house, they were relieved to find it quiet and empty. *Thanks, guys*, thought Demetri. He wanted some time alone with Kristen, outside of the tiny bedroom that had been his since he had moved into the shared house.

Kristen had other thoughts. She wasn't interested in a prolonged talk. She wanted to be with Demetri. She wanted her naked body against his. To let him know her desires, she stood in front of him, took his hands in hers and guided them to her breasts. That was all the invitation Demetri needed. All the loneliness and frustration he had been experiencing for months was released.

Clothes went flying as they headed for the twin bed they would share for the next ten days. There was a moment or two of awkwardness between them that disappeared quickly as they reacquainted themselves with each other. Their lovemaking was frantic, short-lived, and brought them both to ecstasy. When they came up for breath, they laughed at their utter lack of inhibition.

"You animal, you," Demetri teased Kristen. After a hesitation, he added, "I like it, very much." They both laughed.

"And I love you very, very much," he added. "I can't tell you how much I have missed you. You have been all that I have thought about. Everything I have done has been for us."

"Demetri, you will never know how much I love you. I have just been going through the motions at school. I have done okay in my classes, but it's you who has been distracting me."

"Is there anything I can get you before we sleep?" he asked.

"Just you, forever … and a glass of water, if you don't mind."

By the time Demetri returned to the tiny bedroom with the water, Kristen was asleep. "Good night, *agapimou*, he whispered and gently crawled into bed next to her.

Chapter 16

The next ten days were filled with laughter, love, and lots of sex. They wanted to be together every minute of the day and night. When Demetri went back to work, Kristen went to class one day to observe. She was impressed by his teaching style and the admiration he received from both his students and his peers.

The only tense times they spent together were when they were reminded of Demetri's cousins and the outside pressures on him. When they went into a restaurant, Demetri would inspect the surroundings before allowing Kristen to enter with him. He was also careful to instruct her to keep the curtains shut and not to answer the phone while he was away at work. "I'm just trying to keep you safe," was his explanation. It made Kristen uneasy, but she knew Demetri was handling the situation the best he could.

Kristen tried her hand at domesticity, making a superb Thanksgiving dinner for all the housemates and their dates. "She's a keeper," Christos said to Demetri. "I know," was his reply, which made Kristen blush.

One evening, Demetri drew Kristen into the bedroom for a private talk. He had a serious expression on his face that concerned Kristen.

"What's up?" she asked, with waves of anxiety washing over her.

"My friends have been in touch. They know about you." Kristen stayed silent to let Demetri continue. "They have told me that they are going to leave me alone from now on, which makes me happy. I just don't know if it is really possible. It has been a long, difficult struggle for me. The mistakes I made when I first came here have plagued me for over seven years and may for the rest of my life. Once you become part of their club, it is nearly impossible to get away. Do you understand?

"I'm trying to," was her only response.

"It looks as if my efforts are finally working. Only now am I able to make plans for the future." He hesitated. "Kristen, you are the best thing that has ever happened to me. You have taught me how to love and be loved unconditionally. There were times that I did not think I was capable of loving anyone. You have changed that, and I thank you for it. You have given me a gift far more precious than anything material in nature—those things that I would have done almost anything for ten years ago, and almost did."

Kristen watched Demetri's face. It showed a combination of concern, love, and a little nervousness.

"I have come to realize that we are soul mates. We come from very different cultures. Our religions are different. We live on opposite sides of the country. None of that seems to matter."

"I feel the same way," she was able to say quietly.

"Kristen, I do not want to live without you. There will be problems we will need to work out. I am poor, without much to offer you at this point in my life. But I will work hard and make a future for both of us. What I am asking you, Kristen, is if you will marry me."

Kristen was stunned. She had expected a serious conversation, but nothing like this. She hesitated, wanting her response to be perfect. "I know you are not rich, and I don't care about that. What matters to me is that we love each other, which I do with all my heart. Yes, Demetri, I will marry you!" she said seriously and then a huge smile lit up her face.

It took Demetri a moment to realize she had said yes to his question. Her smile told him that she knew everything was going to be fine. "I do not have a ring for you. This was something that I had not planned."

"I don't care about a ring. All I care about is that we are going to spend the rest of our lives together. It's going to be wonderful," she said, with tears in her eyes. She looked Demetri deeply in the eyes. "We can overcome anything as long as we work together. I truly believe that!"

Demetri had always thought of himself as the protector and the provider, and not necessarily an equal partner with a woman. He understood that Kristen would not be subservient to him, as many Greek women were raised to be, but would challenge him to be part of a two-person team.

Kristen understood that being the wife of a traditional Greek man would be a difficult transition, but Demetri was not traditional. He had been brought up in Greece, but, in his own words, had become a bastardized Greek after spending so much time in the United States. She would not be relegated to the typical role of a Greek wife. She was strong, independent, and with Demetri's encouragement was determined to finish her education. She knew that Demetri was the love of her life. Theirs would not be a typical marriage. They would work, fight, play, love passionately and make a wonderful life together. Neither would lose his or her identity as they learned to become a unit unto themselves. Life would be good.

Chapter 17

*D*emetri gently shook Kristen by the shoulders exclaiming, "Kristen, wake up. Where are you? You appear to be in a trance." Kristen opened her eyes and after surveying her surroundings realized she was back in 2019 in Central Park with an older but just as attractive Demetri. "I'm sorry. I must have become overwhelmed by the memories of how we met," she said quietly. "I am back with you now."

"It is getting late," responded Demetri. "I'll take you back to the hotel where we can pick up Kari and have a casual dinner together."

Kari had been waiting for them and was ready to go out when they arrived at the room. They spent a very pleasant evening telling stories and laughing at each other's jokes before returning to the hotel so Demetri could prepare for his upcoming meeting.

Demetri gave Kari a big hug and Kristen a gentle kiss on the cheek before leaving them at their door. "*Kalinichta* to my two best girls," he said and was gone.

Chapter 18

*D*emetri awoke slowly to the noise of the city with a smile on his face. He had been dreaming of the summer that he had met Kristen. The aftermath of his dreams lingered pleasantly until he returned to full consciousness. The smile quickly disappeared when he remembered his morning appointment. He had purposely attempted to ignore thinking about what he would say to Vassilis, but knew he could not put the inevitable off any longer.

After consuming three cups of coffee to clear his head, Demetri shaved and dressed carefully. Image was important. He wanted to appear totally in control, even though his emotions were running wild. As he slipped out of the taxi, he took one last cleansing breath before entering the office building he had visited just two days previously.

The scene was the same: Vassilis was seated behind his large, heavy desk, flanked by his subordinates. It made a very intimidating atmosphere for visitors, which was done purposely. Vassilis was used to being in charge without question. Demetri was also used to being in charge. He did not let the surroundings deter his concentration or determination.

"What have you decided?" Vassilis asked without preamble.

"Before I give you my answer, let me first say that I have the utmost respect for you. Although we are not blood relatives, you have been like an uncle to me. You were indebted to my family, when my parents saved you from imminent death by hiding you from the Gestapo. Then I became indebted to you for giving me the opportunity to come to the United States and get a good education," Demetri stated succinctly.

"All you have said is true," stated Vassilis flatly. "Proceed."

"I appreciate that you gave me my freedom to live my own life many years ago, and I understand what a gift that was. I have a simple but good life. I am well respected by my students and colleagues. I have lived within the law for over three decades, and I have never revealed your secrets."

"Again, that is true," said Vassilis.

"Now, you ask me to risk everything I have built because you need someone to smuggle an artifact out of Greece. I do not need nor want to know why; it is unimportant. You have threatened me and my loved ones directly if I do not agree to your demands. That is unacceptable," said Demetri with a voice that was controlled, although his heart was pounding.

"It is important to us; that is why we have made such harsh demands," said Vassilis in an equally controlled voice.

"I am sorry, but I have paid my debt to you and will not become embroiled with you or other family members again. Therefore, my answer to you is a regretful no. I will not assist you in the endeavor."

"You understand the ramifications of your decision?" asked Vassilis, his face turning crimson with anger.

"Yes, you have made yourselves very clear, although the threats have been insinuated. Do what you will to me, but leave my loved ones out of this," said Demetri with barely masked fury. "I will see myself out," he said as he left the office with an air of confidence he was not feeling.

"What have I done?" he asked himself when he was out of the building. "What will happen now?"

Chapter 19

*I*t was after nine before Kristen and Kari awoke; it was very unusual for Kristen to sleep late; her busy schedule at home seldom permitted it. Kristen looked out the window of the hotel and saw the bustling traffic below. Her practical side took over. She wanted to be ready for Demetri's arrival. She called room service and ordered breakfast for two to be sent up as soon as possible.

"So what happened yesterday?" Kari asked directly.

"I can't believe how upset I got. It has been over thirty years, and I still haven't gotten over him. I made a complete fool of myself and started crying," replied Kristen.

"There are issues you have never resolved, which is why you are so upset. You will feel better if and when you and Demetri can talk things out," said Kari.

"When did you become the smart sister?" asked Kristen as she hugged Kari affectionately.

How could her life have changed so entirely in one day? What would become of them? She had a busy practice in Arizona to return to. She wasn't a twenty-year-old who could fly off to unknown parts of the world on a whim. She had responsibilities. And how could she allow herself to be vulnerable again? She had loved Demetri with her whole being. She would gladly have given her life for his, if the situation had presented itself. That had never changed. The love she felt for him had never diminished, even though she had married another man. Her love was kept hidden in the deepest recesses of her being, allowed to surface only once in a while.

She had no doubt about Demetri's love for her, but would this love consume them as a fire does a forest? If they allowed themselves to follow their hearts, instead of their heads, would it end in another disaster? She could not survive that again. It would destroy her. It was then that Kristen decided that things needed to slow down. They must spend the time and effort truly getting to know each other. They had an advantage now. Maturity gave them patience and—she hoped—wisdom, but Kristen questioned that whether or not that was true. The emotions were as strong now as they had been when she was twenty.

As painful as it might be, she was determined to relive that wonderful/horrible year; even if it meant that Demetri and she would once again part ways, at least they would both truly understand their relationship.

"Good morning," said Demetri on the phone at exactly eleven o'clock. "Are you ready? I am double-parked and was wondering if you can come down."

"Sure, I'll be there as soon as I can catch the elevator. What side of the hotel are you on?" asked Kristen.

"I'm in the garage. They were kind enough to allow me to stay here for a few minutes until you arrive. Is Kari coming?"

"No, I'd rather spend the day alone with you. She'll be happy to join us for dinner this evening if we're back in time," replied Kristen.

"Be sure to bring a jacket. Although it's a beautiful day, it can get chilly at the beach," said Demetri. Kristen hoped that the day would prove to be informative as well as beautiful. She was hoping to get some answers to the questions that had haunted her for so many years.

It took less than ten minutes for Kristen to join Demetri, who looked anxious to get out of the city. He knew the way and pointed the car in the direction of Long Island.

"So where should we go first?" he asked.

"Wherever you want; it's your territory," replied Kristen. "I'm sure whatever you decide will be fine."

"Well then, let's head for the beach first. The weather is good now and is liable to change as the day progresses," Demetri said.

"That sounds great," said Kristen, who could not help but stare at Demetri's profile as he expertly maneuvered the car through the traffic.

"What?" Demetri finally said, noticing her looking at him instead of the scenery. "Do I have a bug in my hair or something?"

"No, I was just remembering the time we spent in your Alfa Romeo in Italy on the way to Terracina," said Kristen.

"Ah, Terracina; who could forget it!" exclaimed Demetri.

Kristen was brought back to the present when Demetri called to her loudly, "Kristen, you have disappeared again, Where are you?"

"I'm sorry, the memories of Terracina flooded back. What an incredible time we had together!" sighed Kristen.

"Yes, some of the best of my life, without a doubt," added Demetri. "We are just about to Jones Beach. Would you like to stop and walk a while?"

"Yes, of course. It's good to be back," responded Kristen.

Since it was too cold to swim, they walked the beach until their legs could not take any more. Demetri had brought a blanket from his hotel room and spread it out in the sand. "Sit," he ordered.

"With pleasure," was Kristen's response. "I don't think I've walked that far for a long time. By the way, I wonder what the management at the hotel would say if they knew their blanket was being used for a lascivious meeting," Kristen chuckled.

"They'll never know. I'll return it to my room this evening," Demetri replied, not quite understanding that Kristen was kidding.

The time seemed perfect for Kristen to discuss what had been bothering her. "You know, we have never talked about what happened after Terracina. It still hurts me when I think about it," began Kristen.

"It was a long time ago," Demetri said.

"Yes, I know. But there are things I don't believe I have ever gotten over. Seeing you again has brought back so many memories—the good and the bad. You know, I have always thought of our relationship as the way *A Tale of Two Cities* begins: "It was the best of times, it was the worst of times.""

"That's an interesting analogy," Demetri observed. "Are you sure you want to do this today?"

"If not today, when?" replied Kristen. "It is important to me that I understand what happened. Isn't it to you?"

"We have found each other; it is a miracle. Why bring up the past, now, when we can know each other in the present? We won't lose each other again. Do you remember how I like to write letters?" Demetri asked.

"Yes. I hate to admit it, but I have kept your letters all these years," said Kristen, slightly embarrassed by the admission.

"You have?"

"Yes, I have kept the memory of you for a very long time, although I do not allow it to surface often. It was always too painful," Kristen replied, looking away so he would not see the sadness in her face.

Demetri saw her turn away, took her face in his hands, looked her squarely in the eyes, and said, "No, don't turn away; I want to see everything you are feeling." Kristen's eyes filled with tears that spilled onto her cheeks. Demetri kissed them away.

"See what you've made me do? I feel so foolish when this happens," whispered Kristen.

"Don't feel that way. I am flattered that you still have such emotions for me," he said, which made Kristen feel slightly better.

"Anyway, I have e-mail capabilities now. Would it be all right for us to communicate that way?" asked Demetri.

"I hadn't thought of that, but why not?" replied Kristen, feeling that it was some consolation for his desire not to go into things today.

"Then it is settled. I will write to you as soon as I return to Greece," Demetri said. "We can spend as much time as we need later on."

"I guess this is your subtle way of changing the subject for today. As usual, you're right. Why dig up buried emotions today, when we can just enjoy each other's company?" conceded Kristen. "I just need to know one thing. Did you really love me as much as I thought you did?"

"How can you even ask that?" questioned Demetri. "I loved you as no other. You taught me how to love. I still love you," he added. "We were just not meant to be, then."

Kristen was stunned by the forthright way Demetri admitted his feelings. *What does he mean by "then?"* asked Kristen to herself. Electricity ran through her chest as she thought about it—a feeling she hadn't had in many years. It frightened her, knowing that her feelings for Demetri hadn't changed much, although her life had. "Just one other question, and I will change the subject. If you loved me so much, how could you leave me?"

"I did not leave you, not really," Demetri replied.

"Are you kidding? Yes, you did!" she wanted to scream, but she held her tongue and listened to the rest of Demetri's sentence.

"As I said, there were some things on which I just could not compromise. Kristen, believe me when I say that we were not meant to be at that time."

"I'm sorry," Kristen squeaked through a constriction in her throat.

"Don't be sad. We have found each other again and should be happy." He took Kristen's face in his hand and kissed her gently. "Now, let's walk back to the car and drive awhile."

They had driven for a few minutes when Demetri said, "It's getting late, and I'm hungry. Let's stop for some lunch. Which would you prefer—a restaurant or a diner?"

"A diner, of course. How could I come out to Long Island and not eat in a diner?" asked Kristen.

They ordered hot pastrami sandwiches, which neither one of them had eaten for years, and laughed at the stories they told each other. They felt at ease with each other; almost as if they had been together for years instead of just a few days. Time seemed to disappear, and they realized that two hours had passed.

"Time goes by so quickly now. I have noticed it more now that I am older," said Demetri. "My father always told me that it took him thirty years to get to the age of thirty-three, and about two weeks to go from thirty-five to eighty." After a moment's pause, he added, "I miss my father. He was very important in my life." Kristen remained silent.

After a moment, Demetri said, "Let me take you back to the hotel and give you a couple of hours to rest. All three of us will have dinner together again this evening. Is that all right with you?"

"It sounds perfect; you must have been reading my mind," replied Kristen.

Their trip back to the city was uneventful, and their light conversation continued until Demetri dropped Kristen off at the entrance of the Waldorf. "I'll see you at eight thirty," he said and drove away.

Kari was waiting for Kristen as she opened the door. "Well, how was your day?"

"It was good, although nothing was resolved. The timing wasn't right. We're going to e-mail each other when he gets back to Greece," Kristen said innocently.

"Oh, so this is going to continue beyond this evening?" asked Kari with a sarcastic expression on her face. "Is that wise?"

"Now, don't be like that. Yes, it's okay. We can't have it any other way. Besides, there's safety in being six thousand miles apart," replied Kristen, trying to believe the words she had heard herself say.

"If you say so," added Kari. "Just remember I warned you."

"I'll be careful; at least I'll try to be," promised Kristen.

"Hey, lighten up; I'm just giving you a hard time. You know I love Demetri now as much as ever. I'm just amazed that after all this time you two still feel the way you do toward each other. It's almost as if someone or something is trying to get you back together."

Dinner was filled with laughter over good times, both present and past. Kari loved being with Demetri again. She still felt like the protected younger sister in his presence, although she was almost fifty years old. He made her feel young again.

When dinner was over and the short walk back to the hotel complete, Kari excused herself once again. "Demetri, don't be a stranger. I loved seeing my big brother again," she said as she gave him a big bear hug. He reciprocated with a kiss on her cheek.

"It's been wonderful," he whispered in her ear, "and it's not over."

"Good," Kari replied. "We have both missed you terribly. Good night and have a safe journey," she said and left.

"Let's walk a little more," suggested Kristen. "I am not ready to say good-bye."

"Let's not say good-bye. Let's just leave it until later," said Demetri. "I hate good-byes."

They walked for another hour, talking and holding hands. When they arrived back at the hotel, Kristen began crying in spite of her vow not to. "I just can't help it," she said desperately.

"I know," replied Demetri, brushing the tears from her face. He kissed her with the passion she remembered. It wasn't sexual, but a way for Demetri to communicate the love he was feeling for her without saying the words; the words that were not right for him to say under the circumstances.

He turned and left her at the door. She watched him leave until he turned the corner and was gone. Kristen began crying in earnest then. When she opened the door, Kari asked, "What's wrong?"

"I'm just being silly," Kristen replied. "I just did not think all of this would affect me as much as it did, that's all."

"I'm a bit surprised myself, but nothing really surprises me when it comes to you and Demetri," said Kari.

"Let's not talk about it tonight; I need some sleep. So what do you want to do tomorrow?" added Kristen, letting Kari know that the subject was closed for the evening. Kristen just could not face it tonight. There would be time in the future to analyze what had happened over the last few days—sometime in the future, but not now.

Chapter 20

"Would you mind too much if we changed our reservations and flew home later today?" Kristen asked Kari. "I feel I need to get home and once again have some normalcy in my life."

"Not at all," Kari replied. "I don't think I could stand another museum anyway."

"Thank you Kari, you're a great sister," she replied as she picked up the phone to call the airline.

Kristen felt a deep sadness as the Airbus lifted off LaGuardia Airport's runway. The memories of Demetri were too vivid in New York; she would be able to suppress them when she returned to her busy schedule. At least that is what she hoped.

It took two weeks, but Kristen was able to fall into her normal routine. She returned to work at her practice during the day, and in the evenings and on weekends cared for Richard. He had been relatively well, so Kristen had been able to spend some quality time with him, and they even found time to have some fun together, instead of merely running from one appointment to another for tests or treatments. Unknowingly, Richard made Kristen feel guilty when he was especially attentive and considerate of her. She felt undeserving, especially when her thoughts drifted to Demetri. She kept her secret well. There was no point in telling Richard about Demetri. She would never want to hurt him, and it would serve no purpose. Richard had been a good husband, and she cared about his well-being.

At the same time Demetri had returned to Athens. He felt uncomfortable being away from the university during the term and missed being in the classroom with the bright, young adults who challenged him every day. He knew there would be a small mountain of paperwork waiting for him on his desk after his absence and realized that being busy would keep his mind from wandering to Arizona.

But as busy as he became, his thoughts often turned to Kristen. True to his word, as soon as he returned to work he e-mailed her his impressions of being back at the university. He purposely kept the e-mails light and did not talk about their relationship.

Kristen enjoyed getting e-mails from Demetri. They were so different from the passion-filled love letters he wrote in 1987, but they still showed his personality and concern for her. She noticed that Demetri was keeping things fairly impersonal and appreciated his efforts. There would be time later to hash through the unresolved issues. Kristen looked forward to hearing from Demetri on a daily basis and responding to his questions as well as asking her own. Two months went by without a break in their communication.

In January, things began to change. Kristen began getting strange calls at all hours of the night, and the line would be dead when she answered the ringing phone. Then, after a couple of weeks, she was stunned when she received veiled threats like, "We know who you are," and "How was your trip to New York?" At first she did not share her concerns with Demetri, not wanting to bother him, but when the caller said, "I wonder if your husband would like to know about your trip to New York," she contacted him immediately. She no longer felt she could ignore the problem and knew that Demetri needed to be involved.

Demetri told Kristen that he had also been receiving threats. His concern had increased as the threats became more specific. The threats infuriated him, but he had felt he was able to ignore them until Kristen informed him of her concerns.

"They have threatened to tell Richard about you. How could they know so much?" Kristen asked Demetri. Demetri wasn't sure. Had they been followed those days in New York? Had they hacked into his e-mail? Whatever the reason, they knew about Kristen and were going to use her as leverage—exactly what he had wanted to avoid at all costs.

"I don't know, but this needs to be taken seriously," responded Demetri. "Has anything else happened to you?"

"Not that I am aware of. I don't think I am being watched. I usually can feel that, remember?" she replied.

"Let me deal with this, and I will get back to you," Demetri said.

The e-mails from that point on became more concerned with the immediate problem than with their relationship. Demetri, in his usual way, felt that he should be able to control things without help or suggestions. Kristen understood that Demetri's stress level was becoming increasingly intolerable and that he was trying to protect Kristen by withholding information, which only made matters worse. Kristen worked to make Demetri understand that excluding her was a mistake. If he felt it would keep her from being involved in this unsavory situation, he was wrong; she was already involved. But Kristen could not seem to get him to understand that two heads were better than one in this situation.

Desperate times called for desperate measures. Although the nine-hour time difference made phone calls difficult to arrange, Kristen called Demetri when she received his message.

"I read of your problems and am glad that you have confided in me," she began.

"I would not have burdened you with this, but I knew you would understand the situation," was his reply. "You have become involved, and I don't know how to undo things."

"Don't worry about it. Let's figure things out," she said. Demetri was surprised by Kristen's clear and rational analysis of the situation.

"All right," she began. "I now know that your meetings in New York were related to today's situation, am I right?"

"Yes," Demetri replied.

"Okay, then tell me about it—not the details, just the demands," Kristen insisted. She had put on her professional hat and would not allow Demetri to gloss over the facts.

"They want me to smuggle a precious icon out of Greece in my boat."

Kristen did not let her shock sway her from her next statement. "In medicine, we always ask questions before deciding on a specific treatment plan. I am going to ask the same questions of you now, and perhaps we can come up with a solution, all right?"

"Go ahead," agreed Demetri.

"The questions are as follows," she began.

"What are the risks? What are the benefits? Do the benefits outweigh the risks? On a personal note, could this involve physical violence or bodily harm to you or anyone else?"

"Good points," conceded Demetri after thinking for a few moments. Kristen felt that this was Demetri's way to avoid answering her.

"Answer the questions, Demetri." Kristen was on a roll and could not be dissuaded from asking more questions. "But before you do, I have another. Why did you say no to begin with? This may seem like a funny question to ask, but is it because you would have said no to any request they made; or is it because it goes against your values and beliefs to do something illegal? Think about all these questions and get back to me. I will be waiting," she said. "And Demetri, remember that you're not alone in this."

His response came the next day by e-mail. "Your questions helped me to think things out a bit more rationally. The answers are as follows: the risks include possible imprisonment and loss of my professional standing and my job, which I love. I believe the risk of getting caught is minimal, since I am totally familiar with the country, and people are accustomed to seeing me in my boat. I doubt that there would be any physical risk involved, either to myself or to any others. The benefits would include being free from my cousins' hold once and for all time. They have promised this, and as you know, a promise is never broken. They have offered me one hundred thousand dollars, which would free me of my financial troubles. The benefits could possibly far outweigh the risks if the mission was carefully planned. Compliance is mandatory. I have no choice but to do as they ask. The reasons I have refused my cousins are complicated and are related to both of the statements you made. Although I am a follower of the Greek Orthodox faith, I do not have an overwhelming feeling that the loss of one icon is of great significance," he continued.

She picked up the phone and called Demetri. After opening greetings, Kristen got down to business. "Where is the icon?" she asked.

"It was stolen a long time ago and is hidden away in the mountains," he replied. "It is unlikely that anyone is actively looking for it now."

"How would you obtain it? Would you have to pick it up?"

"I am to go into many shops around Greece, like a tourist. One of those shops will be giving me an extra package. It is that simple. Then I am to take it to an island off the southern coast of Croatia, where I will hand it over."

"Accept their offer. I will help," replied Kristen after a few seconds of silence.

Demetri was stunned when he heard her words. "I cannot ask you to do this for me!" he responded.

"You did not ask; I offered. It would be much less suspicious if a couple is seen traveling as tourists through Greece and doing great amounts of shopping than if you attempt to do it on your own."

"That is true," Demetri replied. "But why would you risk everything you have there to help me?"

"Do you remember when I told you I would gladly take a bullet for you, meaning I would trade my life for yours? Well, that hasn't changed!" she said emphatically. "I would be honored if I could help free you of this terrible obligation. Besides," she said lightly, "I need some adventure in my totally boring life," hoping to give some levity to the conversation.

"There is only one condition," she continued. "Richard must *never* find out anything about this! And another thing," she added. "I am involved already, so I will not take no for an answer. I did once with you and have regretted it ever since. Let me do this for you!"

Kristen's words touched Demetri deeply. It astonished him that someone would be willing to go to such lengths for him—even Kristen. After thinking for a minute, he could see the advantages of having her along. Yes, it would seem much less suspicious; and it would give them time to be together again, which was a very enticing idea.

After some hesitation, he answered simply, "Yes. Thank you."

"So it is decided," Kristen said after she got over the shock of Demetri agreeing to her offer. "Tell your cousins to stop the threats, that we will do as they ask. We will do it together. You tell me when, and I will make arrangements to be there. I don't need to know anything more. I still trust you implicitly."

"The less you know, the safer it will be for all of us. I will be back in touch," replied Demetri. "And Kristen, thank you!"

"You are welcome. Now, I need to get back to work," she said in her most professional voice, although she was feeling anything but professional. What had she agreed to? What ramifications would her words and actions have? She quickly told herself that the die was cast, and there was nothing to be done now, so she had better do what she said she needed to and get back to work, which she did.

Chapter 21

*O*nce the decision was made, the threats stopped. Kristen was able to concentrate on her daily life without constant anxiety every time the phone rang. Life got back to normal, with the exception of the mission looming ahead of her. She bought a language course and practiced her Greek whenever she had a few minutes to spare. Otherwise, she relegated the upcoming mission to the back of her mind.

Demetri and Kristen's relationship had changed. Kristen's insistence on joining him was the first time she had taken the lead, the first time her decision had overruled his. Before that, Demetri had made all the decisions and called all the shots, as Greek men are accustomed to doing. It was good for both; the relationship had become more balanced.

Although the e-mails continued, priorities had changed. There was no longer a sense of urgency regarding their relationship. There was no more talk of reliving their youth or analyzing their past and present relationship. They were working toward a common goal as partners, not as love-starved adolescents. They decided that the mission would take place in the late summer when there were thousands of American tourists swarming Greece and when it was normal for Demetri to be away from work and out in his boat.

Summer was also a good time to get away from Tucson, where the temperature often rose above 100 degrees. Kristen arranged to be away from work for two weeks and felt guilty about lying to Richard regarding the real reason for her trip. He was unable to travel and had encouraged her to go on her own when she suggested that she needed some rest and had always wanted to return to Greece. Kari was suspicious when she heard of Kristen's solo trip but did not delve further when Kristen made it clear that it was none of her business and to please drop the subject.

Kristen secretly made sure that all her financial and legal papers were in order, just in case the mission did not go as smoothly as she had hoped. Beyond that, Kristen left all the other arrangements to Demetri.

The months passed quickly. The day came for Kristen to leave for Greece. Richard's health was as good as it had been in months, and Kristen was hopeful that it would continue. "Please God, take care of things here while I'm gone," she prayed.

The flights from Tucson to Atlanta and then to Athens were on time and uneventful. *If you can call flying to a destination where you are going to be perpetrating a felony uneventful,* Kristen thought. She had even been upgraded to business class on the transatlantic flight, which seemed like a good omen. It allowed her to get some rest on the long flight and to be refreshed upon arriving in Athens, despite her extreme state of nervousness over what she was about to do. As the plane made its final descent, Kristen said another prayer. "Please keep us safe on this very dangerous adventure," she whispered.

Immigration and custom formalities were almost nonexistent. Kristen was one of the first to disembark the plane and the first to have her passport stamped. *It's been a long time. I hope I am not making the biggest mistake of my life by coming here under these circumstances*, she said to herself as she retrieved her suitcase from the carousel and wheeled it through the door that led to the International Arrival lounge. She was not surprised to see hundreds of people anxiously awaiting their loved ones' arrivals; but there was only one face she was interested in finding.

Demetri was standing twenty feet from the entrance, slightly away from the main crowd. When their eyes met, Kristen saw his expression change from concern to happiness. As always, he stretched out his arms to her as she approached, and she fell into his warm embrace. "*Yasou,* Kristen. It is so good to see you. You are looking well. How was your flight?" he asked.

Kristen could not speak for a moment; she was so overwhelmed by seeing Demetri again. She let his embrace comfort her as if she were a child for a full minute without moving and then pulled away. "It was perfect. And you, Demetri; you look as good as ever," she said, though she noticed the signs of fatigue he could not disguise. She understood the stress he was experiencing and that the effects would be visible only to someone who knew him as well as she did.

"*Pame*, let's get out of here," Demetri said as he reached for Kristen's bag. "The car is parked close by. We will drive out of Athens and stop for coffee where we can talk."

"It's good to see you have a car that's bigger than a postage stamp," Kristen teased when she saw the large sedan he was driving, knowing that he preferred small, sporty cars.

"It is a rental. We need room for all of your purchases, remember?" he replied with a slight smile. Traffic from the airport was hectic, and Demetri needed to concentrate on his driving, so conversation was sparse until they stopped at a café. They ordered coffees, which were served with a glass of water that Kristen finished in one swig.

"I'm so thirsty. I had no idea how dehydrated I could become so quickly in the heat," she said as Demetri asked the waiter to bring more.

"So how are you?" asked Demetri, looking deeply into Kristen's eyes.

"How am I? How are you is a more important question! You look tired," she replied.

"It has been very stressful. I did not want to involve you in all of my problems, especially this, but it was beyond my control. I am very sorry," he said.

"Don't be. You know I would do almost anything for you Demetri; this is the way I can prove it," she said. "Besides, my life has been quite boring for a long time now, and I needed some adventure, although this is not exactly what I had in mind."

"How is Richard?" asked Demetri with sincere concern.

"He has been good for the last few weeks. It was he who encouraged me to come to Greece, although he has no idea of my true motivation in taking this trip. He believes I just need some rest and knows how much I have always loved Greece. It is important that the charade never be exposed, for all of our sakes."

"You have my promise. Now, we must talk about the days to come," he said, after making sure nobody could hear their conversation. "We have ten days to accomplish our mission. During the first days we must appear as typical Greek-American tourists enjoying the "old country." We will travel to Tsangarada in the mountains east of Volos today, if you can stand the drive after such a long journey."

"Anything you arrange is fine with me," Kristen replied.

"Thank you for that. I will not let you down. You will like Pelion; it is a very beautiful place where the mountains meet the sea," Demetri said.

"Does it look anything like the Amalfi coast in Italy or Terracina?" asked Kristen, trying to form an image in her mind of what Pelion would be like.

"No, Terracina was only a beach; this is more mountainous," replied Demetri. Hearing the word *Terracina* brought back memories to both.

"Terracina; how young we were then," she replied without finishing her thought.

"Yes, but, Kristen, we must think about the present. It is important that we focus on what we have to do," he said in response to her obviously wandering mind. His words brought her back to reality.

"We will stay there for two nights and play the role of tourists, sightseeing and buying many souvenirs and works of art. Everyone will think that we are a married couple and we should act that way. I will present my American passport wherever it is requested at the hotels. There is no reason for you to relinquish yours," said Demetri, getting down to business. "If someone sees that your name is different than mine, we will explain that you kept your maiden name for professional reasons. It is unusual in Greece, but they will understand and not question it further," he explained. "We will have to share a room. Is that a problem?"

"Of course not," she replied, although she wondered how they could spend the next two weeks together in such an intimate environment without fanning the flames they had always felt.

"I want you to know, Kristen, that my feelings for you have not changed. I still love you as I always have, but nothing will happen between us unless both of us want it to. I respect your marriage, as well as our friendship. You are doing something for me that nobody else ever could, and I thank you with all my heart. You can trust me," said Demetri with total conviction.

"I have always trusted you, you know that, Demetri," Kristen responded. *It's me I don't trust to be with you*, she thought but did not say out loud.

"After Pelion, we will drive to Delphi. Do you remember it? You were there once," he said.

"Actually, except for pictures I have seen in books I don't remember much. My mind was consumed with other things, namely you, at the time," admitted Kristen.

"It is high season, and there are literally thousands of tourists in Delphi on any given day. We will be just two of those tourists buying rugs and paintings and other items along the way. The difference is that at one of the shops we will also be given the icon wrapped as a purchase. For your protection, you must not know anything about the icon, and you will not know where or when the transfer will take place. You will just believe that it is another one of your many acquisitions. If you are unaware of the details, it will be easier to play our roles without suspicion," Demetri told her.

"I understand," relied Kristen.

"It is vital that nobody suspect us in any way, especially in the hotels. We must appear as normal as possible."

"I understand that too," responded Kristen.

"Then we will go to Corinth, where my boat is ready for our sea journey. We will transport the icon, as well as all of your purchases, in the boat to our destination in the Adriatic Sea. It is that simple. For all intents and purposes, we are just a couple on vacation—nothing more or less. Do you have any questions?" he asked.

"How much danger is there?" she asked.

"None, I hope," he replied.

"What about customs with the boat?"

"The icon was taken a long time ago, and the police are no longer actively looking for it. Although the boat can be searched, it is unlikely for us to have problems, under the circumstances."

"It sounds fairly straightforward to me. Will we be followed or observed during our mission?" asked Kristen, not wanting to be freaked out if her sixth sense acted up.

"It is possible, but unlikely. I have been in close contact with my cousins over the last few weeks, and everything is arranged," he added. "And Kristen, I want you to know how much it means to me that you are willing to risk everything to do this for me."

"*Tipota*, it is nothing," she said, although she knew that it was a lie. It was everything. If things went wrong she could lose her medical license, she could be put into a Greek prison and, most important, disappoint Richard. It was a huge risk, but one she was willing to take to help Demetri to be free.

"All right then, *pame*," said Demetri as he set a five-Euro note on the table and held out his hand to assist Kristen out of her chair.

"One thing I need first," said Kristen, hesitantly, "a kiss for luck."

"Of course," replied Demetri, and he gently and slowly kissed the lips he loved so much. A wave of emotion came over both of them as the connection between them was once again completed.

"This may be more dangerous than just risking prison," Kristen whispered to Demetri.

"Yes, but you have my promise, the danger will not be instigated by me," he said quietly as their eyes met.

The drive to Pelion was long but interesting for Kristen. She observed that Greece looked very much like parts of Arizona—dry, with steep, craggy mountains, but different foliage. Instead of cacti and barren rocks, there were olive groves and evergreen trees as well as scrub brush covering most of the steep cliffs. Kristen also noticed that many of the agricultural areas were irrigated with modern-looking equipment. *Things have changed here*, she thought to herself. She would make a conscious effort to explore those changes during her time in the country she liked so much.

In spite of her desire to take in all the scenery, Kristen's fatigue overcame her, and she slept most of the trip. Demetri stole quick peeks at her when the road was relatively calm, which was not often. He felt lucky that this beautiful woman was once again in his car and in his life. No matter the situation, he was grateful for whatever time they had together.

As they were passing through Volos four hours later, Demetri gently touched Kristen, who awoke and yawned. "Oh, my goodness, how long did I sleep?"

"Most of the way. We are in Volos and will be heading into the mountains. I thought you would like to see the scenery and was afraid you might not sleep tonight if you slept longer," Demetri replied.

The scenery had changed completely since Kristen had fallen asleep. It was no longer barren; the mountains ahead were hardly visible for all the trees.

"What kind are they?" she asked, noticing furry-looking balls on many of the limbs.

"They are all sorts of shade trees, but mostly chestnuts. This region is world famous for them. As a matter of fact, the chestnuts that the New York street vendors sell probably are grown right here," he said. "There are many fig, apple, and other fruit trees as well."

"I did not expect to see such lush mountains," said Kristen.

"People think that Greece is only the Acropolis and the Aegean Islands, but it is so much more," Demetri said, sounding a little like a travel advertisement.

As they arrived in Tsangarada, Kristen exclaimed, "Whew, what a trip. I need a shower and to stretch my legs in the worst way! Can we take a walk after we check in and freshen up?"

"Of course," Demetri agreed, leaving the car and strolling to the entrance of the small hotel after helping Kristen with her bag.

And the adventure begins, thought Kristen as she followed closely behind.

Chapter 22

"The hotel is very nice," commented Kristen as they were led through the tiny lobby to their room.

"Wait until you see the view," said Demetri. "I chose the hotel carefully. It is nice, but one where Greeks stay, not rich foreign tourists. We want to blend in as much as possible."

"What about the fact that I will be speaking English to you?" asked Kristen, with a bit of concern in her voice.

"That is all right. We just need to make sure our conversations in public are that of an old married couple," he instructed.

"Oh, you mean that we shouldn't talk to each other at all?" she said with a smile and a twinkle in her eye.

"Is that what you think of old married couples?" he asked. "Perhaps you are right. So many people seem to run out of things to say to each other. Do you think that would have happened to us?"

"I doubt it, but I guess we'll find out in the next few days when we play the role," she added, still smiling brightly.

"Oh, Demetri, this is beautiful," Kristen exclaimed as she opened the shutters of the door leading to a small balcony. "We are in the mountains but have an incredible view of the sea. Unbelievable!" The hotel sat on the upper edge of Mount Pelion, densely covered with large deciduous trees. The sea, a thousand feet below, looked like a color wheel of blues, ranging from the lightest of turquoises to a deep navy. Kristen's breath was taken away.

"So you are happy with my choice?" he asked. "We could have stayed closer to the beach, but I thought you would like being in the mountains. I hope you are not disappointed."

"Are you kidding?" she exclaimed. "It's perfect! I could not have asked for more if I was on a honeymoon."

"But we are not," said Demetri seriously. "We must always remember that."

"You needn't remind me," she said with the mildest irritation. "I understand the situation perfectly." Demetri always had a way of bluntly making his opinion known. "At least there are two beds. That will solve one problem. Don't people in Europe sleep together?" she asked as she looked at the twin beds that were pushed together, but made up separately.

"You will find many differences between America and Greece," added Demetri. "I hope you will appreciate and enjoy them." Kristen knew she would.

"All right, Master, what are the plans?" Kristen teased as she bowed deeply. Demetri could not help but smile when he replied, "This evening and tomorrow, we are just vacationers. We can do whatever pleases us."

Kristen and Demetri both knew that his words were hasty. No, neither of them could do what would really please them. There was a moment of silence when Kristen said cheerfully, "In that case, I'd like to get cleaned up and then explore this beautiful village. I realize it's too early to eat dinner, but perhaps we could have a snack. I'm really hungry."

"Your wish is my command," Demetri mimicked Kristen's former bow. "While you are in the shower, I will find something delicious."

More delicious than you? Kristen thought to herself. Then, *Stop it, you promised not to have those kinds of thoughts!*

Kristen had just finished dressing when Demetri opened the door with the key. "I apologize for not knocking, but married people don't usually do that, and as you know, we are old married people."

"That's quite all right. What's in the bag?" replied Kristen, hoping for something sweet. She wasn't disappointed.

"They are Greek cookies I found at a nearby bakery that are dipped in honey. I think you will like them," Demetri said.

Kristen carefully took one and bit into it. The cookie itself wasn't very sweet, but the honey and a sprinkling of ground nuts made the perfect combination. "They're wonderful," she said as she took one more for the road.

"Where to?" she asked simply.

"I thought we would walk to the main square and see what is going on there," replied Demetri.

"That sounds great to me," Kristen said as she picked up her purse on her way out the door.

Their first evening together was spent as any tourists would have spent it, although the village was very small, without many people. They walked to give Demetri a chance to show Kristen the village, had a leisurely iced coffee, watched others stroll by, explored a few shops that were of interest to them, and found a lovely *taverna* for dinner at nine o'clock, as night was just beginning to fall. Nine was still a bit early for the natives to dine, but the tourists, especially the British and Americans, liked to eat earlier, and the *taverna* was open, although not busy.

"This is unbelievable! How did you ever find such a beautiful location?" exclaimed Kristen. Kristen saw that the *taverna* was tucked into a corner of a village square that also had a small and very ornate church, a fountain spewing pure cold water, and a huge tree to shade diners from the midday sun, all overlooking the sea below. Kristen was able to see houses located on the mountain below her that seemed quite old and had the traditional slate roofs. Her enchantment showed on her face, and Demetri was pleased.

"You forget that this is my country; I have lived here many years and have had time to explore. I am just happy that you like it. I thought you would." Demetri ordered for them, carefully choosing dishes he knew Kristen would enjoy, but wanting her to experience the local cuisine.

"This is so good. What is it?" asked Kristen between bites. "I think it has nutmeg in it."

"Yes, it probably does. I hope you don't mind, but I ordered the stewed rabbit for you, without your knowledge. I did not know if you'd try it if you knew what it was," he explained.

"I was wondering what all those little bones were. I hate to admit it, but it's delicious. What other little specialties do they have here that I should know about?" Kristen asked. "Or should I ask? Maybe it is better that I don't know!" she laughed.

Their conversation was lively and pleasant, but controlled—first, because they were in public, and second, because they were still figuring out what topics were acceptable under the present circumstances. They both understood how vital it was not to cross the line into intimate; and they also knew how difficult it was going to be.

During dinner, Demetri kept an eye open to see whether anything was out of the ordinary, whether there was any sign of being followed or of danger. Nothing felt or looked strange, so he let down his guard just a bit. *I must keep sharp at all times*, he told himself.

There was a moment of awkwardness when the two arrived back at the room, and it was time to settle in. Kristen brought things down to earth by saying, "Would you mind if I telephone Richard? I told him I would call and let him know I arrived safely. It won't take long."

"Of course not. Should I leave you alone?" he asked.

"No, not at all. Just please don't start the shower or flush the toilet. That would be a little difficult to explain," she giggled to him as the invisible wall that had existed between them tumbled down.

Kristen was able to get through to Richard on the first try and had a brief and friendly conversation with him. "Yes, the flights were perfect. Yes, I arrived without a problem and am having a great time my first day here. No, I'm not too tired, and yes, I'll take care. Are you sure you don't want me to call you again while I'm here? In that case, I'll talk to you in two weeks, when I see you at the airport. Love you too. Bye." Kristen had been careful not to lie openly to Richard on the phone, but she felt a twinge of guilt by only telling him half truths.

Demetri had felt uncomfortable listening to the conversation. He figured that Kristen had made the call purposely to remind him of their new relationship. He also noted that there was something lacking in the communication between Richard and Kristen. Was it passion? They seemed more like brother and sister talking than husband and wife. He quickly put that thought out of his mind.

"Do you need another shower or are you all set?" Demetri asked considerately.

"I'm fine. You go take a shower, and I'll put on my PJs. When you finish, I'll wash up."

Demetri was on his bed when Kristen came out of the bathroom. She remembered that he liked sleeping in the nude, but tonight he was wearing a conservative pair of boxer shorts. She could not help but admire his appearance, especially knowing he was nearly over sixty.

He still had an athletic body that sent waves of desire through her. Kristen walked with regret over to her own bed and got in. "Good night, Demetri."

"I wanted your first night in Greece to be special," he whispered.

"It was! Thank you for a wonderful day."

"There is no need to thank me for anything. It is you I should be thanking, over and over again. Good night, *agapimou*," he said softly as he turned out the light. Kristen knew the meaning of *agapimou*: my love. Chills pierced her body when she heard Demetri let the word slip. "No, don't," she told herself. "You promised to keep your cool." It took all her strength not to creep quietly over and join Demetri in his bed, but she kept her resolve and fell asleep alone.

"*Kalimera*, Kristen," Demetri was saying as she slowly opened her eyes. "How did you sleep?"

"Fine, I guess. But Demetri, how you snore! I had forgotten about that!" she said with a smile. "I had no idea that this mission was going to include a nightly interlude. Perhaps I would have thought twice about it if I had remembered."

"I am sorry. There is nothing I can do about that," he replied seriously.

"Hey, lighten up. It will just solidify to others that we are an old married couple and sleeping instead of doing more interesting things," she said with a laugh, and Demetri laughed too.

"So what's on today's agenda?" asked Kristen.

"I have some phone calls to make privately after breakfast. Then I think we should spend some time at the beach at Agio Ioannes and then hit the shops. Remember, we are spenders. And, by the way, I have been given plenty of money, so you can buy anything you desire," he added.

"Exactly what a woman loves to hear from her husband," replied Kristen, again with a smile. "Just let me know if there is anything specific you need me to do; otherwise I will just act naturally."

"Good. Let's get ready." Demetri suggested.

The short but extremely steep and narrow drive down to the shore was a new experience for Kristen. Demetri had backed the car up twice to allow an oncoming bus and a large truck enough room to make the hairpin turns. "I'm glad you are driving and not me," she said, trying to keep her nausea from showing. "What incredible scenery! I don't think

I've ever seen anything like this." The villages were barely visible among the large trees. "I know there are rocks in the mountains, but the foliage is so thick I can't see any."

"Did you know that this road did not exist when we first met? It was only built in the eighties. Before that time there were only paths. How things have changed here in the last thirty years," commented Demetri.

And some things don't ever change, thought Kristen to herself, looking at Demetri's profile.

They arrived in Agio Ioannis to find the normally calm sea raging with five-foot waves pounding onto the beach. "This is very unusual. There must be a storm coming in. I guess we will not be able to swim today," said Demetri. "I am sorry."

"It's not your fault. As long as I don't have to be in one of those," she said, pointing to the small fleet of fishing boats bobbing on top of the unsettled waters, "I'm fine." Kristen had always been prone to motion sickness and hadn't recovered from the wooziness she had felt in the car. The thought of being in a tiny boat in the heavy surf made her nausea worse. "Why don't we explore the village first? If the weather improves, we can go swimming later."

Agio Ioannis' shops, *tavernas*, and small hotels lined the narrow strip between the mountain and the sea, spilling up the hillsides. Kristen was glad to see that there were no high-rise buildings spoiling the landscape, and that there weren't masses of people.

"I'm surprised there aren't more people," she commented.

"This is still a well-kept secret, even though it is close to Volos. And it is relatively cool and very windy today. Maybe people decided to stay in this morning," he suggested.

Kristen stared at the water, which changed colors along with the intensity of the sun. "The colors are amazing," she exclaimed. "The blue of the sky and the sea, the whitecaps of the waves, the green mountains, and the red tile roofs are so intense." Her senses were heightened by the new sights, smells, tastes, sounds, and touches. The feeling of Demetri, even just casual contact, made Kristen's skin tingle.

"What's in there?" Kristen pointed. She did not wait for an answer but entered the store and looked closely at the very colorful jars lining the shelves of a shop. "Oh, it's fruit!" Kristen bought three jars without knowing exactly which fruit was in each jar.

Demetri was amused at the purchase Kristen made. "You will have to do better than that," he smiled. "You hardly spent anything."

"It's my turn to be sorry. You see, I am always too busy at home to shop, so I am not in the habit. As a matter of fact, in Tucson Kari has to literally drag me to the mall."

"That is what a husband really likes to hear!" laughed Demetri, remembering what Kristen had said earlier. Then he asked, "How is Kari? I miss my Little One."

"She's fine and is completely unaware of this little mission of ours. She tried to get me to talk when she found out I was coming to Greece alone, but I totally refused. Aren't you proud of me?" Kristen smiled.

"Yes. I know how difficult it is for you to keep anything from Kari. Does she know that you will see me?"

"She suspects. Why else would I come to Greece? She knows I would not come to see ruins I have already explored, but she knows nothing specifically. I left a letter explaining the situation in case something bad happens in the next few days. She swore that she would not open it unless my return was delayed," Kristen explained.

"Wise of you," he noted. "I have nobody in whom I can confide except you, and you are here." Without consciously thinking about his actions, he took Kristen's hand and squeezed it. When he realized what he had done, he pulled his hand away.

"No, don't. It's okay," she said as she gently took his hand and kissed it. Demetri was touched by her sincerity and warmth. They looked deeply into each other's eyes before breaking away slowly. "Okay, dear friend, let's go get some lunch and then maybe we can go for a swim," Kristen suggested.

The rest of the day was like a slice of heaven. The weather became sunny and hot, and the surf calmed enough that they were able to swim safely. Kristen was careful to apply a lot of sunblock, knowing that it would be unwise to get sunburned. It wasn't long before she and Demetri were happily diving into the waves.

"You still swim well," remarked Demetri, seeing the ease in which she cut though the sea water.

"I have always loved to swim. Do you know I have a pool in Tucson?" asked Kristen. "I try to swim at least four times a week, even in the winter. One of the luxuries I allow myself is to heat the pool all year round."

After two hours of swimming and sunbathing, Demetri asked Kristen if she was interested in walking for a while.

"Sure. Where should we go?" Kristen asked.

"Let's go explore more of the shops," he suggested.

"That is the first time I have ever heard a man suggest a long shopping trip," she teased, although she understood Demetri's motivations.

Many of the shops looked the same to Kristen, since they all seemed to have much the same merchandise. Demetri made suggestions as to which shops would be good to explore and encouraged her to buy anything that she seemed especially to like. Kristen wasn't used to having carte blanche but easily got into the spirit of her assignment and purchased four oil paintings on canvas from a local artist. Demetri took charge of all the transactions, interacting with the merchants, paying for the purchases, and handling the packages when they left the shop, as well as carefully placing them in the trunk of the car. Kristen at first felt like a princess but then realized that Demetri was preparing her for Delphi's many shops. *This is the kind of boot camp I could really get used to*, she said to herself, but she realized the fun was about to turn serious. She told herself to enjoy it while it lasted.

Demetri's cell phone rang. After a short conversation, his mood changed.

"Is there something I should know?" Kristen asked with concern after Demetri finished the call.

"No, there is nothing," replied Demetri. "Remember, the less you know, the better it will be."

Something had transpired, but Kristen had no idea what. Because she was so in tune with him, only she saw the subtle change in Demetri's mood; nobody else would have noticed. She put on a happy face and said, "Perhaps we should take a rest. I am feeling a little tired after yesterday's long trip."

"That sounds wise. I will take you back to the room, where you can sleep for a while. I have things I need to do alone," said Demetri firmly.

Kristen knew that the good times were to be short-lived. Something had happened that she did not understand, and she knew not to pursue it further. Demetri would let her know if she needed to be advised.

She lay down, but sleep did not come easily as she contemplated the challenges and possible dangers to be faced in the days to come.

It was hours before Demetri returned to the room, looking tired and stressed. "There has been a complication. The icon had to be moved," he said simply. "Instead of Delphi, we will be driving into the mountains in western Greece near the Albanian border to a village called Metsovo. We will have to leave early in the morning."

Kristen looked deeply into his eyes. "Are you okay?" she asked.

"Yes, I am fine. I just need some sleep," he replied. "And Kristen, thank you again for being here."

Kristen left the hotel for a few minutes and purchased two gyros and a Greek salad to have for their dinner. She was gone less than twenty minutes, but when she returned to the room Demetri was sound asleep.

"He needs sleep more than food," she said as she quietly ate and then prepared for the next day by packing up their belongings.

"Good night, Demetri," she whispered as she kissed his forehead. "May God bless us both," she added as she slipped into bed and fell asleep immediately.

Chapter 23

Since Kristen had packed everything the night before, she and Demetri were able to leave the hotel efficiently after purchasing two cups of coffee from the hotel restaurant just as the sun was rising. It promised to be another hot and sunny day. There was little conversation; Demetri was concentrating on the road, and Kristen did not want to interrupt his thoughts.

Although they drove through Volos before the morning rush hour, dodging the unpredictable traffic was difficult. "I remember the driving to be crazy when I was in Greece many years ago," Kristen finally said. "I see that some things don't change." Her statement was meant to ease the tense environment in the car.

"You are right. I used to think that the traffic on Long Island was insane, but it doesn't hold a candle to the drivers here," replied Demetri, who seemed to come out of a trance. "I am sorry I have been so quiet, but I have been thinking,"

"Is there anything you can tell me or anything I can do?" Kristen asked.

"I think you should know that the police were alerted to the whereabouts of the icon and are looking for it. I don't know how they found out about it after all these years. There must be an informer in the inner circle here in Greece. That is very dangerous to everyone, including us. We may have to retrieve the icon in a different manner than first planned and it may mean more risk for you. Are you still willing to go through with this? If not, I can drop you off now and put you on a bus to Athens."

"I appreciate your concern, Demetri, but if I can be of help to you, I am not willing to leave just because the risk is higher than expected. The question I am asking is: can I be of help?" she asked.

"More now than ever, I'm afraid," he replied, with concern but also relief in his voice. "They will not suspect a woman of this. I may need you to go out on your own. Are you willing to do that?"

"I told you before, and I'll tell you again: I will do whatever it takes to free you from this bondage. I need you to tell me exactly what needs to be done," said Kristen.

"I don't know now, but I'll know more after we arrive in Metsovo."

They rode in silence, with both of them engrossed in their thoughts. They continued the trip, driving through Trikala, a busy modern-looking city, and then began to climb into the mountains. They passed Meteora, with its monasteries built into the two-hundred-meter cliffs, and on to the winding roads that led to Metsovo, high in the mountains. Kristen had silently watched the scenery and marveled at how rugged Greece is. She saw the tiny villages snuggled into the sides of the steep mountains, and wondered how the inhabitants were able to move around, especially in winter. *Surely there must be roads, but I cannot see them or imagine how they were built*, she thought. The answer to her question came as Demetri turned the car off the main road. The road leading into Metsovo was hardly wider than a single lane, was very steep, and was paved only in patches. Demetri had to pull over to let traffic pass in the opposite direction numerous times on their two-kilometer drive into the town.

"We will get settled into the hotel here, and I will have to leave you. Feel free to walk around the village and become acquainted if you wish. I will call you on this when I need you," he said, handing Kristen a cell phone. "Keep it on at all times," he instructed. She nodded. "There is a number programmed into the phone. Call it only if there is an emergency. The person who answers will give you instructions if I cannot. Here is my number. Do not call it unless you have no other choice. I will try to stay in contact with you."

They checked into the Bitounis Hotel, a family-owned, C-class hotel away from the central square of the village. Kristen was enchanted by the homey atmosphere, as well as the handwoven tapestries on the walls and in the seating areas, and the beautifully carved wood ceiling and furniture. *I could swear I'm in Switzerland*, she thought, *except that everyone here speaks Greek.*

Their room was small but immaculately clean and had all the modern comforts: a bath, a hair dryer, a TV, and a phone. What impressed Kristen was the incredible view from their small balcony. She was able to see the steep mountains they had just driven through, plus the houses of the village densely perched below. Had circumstances been different, she would have loved to spend a week or two getting to know the area.

"It is important you remember that we are married and tourists, especially in these small hotels. The people here will notice when you come and go. They may even wonder why I am leaving you alone so soon after arriving. I would recommend you tell them I am having some minor car trouble that needs to be fixed. That should appease their curiosity," said Demetri.

"Is there anything else I should or shouldn't do?" she asked.

"It is all right to go to the shops and have the merchants show you their wares. Buy something, but not too much. You will be asked where you are from. Tell them the United States but your husband is Greek, and you are visiting together. Many shopkeepers will not speak English, so keep things simple. Smile and be friendly, like you always are. I will be back as soon as possible. If it gets late, pick up some dinner or go to the *taverna* across from the hotel. Don't worry about me; I will eat when I can."

"Demetri, be careful," Kristen said as she fell into his embrace, which felt strong and soothing. She hesitantly moved away when he said it was time for him to leave.

"One kiss, please Demetri, before you go," Kristen pleaded.

"Of course," he said as his lips met hers with all the tenderness he was feeling toward her. "Until later, then," he said softly as he opened the door and was gone.

Kristen was filled with concern and anxiety. She felt panic but suppressed it, just as she had learned to do in the emergency room at work. *Panic helps nobody*, she told herself. *You need to pull yourself together*. In spite of herself, tears filled her eyes as she saw Demetri leave. "Go well," she said quietly, as if praying.

The day was still young, and in spite of the heat, Kristen decided to explore the village. She stopped in the lobby where Tolis, the owner's grown son, was happy to answer questions. "What is good to see in the town?" Kristen asked slowly, not knowing whether he would understand her.

In excellent English he replied, "There is a museum that is very nice, an art gallery, and you must visit at least one of the three monasteries."

"How far is a monastery?" asked Kristen, thinking that would interest her more than the other sights.

"It is in that direction," he said, pointing toward town. "Follow the signs. It should take you fifteen minutes to walk down, and who knows how long on the way back. You see, it is a very steep walk," he said with a slight shrug of his shoulders and a smile. "Be sure to wear good shoes if you go there.

"Metsovo is a very nice village where we make many things to sell," he continued. "We are famous for weaving and wood carving. Also, Metsovo has many kinds of cheeses that are made here," he added proudly.

"I can't wait to see the shops. When I travel I like to buy good quality items indicative of the areas I visit," Kristen added for good measure.

"You won't be disappointed. There are many fine shops here," Tolis said. "Where is your husband? Is he going with you?"

"No, he took the car to have it fixed and should be back soon," Kristen said, glad that Demetri had prepared her for the inevitable questions.

"I have a cousin who fixes cars, if you would like me to call him," Tolis offered helpfully.

Kristen had forgotten that Greeks always had cousins, especially in a small hamlet like Metsovo. "Thank you very much, but I think he has already contacted someone," she said vaguely. He seemed to accept her explanation without question.

"Good. If you want to eat, I recommend the *taverna* across the street. The food is good, and the prices are better than the ones around the square that get many tourists," he added.

"Thank you. Oh, by the way, is the water safe to drink?" asked Kristen.

"Yes, sure, it is very good. You will see springs around the village. They are all pure and safe. Enjoy your stay here," he said as Kristen thanked him and headed out the door.

The people are very friendly here, thought Kristen. *I hope that extends to icon smugglers as well*, she thought as she stepped out of the hotel, past the small patio garden filled with white petunias and red geraniums, under the stone arch that served as the entrance to the property, and began walking down the steep, slippery cobbled road into the center of the village.

She looked up and saw the layers of homes above where she stood. Most were built of the native rock on the lower levels and stucco on the second or higher stories. Although many of the houses rose up four stories, she noted that the main entrances were on the third level. "I don't suppose they have elevators," Kristen commented to herself. She was enthralled with the fine woodwork of the house windows and doors. *Beautiful*, she thought as she continued to inspect the houses that were so different from the ones in Tucson. Many had ornate wrought iron railings on balconies overhanging the road. Kristen was most impressed by how colorful everything was. Nearly every house had window boxes or hanging plants of bright reds, purples, and oranges. *It's exactly what I thought an alpine village would look like*, she commented only to herself.

As she continued her stroll, Kristen passed shops filled with beautiful, handmade wooden bowls, spoons, flutes, wine barrels, vases, and carvings of animals. She was amused by one shop that had a potpourri of old items hanging on a wire fence including brass cow and sheep bells, old wooden wagon wheels, a carved wooden pitchfork with three tines, bridles, rusty sickles, old gas irons, a number of metal utensils that Kristen could not recognize or begin to know what they were used for, and some very weatherworn woolen clothes. The word *eclectic* came to Kristen's mind as she passed the shop.

At least the small business is alive and well in Greece, Kristen thought. *It's a shame that the little guy has been forced out of business in the US*. She liked the idea of walking to the different shops and purchasing daily items from one's neighbors. It became clear to Kristen that Metsovo was not only a village, it was a community. *Bravo*, she thought.

The petrol station consisted of three gas pumps at the side of the very narrow road, with a small adjoining room to hold oil and other items needed by the numerous motorists in the town. A middle-aged man sat next to one pump, patiently waiting for his next customer.

Life teemed everywhere. The village was noisy with cars and motorcycles passing by, children playing and arguing with their parents, the sounds of construction, people greeting each other with *yassas* and *kalispera*, and music from the numerous cafés she passed.

The main square of the village seemed to Kristen to be in a state of controlled chaos, where people and motor vehicles crossed wherever they liked, buses stopped to pick up passengers and their baggage in the middle of the road, and dogs and cats scurried to stay out of harm's way. *Chaos, yes,* observed Kristen, *but it seems to work. Everyone seems content.*

Kristen passed a supermarket, and her survival instinct clicked in. *Why am I wasting time sightseeing when I should be preparing for a possibly treacherous and dangerous journey?* she asked herself. *You have been stupid,* she scolded herself. She entered the market and searched the shelves carefully. She bought foods that would be nourishing and easy to keep, including canned moussaka, meatballs and dolmas, a bag of almonds, packages of crackers and cookies, a heavy loaf of peasant bread, a large slice of Metsovo cheese, and a number of bottles of water. She also purchased two flashlights with batteries, a cigarette lighter, and a small sewing kit. *Dad would be proud,* she thought as she went through a mental checklist of emergency necessities, *except he would roll over in his grave if he knew that I had knowingly put myself in danger.* The thought amused Kristen, especially since her father was still alive. *I just hope he never finds out about all of this!*

Kristen made stops at numerous shops and purchased miscellaneous necessities and souvenirs before stopping at a pharmacy, and while she bought the essentials for a first-aid kit, she conversed with the pharmacist, who had been educated in London and spoke English well. She was surprised to find that she could purchase many drugs without the prescription that was necessary in the States, which she did. "Better to be safe than sorry," she said, remembering the training her survivalist father had given her all her life. She had brought a blood pressure cuff and stethoscope with her on the trip, feeling naked without them, and felt that she was fairly well prepared for any minor injuries she might face.

Getting all the provisions back to the hotel turned out to be a problem. Kristen was very pleased when the pharmacist said, "Here, let me take you back to your hotel in my car."

"*Efharisto poli*," Kristen called to the kind man as she entered the hotel. *What a nice thing to do*, she thought as she carried her heavy load through the lobby.

"*Kalispera*," she heard Tolis call to her. "Such a heavy load; are you going camping?" he inquired. His question reminded Kristen to be careful with her answer.

"No, we are going to have some picnics while we are here," she heard herself say. It seemed to make sense to Tolis.

"*Kala*," he added. "Just be careful of snakes. Some around here are very poisonous."

Kristen shivered at the idea of running into a snake, especially one that could be venomous.

"Thanks, I'll try to be careful," she called back as she went down the hall to their room.

Kristen spent part of the afternoon packing the provisions into the backpack she had brought with her, so that they could be easily carried. She felt good about doing something positive to help, and keeping busy kept her from worrying about Demetri.

She became restless and decided to take a walk to the monastery that Tolis had mentioned. She put on her best walking shoes and proceeded to stroll through the village before heading down the mountainside. She could not resist stopping at many shops that displayed the handwoven tapestries she had admired in the hotel, and bought items from many merchants, knowing they would make great gifts as well as additions to her home decor. *Demetri would be proud of me*, she thought as she asked the last shop owner to package her purchases and explained that she would pick them up on her way back to the hotel.

"*Entaxi, efharisto poli*," the shopkeeper replied as she waved good-bye to Kristen.

As she headed down the road toward the trailhead to the monastery, Kristen's sixth sense stirred. She looked around to see any unusual behavior and saw a young man walking toward her. She turned and quickened her pace, hoping to lose him in the crowds of tourists in the square. His pace matched hers until she lost sight of him among the throngs of people. Relieved to see that he was no longer following her, Kristen slipped out of the crowd and headed for the path. She was startled when she bumped into the same young man she had been avoiding. Panic overcame her. There was no escape. She saw that the stranger had a small package tucked under one arm. Could it be a gun? Would anyone in the village want to harm her? Rational thinking was impossible at the moment. She began to run away as the young man called to her.

"*Signomi, Kyria*," he called to her. "You forgot your purchase in my mother's shop, and she asked me to find and give it to you."

Relief and embarrassment flooded over Kristen. "Of course," she said as she reached for the offered package. "Thank you very much." She felt very foolish as the boy disappeared back into the crowd. *My imagination is getting the better of me. I need to calm down and trust that all will be well*, she said to herself.

After a few deep breaths she determinedly headed for the trail that would take her to the monastery. The path passed many of the villager's homes via steep steps carved into the mountainside. *Now I know why I have not seen any fat people in Metsovo*, Kristen said to herself. *They stay in shape by walking up and down these mountains every day.* She continued to follow the steps past the homes and a small church to a cemetery.

She stopped to view the graves that were so different from ones in the States. Each grave was built above ground level, with a picture of the person in a small shrine and the person's name, the date of death, and how old the person was at the time of death, but no birth date. Kristen remembered that Greeks did not commemorate birthdays as Americans do but their Name Day instead—a day when Greeks named after saints (and most are) celebrate their saint's special day once a year. *Perhaps that is why there are no birth dates*, she speculated.

After leaving the small cemetery, Kristen was determined to make her way to the monastery without any more distractions, which she did. Her knees bothered her from the steep grade, and she wondered how she was going to make the long climb back uphill. At last, the monastery named after St. Nicholas came into view. "I'm so glad I came!" Kristen exclaimed as she gingerly opened the large wooden door that served as the entrance. A bell clanged, notifying the caretakers that they had a visitor.

"*Ella*," she heard as she poked her head through the door and saw the inner courtyard. The monastery wasn't big or elaborate, but Kristen felt a sense of peace there she had not felt in a long time. She was shown around the small but extremely ornate church, and, although she did not understand the Greek explanations, she did understand the holy nature of the surroundings.

After seeing the monk's living quarters and taking a number of pictures, Kristen bought a book and thanked her hosts profusely for the wonderful tour. "I am so glad I made the effort to see that!" she said, knowing that few visitors to Metsovo visited the monastery because of its remote location. "I wonder if I'll be as happy when I get to the top of the mountain," she laughed, and began the rigorous climb. When she returned to the hotel, after retrieving her purchases, she was tired, and her muscles were quite sore. Upon opening the door to their room, she immediately noticed that Demetri had not returned in her absence and tried unsuccessfully not to worry.

Chapter 24

*A*s Kristen explored Metsovo, Demetri drove to Perivoti, a tiny village, where he was instructed to wait. Although it was close to Metsovo, it took over an hour to drive the twenty-five kilometers over the rough, mountainous roads. He was met by a dusty, middle-aged man, who introduced himself as Stavros as he signaled Demetri to get on the back of a decrepit motorcycle. "Your car will be safe here," he said in broken Greek. "I will return you to it when your meeting is over."

Demetri had no choice but to obey. *Stavros must be Vlach,* he thought to himself. *Greek is not his first language.* Vlach was a language that originally derived from a combination of Latin and ancient Greek and was only spoken in the high mountains of northwest Greece. It was dying because it was a language that had no written form, and the younger generation preferred to speak the more modern and acceptable Greek.

The ride went from being merely uncomfortable to excruciatingly painful to Demetri's back when they left the semipaved street and turned onto what seemed more like a rocky rut-filled goat trail than a road. He said nothing as his pain increased with the elevation. It was clear that no cars could navigate the steep, rough terrain, and, except for some goats, Demetri saw no signs of life for nearly an hour before the motorcycle came to an abrupt stop. "We are here," mumbled Stavros, who pointed to the entrance of a cave. "Go," was all he said. Demetri stiffly climbed off the motorcycle and entered the cave, not knowing what to expect.

Inside, there were five men approximately Demetri's age sitting in a circle, with a lantern as their only light source. They wore the traditional costume of the region: white wool trousers, a black blouse with an embroidered black wool vest, a black pillbox cap, and black shoes with black pom-poms. They were smoking self-rolled cigarettes, and when they saw Demetri, they signaled him to join the circle.

"You have been chosen to help us in our quest," said the group leader in Greek to Demetri. "We welcome you as a friend. You may call me Costa." Demetri was visibly relieved when he heard the words, since he had been picturing all sorts of horrible possibilities. "I am sorry we had to bring you so far, but it is necessary. After successfully hiding the icon for years, we have been exposed. The person who exposed us has been dealt with and will give neither you nor us any more problems." Demetri could imagine what kind of punishment such a person would receive and was glad that he had not been around to witness it. "However, the police know about the icon. We have had to move quickly to hide it until you can take it with you." Demetri had been aware of that information and wondered what would be expected of him next.

"Is the icon safe?" Demetri asked.

"Yes, it is safely hidden. The danger will come when it changes hands. We hear you have a friend with you. Who is she and how is she involved?"

"She became involved when my cousins used her as leverage to get me to agree to do this. She understands the risks of helping me and is totally reliable. I have known her for over thirty years, and she is willing to risk everything to make this a success," said Demetri confidently.

"Good. She can help us and is welcome," said another of the men, who remained nameless.

Demetri knew he shouldn't ask, but he could not help but inquire, "Why are you doing this?"

"Since you are risking your life, I will tell you," Costa said after a moment's thought.

"We owe our lives to your cousins," Costa began. "After World War II, this area was infiltrated by Communists. You may know about that."

"Of course I know about it," replied Demetri. "You forget that I lived in Greece during that time, and I had relatives who were killed by the Communists."

"Your cousins, after they were smuggled out of Greece with our help, protected us and our families when we faced certain death. Many years ago, they asked us to steal this icon and hide it until a time came when it could be smuggled out of the country. We did it gladly. It is a small price to pay for what they did for us," continued Costa.

"One more question. Why now?" asked Demetri.

"The icon is the one your oldest cousin prayed to when the Communists were hunting him, and he believes it saved him. He is getting very old and would like to have it with him on his deathbed. Although we do not know for sure, we believe that there are diamonds and other precious jewels hidden inside the frame. You see, it is not only a matter of your cousin's soul; the icon is probably worth millions of dollars. We only care about its spiritual value; the other only causes us trouble. Do you understand?" asked Costa.

"Yes, I understand, thank you," replied Demetri. "Tell me, what do you need me to do?"

"We will know more in a day or two. In the meantime, prepare yourselves for what may be a difficult journey. Also, continue to play the part of tourists. You will be given the location to pick up the icon. Once that is done, you will receive other instructions. Do you have questions?"

"No, not at this time," Demetri replied.

"Good, then go back to Metsovo. We will be in touch," Costa said, gesturing toward the cave's entrance.

The ride down the mountain to the car was even more miserable than the ride up, but Demetri did not notice. His thoughts were of his cousins and the difficult days ahead, and of Kristen's constant belief in him. He was determined neither to disappoint her nor to let any harm come to her.

Chapter 25

"Thank God you're back," cried Kristen as Demetri opened the door Kristen had purposely left unlocked. "I was so worried."

"Things went as well as can be expected, so you needn't have worried, but I appreciate the thought. I will tell you about it in awhile," he replied. "What I need now is a shower and some Ibuprofen. My back is killing me."

"I can supply you with the Ibuprofen. Do you need something stronger? Remember, I'm a doctor," Kristen inquired.

"No, I think I'll be all right after I rest awhile," Demetri said as he headed for the bathroom. After he finished showering, and while he toweled off his wet hair, Demetri popped his head through the door's entrance and asked, "What did you do this afternoon?"

"I began to explore the village. It is very interesting and quite pretty," she began. "And, since I did not know whether or not we would be leaving immediately, I bought food, water, and some basic necessities in case things get rough. I arranged them in a backpack and have them ready to use at a moment's notice."

Demetri smiled, "You are your father's daughter. It was very wise of you to do that, and I am ashamed to say I hadn't thought of it. I hope there will be no need for the provisions," he said, not really believing his words. He believed that Kristen's planning might actually help them out tremendously.

"So what now?" asked Kristen, although she was distracted by the sight of Demetri crossing the room with only a towel wrapped around his waist. Kristen felt a surge of desire that she suppressed.

"Now, we wait," he replied unself-consciousnessly. "We continue to play the role of married tourists until I hear more."

"So we will be staying?" asked Kristen happily. "I think I'm really going to like it here."

"Yes, at least for a day or two. Enjoy things now, because they may become dangerous very soon," he added.

"I will," said Kristen, with determination in her voice. "Now, rest."

The sun had set when Demetri awoke. "I feel much better. Thank you for the medicine and letting me sleep. Would you like to see more of the village?" he asked.

"Yes, please. You can serve as my guide, since you have been here before," Kristen added.

"I have only been here in winter. It looks very different in the summer," he replied.

"That's okay; we'll have fun discovering it together, then."

They set out on foot on the now familiar road to the main square. Demetri noticed that Kristen devoured the new sights and sounds as a hungry child would a candy bar. "It is very unusual for a foreigner to have such an interest and understanding of our culture. I am impressed," said Demetri.

"You forget, I was Greek in a former life," she teased.

"Oh, that explains it," said Demetri, going along with the joke.

"Let's walk to the square first and just sit and watch for a while; then we can find somewhere to eat," suggested Kristen, and Demetri agreed.

The festive atmosphere of the village at night was a stark contrast to the chaotic mood of the daytime. Couples of all ages, many accompanied by children, strolled toward the square. Children played and ran around, while the adults—many very elderly—sat on benches around the perimeter, chatting with their lifelong friends and relatives.

"Is there a party?" asked Kristen.

"No, this happens nearly every night," Demetri explained. "Life here is simple. People congregate each evening to pass the time and gossip with their friends. It is a tradition."

"One that I like very much!" exclaimed Kristen, watching the older women sitting quietly watching the children or conversing. Many of the women wore the traditional costume of the area: full-length dresses with close-fitting bodices, velvet sleeves of varying colors, a handwoven wool skirt covered by an apron, and a scarf worn over long braids flowing down the women's backs.

"I read in *National Geographic* that there are certain things that long-lived cultures have in common: good diet, regular exercise, and a strong feeling of family and community. I see community here, which is missing in most places in the U.S. now," Kristen commented. "Life in the mountains, especially in winter, must be very hard. Look at the hands of the women," she added. Many were large and appeared to be afflicted with arthritis.

"It is from years of physical labor that they have endured, especially more than twenty years ago when life was very difficult. And remember, many of the older women gave birth to ten or more children," said Demetri.

"I admire their deep roots and the simplicity of their lifestyle," began Kristen. "I, who have all the education and freedom to come and go as I wish, envy the simple but proud and stable lives these people live. Can you believe it?" asked Kristen. As if to explain, she added, "Sometimes the stresses and complications of everyday living get to me. There never seem to be enough hours in the day to get everything done, and I wonder why I stay in the rat race."

"That is especially true since your husband has been ill," said Demetri, causing a streak of guilt to slice through Kristen.

"Yes, it has been stressful; and practicing medicine isn't what it used to be. I went into medicine to help people, but now all that seems to matter is the financial bottom line. Medicine has become big business and not a service anymore … at least in the US. I cannot know what it is like in Greece," said Kristen, thinking aloud.

"I don't know much about it," added Demetri. "I avoid doctors as much as possible," he said and gave her a sly look. "Except one special doctor who knows how to make me feel very good."

"Oh, sir, you make me blush," Kristen said, presenting her version of a Southern belle by using a Southern accent, fanning herself, and batting her eyelashes.

Their eyes met, saying more than their words could. Kristen broke away, concerned about the intimacy of the moment. Demetri was too alluring, too available, and way too dangerous.

"Are you ready to eat?" asked Demetri. "Let's test your Greek. Answer this question. *Ti the thellate na fate?*"

Kristen answered in English without thinking that Demetri had asked the question in Greek: "Anything would be good. How about lamb?"

"*Bravo*, Kristen!" Demetri said in a pleased voice. "You have been studying."

Kristen blushed a little and smiled proudly.

They found the *taverna* across from the hotel that had been recommended to them and settled into a table on the small patio adjoining the road. "This is very romantic," Kristen said. "If circumstances were different, I'd say it was the perfect place for a honeymoon."

"But we're already an old married couple, remember?" Demetri reminded her.

"Oh, yes, I forgot," she said, smiling as the salad was placed in the middle of the table. They began eating with relish, as both were very hungry.

After they finished dinner and were sipping coffee, Kristen said, "I don't know which was more delicious, the veal or the lamb."

"They were both delicious, just like you," Demetri let slip.

Kristen looked at him sternly.

"I'm sorry," said Demetri. "I got carried away."

"I'm not angry," Kristen quickly explained. "It's just that you are too attractive to me. I am having a difficult time being good with you so near. It's killing me, but we promised, and we need to stay focused, remember? Oh, Demetri ..." she sighed without finishing her sentence. She did not need to; her eyes said everything.

They made the short walk back to the hotel in silence, both engrossed in their own thoughts.

"We'd better get some sleep," Demetri said as they reached the room. "We don't know what tomorrow may bring."

Chapter 26

At two o'clock the next afternoon, Demetri's cell phone rang. "*Ne*," he answered. Kristen watched as the conversation took place, not understanding much that was being said in rapid Greek. "We must go," he said turning to Kristen.

"When?" asked Kristen. "Should I pack the suitcases?"

"No, we will not be checking out until tomorrow, as originally planned," he said. "But I must take a long walk today. Plans have changed. Costa and friends do not want to involve any of the merchants in the area. I will have to pick up the icon at an abandoned monastery called Zoodochos Pigi. It is not far outside Metsovo and I can drive part of the way there but must walk the rest of the way and back. It may be very difficult, and I must not be seen by anyone."

"What do you mean by 'I'?" asked Kristen sternly. "The correct term is 'we.'"

"It will be a difficult trip. I cannot ask you to go with me," Demetri explained.

"That's BS! The first rule of hiking is that you never go alone. I want to go and you cannot dissuade me," she added emphatically.

"Okay, okay," Demetri said, raising his hands in a gesture of surrender. "I should have known better than to exclude the best Girl Scout in the world. You are always prepared!"

"That's better," huffed Kristen with an impish expression on her face. "What should I tell Tolis if he asks where we are going?"

"Tell him we are going to take a drive to Zagorohoria and will hike the gorge there," he replied. "Tell him that we will take a picnic and be out for the rest of the day and won't be back until late tonight."

"*Entaxi*," Kristen said without realizing that she spoke Greek. It was becoming second nature to her in a very short period of time.

"It will be a rough walk, so be sure to wear your strongest shoes," he reminded Kristen, who did not need reminding. She was used to hiking in the mountains of Arizona, where you would not dream of walking without proper boots.

Tolis was at the front desk as Demetri and Kristen were leaving, with Demetri carrying the pack.

"So you are going out?" he asked pleasantly in English.

Kristen replied just as pleasantly, "Yes. We are taking a car excursion to the gorge and hiking it. We will stop on the way and have something to eat."

"You will like it; it's very different from Metsovo. It is getting late. Perhaps you should go tomorrow," he advised.

"We can't go tomorrow, so we'll take our chances today. Thank you for your advice," said Demetri politely.

"We will see you later then," Tolis said conversationally.

"We may be in very late. Do you lock the doors at a certain time?" Kristen asked.

"No, we always have someone here," Tolis replied.

Darn! both Kristen and Demetri thought to themselves. There would be no easy way of carrying the icon into the hotel.

"Okay, then, we'll see you later," Kristen said cheerfully.

"*Kalo taxidi.* Have a good trip," Tolis called to them as they left to get into the car.

"You did very well," said Demetri to the visibly shaken Kristen.

"I hope that lying never gets easy for me," she added.

"Let's hope you don't need to once this mission is finished," said Demetri, trying to console her. "It's necessary right now."

"Where are we going?" Kristen asked as Demetri started the car.

"Not far by car. Then we will walk," he explained.

As they drove, the mountains in and around Metsovo became high and rugged. "This reminds me so much of parts of Colorado and Arizona," said Kristen. "If I didn't know better, I'd swear we were outside of Holbrook. The mountains are so dry, yet covered with scrub foliage. And so rocky!"

"Aren't mountains usually rocky?" teased Demetri. Kristen was mildly surprised that he had made up a joke.

"Very good!" she said appreciatively. Demetri smiled as he continued to watch the road.

The terrain changed from white rocks to red clay. "Now, this looks like southwest Colorado," she commented. "Someday you'll have to come and see it. It's magnificent!"

"I'd like that" was all he said. "The monastery is located at a place called Red Rock. I guess it doesn't take a genius to understand why."

They turned off the main road onto a dirt road that was rough and rocky. *I should have rented an SUV,* Demetri chided himself. "If this road gets any rougher, we will have to walk a great distance," he said aloud to Kristen. "Nobody uses this road, so the chances of us being seen are small. Keep your eyes open, though, and let me know if you see anything unusual."

They traveled another two miles before the road deteriorated to a path. "This is where we begin walking, after I find a place to hide the car," Demetri said, looking around. He spotted a crumbling rectangular building that might have been a small barn at one time. He pulled the car behind the wall so it was hidden from the road. Luckily, there were trees surrounding the area, and Demetri felt that the car could not be seen from most angles. "That is the best I can do," he said. "We will just have to hope nobody sees it. Give me the backpack."

They began walking slowly up the rough path in the heat, and although Kristen had tried to get into shape for the trip, she needed to stop occasionally to catch her breath. "Wow, this is a hike and a half," she exclaimed. "At least it will be downhill on the way back."

They were both glad that Kristen had had the foresight to bring the backpack with water and provisions. They stopped often and drank the water, even though it was no longer cool, and then continued on their way.

Suddenly Kristen screamed.

"What is it?" Demetri asked.

"Don't move. There is a snake just in front of me," she said quietly.

It was approximately four feet long, an inch in diameter, and brown with dark-brown markings.

"I don't know if it's poisonous or not, but I don't want to take any chances."

The snake became aware of their presence and quickly slithered away.

"I sure am glad that snake wasn't the aggressive type. Did you see how fast it was? We wouldn't have had a chance!" She gave a visible sign of relief, collected her wits, and began walking.

Demetri watched Kristen and admired the way she was able to handle the unexpected situation.

They finally arrived at the monastery—hot, sweating, and breathless. Kristen looked around at the ruins and said, "This must have been an amazing place at one time. Look at the view! And feel the cooling breeze up here."

"*Zoodochos Pigi* means the Fountain of Life," Demetri explained. "It seems ironic that a place with such a name would be left to die," he said poetically.

"You are still the romantic, aren't you?" commented Kristen, not trying to be funny.

"Yes, I still am, sometimes," he replied.

The monastery was surrounded by a six-foot stone wall. The chapel was just inside the front entrance with the two-story living quarters beyond. The roofs were missing from most of the natural stone buildings, and many of the support beams were rotted, causing the upper stories to collapse into the lower areas. The chapel had no door, so Kristen and Demetri were able to see inside without difficulty.

"I wonder who lived and prayed here," commented Kristen. "And what their lives were like."

"There are old monasteries all over Greece," explained Demetri. "The monks lived very simple lives of prayer and contemplation. They grew their own food, made their own wine, and lived separately from others. Many monasteries have been closed and left to decay because people do not want to live this kind of life anymore."

He is always the teacher, thought Kristen admiringly. "Thank you for the lesson; it was very interesting," she said. "Sometimes I think this kind of life would be easier," she said, thinking of all the stresses in her life.

"If it was easy, more people would want to live it," said Demetri.

"You're right," said Kristen. "Okay, we're here; now what?"

"I was told that I would find the icon in the bell tower. Let's go," said Demetri as he climbed over the loose rock.

"Be careful," said Kristen with concern.

The icon was exactly where Demetri had been told it would be. He carefully removed it from its protective packing and held it up for Kristen to see.

"It's not as big as I had imagined," said Kristen, "which is a good thing."

The icon looked very old, the gold leaf peeling away from the ancient-looking wood and its thick, rustic frame. It measured only twenty-eight by thirty-five centimeters. It did not look like an image of Christ to Kristen, so she asked, "Who is he?"

"I do not know, and I do not care," said Demetri bluntly. "The Orthodox Church has many icons of saints and martyrs. It could be any one of them. All we need to know is how to hide it."

"It will fit in my backpack," Kristen interjected as she began emptying it of food and some of the water that was left.

"Good, but we must not leave anything behind. They must not suspect that anyone has been here recently," warned Demetri.

"Good point. We can put the food in one of the plastic bags from the grocery store and carry it out separately," she said as she started rummaging through the backpack.

"You are well prepared. I am impressed," smiled Demetri. "Now, let's go." Kristen volunteered to carry the backpack first, over Demetri's protests.

"I'm younger than you are," she retorted. "And don't give me any of that male chauvinist crap about the man being the only one strong enough to carry a burden. I'll let you know when I get tired. We just need to go slowly." Demetri was stunned into submission. He had never noticed Kristen swear before and understood she was serious.

"All right," was all he said, and he handed the backpack to her.

As they began their trek down the mountain, the sky was getting very dark. There was no moon, and the path was very steep, rocky, uneven, and slippery with foliage that had accumulated.

"No, we must not use the flashlights unless we have to. Someone may see us," instructed Demetri as Kristen switched on the light. She immediately extinguished it.

"I understand your concern," she argued. "But I can't see where I'm going."

Just then, Kristen heard a sudden intake of breath and a muffled cry as Demetri stumbled and fell. Kristen heard his groans from below and switched on the light.

"Are you okay?" she cried and saw him lying on the ground twenty feet below the path, barely conscious. She quickly but carefully made her way down to where Demetri lay, assisting in her descent by grabbing the branches of the nearby trees as she went.

The physician in her immediately took command. She first checked to see whether he was breathing regularly, which he was. She then called, "Demetri," close to his ear, but not loudly enough to be heard up the mountain. He reacted to the sound of her voice. "Good," she said.

She then quickly shone the flashlight into each of his eyes. "Also good," she repeated. His pupils were equal and reactive to light. Chances were that he would regain full consciousness quickly. Next, Kristen examined his head without moving his neck and discovered a large gash behind his left ear that was bleeding profusely. She reached into the backpack and brought out the first-aid kit. *Thank God I got this*, she thought, and opened a pack of sterile gauze and placed firm pressure on the wound. She wrapped the gauze with the Ace bandage she had purchased, which kept the pressure while freeing her hands, and she began to look for other injuries. Except for some bruises that were forming and some minor contusions, he appeared all right. Demetri regained full consciousness, and Kristen stopped him from moving.

"You fell and hit your head. I need you to stay still until I can figure out if you have had a neck injury. Just tell me where you hurt," she said in her most professional voice.

"My head and my left arm," Demetri said.

Kristen examined his arm, which was scraped pretty badly but didn't appear to be broken. "I want you to move your fingers," she instructed, and he did. "Now move your feet," which he was able to do.

"Do you feel any numbness or tingling in your arms or legs?"

"No," he whispered to her.

"Okay. I'm going to gently move your head and you tell me if you have any pain." She did and he denied any pain or numbness.

"It looks like you were lucky. You have a pretty severe cut on your head, but I don't think you have a concussion or have damaged your neck or back. Lie there a few minutes until the wound stops bleeding; then you may sit up if you can," Kristen explained.

Demetri did as he was instructed. Within ten minutes the bleeding had stopped and he was able to sit up, although he felt very dizzy. "That is normal. Just stay still until it passes," she said calmly.

Once he was feeling well enough, he slowly stood up with Kristen's help. A wave of nausea and dizziness swept over him, which resolved as quickly as it had appeared. "We can't walk out of here with you in this condition," said Kristen firmly. "We need to go back to the monastery where you can rest, and I can stitch you up."

"But how will you do that?" asked Demetri.

"When you said I am my father's daughter, you weren't exaggerating. I always carry albuterol, epinephrine, and a vial of lidocaine with me in case of life-threatening emergencies. I don't know why, really. I've never needed to use them, but I'm glad I have them now. I also carry a couple of syringes for good measure. I don't have proper suture material, but I do have a sewing kit with me, so that will have to do."

"You are amazing," said Demetri.

"Then, carefully, let's go back and get you fixed up," said Kristen as she wrapped Demetri's arm around her shoulder to give him balance on the short climb up the hill back to the path. "And don't worry, the icon is fine," she added for good measure.

The monastery looked very eerie in the semidarkness, casting shadows from the newly risen moon. They entered what was once the living quarters, in an area that was relatively undamaged. Demetri sat on a large rock and Kristen began working on his wound, first releasing the bandage slowly to make sure it did not begin bleeding again. She then irrigated the wound with the bottled water. "This is going to hurt," she said as she injected the three-inch wound with lidocaine. Demetri did not flinch. She then sterilized the sewing needle the best she could by putting the needle in the flame of the cigarette lighter and quickly began stitching.

"I hope you don't mind blue," she said as she began. "It's the only color they had." She hoped that Demetri would find her statement amusing and that it would help to lighten the serious atmosphere.

"I prefer pink, but blue will be acceptable," he replied, and Kristen knew he was going to be all right.

"I'm done," she said about ten minutes later. "How do you feel?"

"I am okay."

"Good. I want you to drink a liter of this water before we begin our trek back. And I want to take your blood pressure." Demetri was pleasantly surprised with all the equipment she had fit in the pack.

"Your blood pressure is slightly low, but that is to be expected. Drinking the water and replenishing the fluid you have lost will bring it back to normal," explained Kristen.

They spent another hour in the cool and dusty monastery before beginning the long hike back to the car. It was two AM when they drove up to the entrance of the hotel.

"Let me go in first with the package and the food," Kristen recommended. If anyone asks, I'll tell them you are unpacking the car. I will go and get you another shirt to change into, since yours is covered with blood. If we are lucky, they will not notice your hair. I will be right back, okay?"

"Good idea. I will be here. There is another shirt just like this one in my bag," Demetri said.

"Wish me luck," Kristen said as she entered the hotel.

Luckily, the person on duty was snoozing in a chair in front of the TV, which was showing reruns of the American version of Hercules, with Greek subtitles. Kristen retrieved their only key hanging from a hook behind the desk and tiptoed into the room unnoticed. She retrieved a new shirt for Demetri, who put it on. They then entered the hotel with the pack slung on Demetri's back and casually called their greetings to the drowsy clerk as they crossed the lobby into the hallway that led to their room.

"Whew, that was a close one," Kristen exclaimed as she helped Demetri remove his clothes and get into bed.

She kissed him lightly on the forehead. "Good night, *Demetrimou*," she said quietly as he fell into an exhausted slumber. "Rest well, and I will see you in the morning."

Kristen took everything out of the backpack and placed the wrapped icon in her suitcase, surrounding it with her clothes. She figured there wasn't a safer place for it at that point. Afterward, she took a brief shower to remove the dirt and relieve her tired muscles from the day's trekking. She slept fitfully until the sound of Demetri's phone ringing woke them both.

Chapter 27

"No," said Demetri sleepily into the phone. He looked around the room, trying to get oriented to his environment. He saw Kristen, and the reality of yesterday's events flashed back to him in a millisecond.

Kristen heard Demetri's side of the conversation but again understood very little. She allowed herself to wake up slowly, not wanting to face the day to come with fewer than four hours of sleep. She looked out the window and saw the mountains perfectly silhouetted by the rising sun. *Beautiful*, she thought.

"Coffee, I need coffee," she said aloud to herself, but there was none available. It would be at least an hour before the breakfast room of the hotel opened. She heard Demetri end the conversation and saw him turn to her.

"Good morning," he said softly. "I did not have a chance to thank you for saving me last night, so I would like to do it now."

"You are welcome. Come over here so I can see my handiwork in the light of day," she requested. He sat on the bed next to her as she sat up and inspected the wound. "Not bad, especially under the circumstances. I can hardly see the sutures, and it looks like there is no infection, although the procedure was hardly sterile. You can wash your hair to get the blood out, as long as you do it gently and carefully."

"Maybe you should wash it for me," Demetri said, remembering Terracina.

"Hmmm," Kristen replied. "I think not. That would be more dangerous than having this stolen icon in our baggage."

"You're right. My head is killing me. Do you have any more of that Ibuprofen?" he asked, changing the subject. She reached into her bag and brought out three. "Eat something with this. There is bread and cheese in the bag."

"Gladly. I'm very hungry," he said.

"And I'm dying for a Starbucks," Kristen added. Demetri looked at her questioningly. "Forget it, you would not understand. Tell me about the call."

"They asked if we had the package. I told them it was with us and that we were not seen. I also told them about my accident and what you did for me."

Kristen got right to the point. "What are we supposed to do now?"

"I don't know if you are going to like this or not," said Demetri hesitatingly.

"It doesn't matter whether or not I like it. Tell me what we have to do to complete the mission," insisted Kristen.

"They want me to go get the boat," he began.

"That makes sense," Kristen interjected.

"And they want you to carry the icon in your baggage and go to the island of Corfu, off the west coast of Greece, where I will meet you," he added. "They believe it will be less likely that the police will look for the icon on a foreign tourist."

"How will I get there?" was all Kristen asked. Demetri was very proud that Kristen had not blinked when she heard what she had to do.

"You can catch a bus from Metsovo to Ioannina, and then another to Igoumenitsa. There you can easily get on a ferry to Kerkira, the capital of the island."

"What will I tell people here if they ask why I am taking a bus, and you are leaving in the car?" she questioned.

"We need to leave the hotel together. Nobody else will question your movements; nobody else knows or cares who we are," Demetri replied.

"That makes sense. Corfu isn't far. I should be there in one day. It will take you two or three to get there. What will I do in the meantime?" she asked.

"It is safer for you to be in Corfu, where there are thousands of Americans. Find a large hotel to stay in, where your actions will not be noticed, and call me on my cell phone to let me know where you are. If you don't get through to me, keep trying. I may be out of range. You also have the contact number I gave you in case of an emergency," he instructed.

"What do I do with the icon until you arrive?"

"That is a good question. I am not familiar enough with Corfu to know if there are storage lockers or not. You may need to take it into your hotel room, but be careful, housekeeping must not have a chance to see it," Demetri thought out loud. "I don't know how else to advise you at this point. I am sorry."

"What happens if I am arrested?" Kristen asked in a manner-of-fact voice, not allowing her concern to show.

"You need to plead ignorance. You have no idea how the icon got in your bag. It must have been put into your suitcase without your knowledge on the ferry. Then use the cell phone number I gave you. They will help until I can be with you. I have made sure there are no fingerprints on the icon. Do not handle it."

"You've got a deal on that. The less I know about it, the better, remember?" she said. Then she asked, "When do we go?"

"There is a bus to Ioannina at 8:30, so we must hurry," Demetri said.

They both got busy. Demetri showered, while Kristen packed their belongings. By the time they were finished, the breakfast room had opened. "I will get coffee and breakfast and bring it up to the room," said Kristen. "I don't want anyone noticing your stitches, although they barely show through your thick hair."

They relished the hot, strong coffee that helped refresh their two weary bodies. As soon as they finished the simple breakfast of bread, cheese, and yogurt, it was time to leave. Demetri turned Kristen toward him and held her tightly at arm's length until their eyes locked.

"How can I tell you how much you mean to me, and how much I appreciate what you are doing for me? Words cannot express my appreciation," and, after hesitating, "my love." He pulled her to him. She raised her face to receive the kiss that might be their last. She did not pull away. She felt the thrill of his lips on hers and was carried away by emotion. The passionate kiss they shared lasted nearly a minute and said everything that neither one had allowed themselves to express in words.

"Go with God," said Demetri. "And may he bring you back to me safely."

"Please be careful, my love," is all she could say. Demetri was touched to his very core when he heard the passion in her voice.

Kristen paid the hotel bill in cash as Demetri loaded the car. "Thank you for everything, Tolis. We enjoyed our stay here very much. I only wish we could stay longer," Kristen said.

"Perhaps you will come back sometime," replied Tolis politely.

"I hope so," Kristen said and secretly thought, *Until then,* yassas.

Demetri turned the car down the hill toward the square. The bus was just arriving as he unloaded Kristen's suitcase. "Here, you better take the backpack. You know how to use it better than I. And here is plenty of money. You may need it," he said, trying to smile.

She accepted both, and Demetri loaded her suitcase with the icon into the baggage compartment of the bus, where they decided it would be safer. He returned to her side. They had said their good-byes and did not want to draw attention to themselves by kissing each other in public. Kristen merely looked back at Demetri as she boarded the bus. Demetri waited for the bus to leave before he got into the car and headed back to Corinth.

"Please God," they both prayed. "Keep us safe."

Chapter 28

*K*risten found an empty seat by the window and settled in. *What have I gotten myself into?* she asked herself. A woman in her late twenties sat next to her. Kristen greeted her with *"Kalimera,"* and the woman acknowledged the greeting but said nothing. As the bus picked up speed, Kristen subtly waved to Demetri, who was watching her with great concern on his face. He simply nodded his head as the bus turned and then was out of sight.

Kristen thought it would be less conspicuous if she appeared to be traveling with another woman and purposely began a conversation with her seat mate. "Do you speak any English?"

"Yes, I do," the woman responded in a distinctly British accent. "Where are you heading?"

"My final destination is Corfu, but I may just go to Ioannina or Igoumenitsa today. I haven't decided," Kristen replied.

"What a coincidence! I am going to Corfu too, but I will make the entire journey today," she said. "My name is Sofia."

"I'm Kristen," she said, feeling greatly relieved to have someone to travel with, at least for a while. "What were you doing in Metsovo?"

"I have family there. It was my mother's sixtieth birthday, and we had a family reunion. I am going to Corfu for a few days of fun before I head back to London," Sofia said. "And you?"

"I had heard wonderful things about Metsovo, and just had to see it during my three-week trip to Greece. My friends wanted to stay by the sea and weren't interested in going to the mountains. I will meet them in Corfu, when they arrive tomorrow," Kristen lied. She thought it sounded convincing.

"Where are you staying?" Sofia asked.

"I haven't figured that out yet. I hope to find a room when I arrive," Kristen said.

"It is high season, but the ferry arrives early in the day, which is good. When you get off the boat, you will see people selling their empty rooms. Many will have brochures or pictures of their hotels and *domatias*, rooms. Make sure you negotiate a good price and insist on seeing the room before you agree to stay," Sofia advised.

"Thanks for the advice. It's been many years since I have been to Greece, and I find things a little intimidating at times, especially since I don't speak the language very well," Kristen said.

"You will find that most Greeks are good to strangers. Hospitality is very important here. If you have a question or a problem, just ask someone," Sofia said. "If you decide to go on to Igoumenitsa, follow me; we need to change buses in Ioannina."

"I may just do that, thank you," said Kristen with some relief as the conductor stopped at her row, asking for her destination. "Ioannina, for now," Kristen said and paid the requested fare.

Ioannina wasn't far from Metsovo, but the ride took almost an hour and a half because of the winding and sometimes steep road. Kristen noticed the scenery changing from high, alpine, tree-covered terrain to a more barren appearance.

"If you decide to stay in Ioannina, and you have a chance," began Sofia, "you should go up to Zagori, where there is a very beautiful gorge. You can get there by bus, or you could take a taxi or hire a car; it's not far."

"Thank you, I may just do that," said Kristen, thinking, *It never hurts to play the role of tourist.* She thought it was ironic that she and Demetri were supposed to have gone there the previous day. "It must be very popular," she continued to Sofia. "I have heard many people speak of it."

As the bus arrived in Ioannina, Kristen noticed a number of policemen checking people's identity papers as they boarded the buses in the busy station. "What's going on?" she asked Sofia.

"I don't know. This is very unusual," said Sofia.

Kristen felt a wave of panic sweep over her. *The police may be looking for the icon,* she thought. *What should I do?*

Just then, a policeman boarded the front of the bus and talked to the driver for a moment. He asked for and inspected identity papers of some of the passengers. Kristen sat with a pleasant smile on her face, although her heart was beating fast enough to cause her chest pain. The policeman stopped next to her row. He looked directly at Kristen and Sofia for a moment, and then said something in Greek that Kristen did not understand.

"He wants to see your passport," Sofia explained.

Trying to control the tremor in her hands, Kristen reached into her purse and handed her passport to the officer. He looked at it intently and then again at her, comparing her picture to her face.

"What is the purpose of your visit?" he said in English.

"I am on vacation," Kristen said as calmly as she could. The policeman hesitated a moment and then looked at Sofia, asking for her papers. Seemingly satisfied, he moved on to the next row.

Kristen's relief was immeasurable, but she realized that she was in big trouble. She had escaped once, but it appeared that the police were less interested in arriving passengers than departing ones, who were being asked to open their bags for inspection. *This is very bad*, she told herself.

"You know what, Sofia? Ioannina looks very interesting, after all; in spite of whatever is going on here. I think I will take your advice and visit the gorge today and catch the bus and ferry to Corfu tomorrow," said Kristen, trying to keep her manner light and cheerful.

"I think you will like it. I have a half an hour before the bus leaves for Igoumenitsa. Would you like to have a coffee with me, and I can tell you about the city?" Sofia offered.

"Yes, that would be nice," Kristen said as they left the bus. "I'm afraid I have a lot of luggage," she murmured as she struggled with the backpack while attempting to get her suitcase from under the bus.

"Here, let me help," offered Sofia, who relieved Kristen of the backpack. "Haven't you learned to travel light?" she asked teasingly.

"I'll never learn, I'm afraid," responded Kristen as she wheeled her bag to the café across the square from the bus station.

After they had ordered two iced coffees, Kristen needed to use the toilet and began shuffling her luggage toward the sign pointing the way.

"Why don't you leave our luggage here? I will look after it for you," offered Sofia.

After hesitating a moment, Kristen realized it would look suspicious to ignore this friendly request. "Thank you, that is very kind of you," she said politely.

"*Tipota*," Sofia replied. "I will watch it carefully until you return."

Kristen tried to control the shaking of her hands as she dialed Demetri's number once she was alone. A recording came on the line and informed her that the party she was calling was unavailable. "Damn!" Kristen exclaimed, but she did not panic. She took a very deep breath and dialed the emergency number. The line was answered after one ring. *Thank God*, Kristen thought as she quietly explained her situation.

"Is the package safe?" asked the person at the other end of the line in English.

"Yes," replied Kristen.

She was given thorough instructions, including where to go to wait to be picked up. "You were right to call. Act naturally and do exactly what I have told you to do, and you will be fine. I will see you within two hours," said the voice, and the phone went dead.

After using the toilet, Kristen rejoined Sofia, who was sipping her coffee. Having someone to talk to, if even for a few minutes, helped calm her nerves. Sofia began explaining the highlights of the city, but Kristen's ears were ringing so badly from fear she could not concentrate on the words being spoken.

"I have to catch my bus," Sofia said eventually as she reached for her purse.

"No, please, let me pay," said Kristen quickly. "I have enjoyed meeting and talking with you so much. Perhaps we will run into each other on Corfu."

"*Efharisto*," Sofia said, adding, "*Adiosas*" as she crossed over to the bus and opened her small bag for inspection before she boarded.

Kristen suddenly felt terribly vulnerable and alone. She did not lose her head, though, and, after paying the bill, she began walking slowly toward a large hotel with her luggage, as she had been instructed to do. She walked into the lobby and explained to the man at the front desk that she was being met by a friend and asked whether it would be all right if she waited there, even though she wasn't checking in.

"*Entaxi*, sure, it is okay," the young man said. "Maybe next time you will stay here instead," he said in English.

"*Efharisto, poli*," Kristen replied and sat on a comfortable sofa close to the entrance. *Greeks are very hospitable*, she thought to herself, relieved to have a cool, relatively safe place to wait.

Kristen's nerves jumped every time someone entered the lobby, expecting her contact to arrive, and praying that the police would not search the hotel. Exactly two hours after her call, a handsome, well-dressed, middle-aged man in a suit and tie entered the lobby. He turned to Kristen, smiled, held out his arms, and called, "Cousin, I am so glad you are here. It has been a long time." Kristen instantly realized who he was, and perpetuated the charade by hugging the stranger as if they were long-lost relatives. "Come with me," he whispered, "you will be safe." Kristen followed, carrying the backpack as he took hold of the handle of the suitcase and wheeled it out the front door.

When they were alone, he said, "I am Alexis. The police you saw were looking for the icon, as you suspected. You were right to call for help."

Kristen was visibly shaken when she realized how close she had come to being arrested. She was also slightly relieved, realizing that she had instinctively known what to do in a crisis.

"What next?" she asked.

"We will get you to the ferry, but not by the main road. We will have to take the very rough mountain roads that go to Igoumenitsa, where we will drop you. We will have to be very careful. There are no tourists where we are going, and you will stand out with your modern clothes and your blonde hair. Once we get to Igoumenitsa, you will look like the thousands of other American and British tourists taking the ferries, and you should be safe. Now, *pame*." She opened the passenger side door of the black four-wheel drive SUV, threw the backpack in the back seat, and fastened her seatbelt as Alexis placed the suitcase carefully in the storage area and started the car.

Chapter 29

"What have I done?" Demetri kept saying to himself, over and over again. "If anything happens to Kristen, I'll never forgive myself. How did she ever convince me to allow her to do this?" he chided himself as he put the car into gear and headed up the steep road past the hotel that led to the main road to Trikala. His thoughts were interrupted when he swerved to the right to avoid colliding with a truck driving in the opposite direction. "*Malaka*," Demetri swore at the other driver as he turned the car back onto the road, this time in Greek since there was no English equivalent. "This is not a good way to begin a long drive."

All went well for another twenty minutes, when traffic stopped ahead. As he drove closer, he saw that the road was blockaded, and the police were searching every vehicle. "What the hell!" Demetri exclaimed. "This is bad, this is very bad," he repeated—not so much for himself, knowing he had nothing incriminating on him or in his car, but out of concern for Kristen's well-being. He considered turning the car around, but knew it was of no use to do so.

"I've been in a lot worse situations than this," he told himself. "Just be cool and do not attract attention to yourself by losing your temper."

When it was his turn to be inspected, Demetri provided the policeman with his Greek identity papers and pleasantly inquired in Greek, "What is going on?" The policeman ignored his question and, after searching the back seat, gestured for Demetri to open the trunk. The many purchases he and Kristen had made were there, but after careful inspection, the policeman did not seem to be interested in questioning him further. "You may go," was all he said.

Demetri closed the trunk and was allowed to proceed without further delay. His heart pounded—not for his own safety, but for Kristen's. He tried calling Kristen to warn her that the police were actively searching travelers but was unable to get a signal.

"Damn," he swore again.

He had no choice but to continue his journey, wondering every minute whether Kristen was safe.

He stopped at Kallambaka and used a landline to try to call Kristen's cell phone. There was no answer. He then called his contact and told him of the incident. "We will take care of it," Demetri heard. "You continue, and we will be in touch when we know something." Demetri had no choice but to comply.

He debated the route he should take to get to Corinth, where the boat was docked. *If I drive to Lamia and then to Itea on the coast near Delphi, I might be able to catch a ferry that will take me there*, he thought. *But there is no guarantee I will be able to get the car on the ferry without a reservation, and I do not know the schedule. It may be quicker if I take the National Road to the turnoff close to Athens and drive through Corinth. At least I am familiar with the road.* He decided on the latter of the two routes.

When he was close to Lamia, he tried calling Kristen again. This time she answered the phone, to his great relief. "Are you all right?" were his first words.

"I am fine," she said, although she did not feel fine. "The police were searching the buses, and I only traveled as far as Ioannina. I had some scary moments, but I am now with friends who are going to take me over the mountains to Igoumenitsa. How are you?"

"Physically I am fine. There was a police roadblock on the way to Kallambaka, but I had no trouble. Mentally, I am very worried about you."

"Don't be. I am in good hands now. Alexis wants to talk to you," she said as she passed the phone to him. The conversation that followed was in Greek. She knew she would not follow it, so she turned her thoughts to other things until the phone was passed back to her.

"It looks like you have a hard journey ahead of you tonight and tomorrow. I am sorry for all of this," Demetri said.

"Let's put it this way," Kristen retorted, "you owe me big!"

Demetri tried to laugh at her attempt at levity but could only say, "I know. Be safe and well, and we will talk again soon."

"Good-bye for now," said Kristen and closed the phone. Demetri's heart ached, knowing the danger to which he had exposed Kristen. *I will make this up to her*, he promised to himself, *if it takes the rest of my life.*

The rest of his journey went smoothly. Although it was almost midnight, he returned the rental car and exchanged it for his own, which he had left parked in their lot. He transferred the purchases from the sedan to the SUV he owned and drove to his boat without stopping at his home. He did not want to be seen by friends or neighbors and have to answer the questions they would ask.

His boat was a forty-foot cabin cruiser that was able to make the long journey, although he had never taken her so far alone. As long as the weather stayed nice, he believed he should have no problem handling her himself. There was always someone willing to help dock the boat at a marina along the way, which was the most difficult part of a solo trip. He estimated that it would take about twelve hours of traveling to reach Kerkira, not including any stops he would have to make. He hoped to be there within a few hours of Kristen's arrival, although he had no idea when that would be. It would depend on how her trek through the mountains went.

He decided to get a couple hours of sleep before setting off at sunrise, but after finding it impossible to keep his brain from spinning, he set out in the darkness. "Please be safe," Demetri said softly as he started the engine and pulled away from his slip and pointed the boat toward Patras.

The next morning was clear and calm. *A good omen*, thought Demetri. *I should make good time.* As he was drinking his second cup of coffee, a great surge of emotion swept over him. He never felt freer and seldom happier or closer to God than when he was on his boat on the calm sea. Although he hadn't always agreed with organized religion, he was extremely spiritual. He asked God to bless his journey, to keep Kristen from harm, and to forgive him for what he was doing.

The day passed uneventfully. Demetri enjoyed being in the sun and loved the feeling of the wind in his hair. Had it not been for his worry about Kristen, the day would have been perfect. He arrived in Patra by early morning, where he filled the fuel tank and pointed the boat north.

It had been years since he had seen the west coast of the mainland, and he marveled at the beauty of the coastline and of the islands of varying sizes that he passed.

Demetri studied the environment, something Kristen had taught him to do in Metsovo. He saw the calm, deep-blue water that was without whitecaps, the sail boats and powerboats that passed, leaving wakes that reminded him of the contrails jet planes create in the sky. He viewed the rugged peaks of the mountains, which looked like distant shadows instead of hard granite and marble, knowing that Kristen was there. He felt thrilled when he spotted a pod of dolphins racing in front of the bow of the boat, something that occurred often for him, and something he always considered a sign of good luck. Had it not been for the reality of the mission, Demetri would have felt the happiest he had in years.

He decided to make a quick stop in Fiscardo, a small yachting village on the northern tip of Kefalonia. He knew he would be able to obtain fuel and a good meal, both desperately needed.

"If only Kristen could be here with me, this would be perfect," he said to himself as he jumped from the deck onto the pier with the help of a fellow sailor.

"Where can I get fuel and Ouzo?" he asked his new acquaintance.

"Everything you need is right here," the man replied.

"If only that were true," said Demetri to himself as he strolled to the nearest café.

Chapter 30

*A*s Kristen rode out of Ioannina with Alexis, it suddenly occurred to her that she was completely at the mercy of strangers. *I have no choice but to trust them,* she thought. *What else can I do? And besides, what would they want me for, white slavery? I think I'm way too old for that,* she laughed quietly to herself. Her instincts told her that she was in good hands and that she would arrive in Corfu safely, so she ignored her other thoughts and began to relax.

"Where are we going?" she asked Alexis. The moment the words flowed from her mouth, she knew it was a silly question. She had no knowledge of the area, so place names would have no meaning for her. She quickly added, "Never mind, it doesn't matter."

"The plan is to take you out of town, where you will be met by other friends, and I will say good-bye to you," said Alexis. "They know the mountain roads and will see you safely to your destination."

"I see, thank you," said Kristen.

"They are very good and simple people. They speak very little English and you may have difficulty understanding them. Trust them. They will take good care of you and the package," he added.

It wasn't long until Alexis drove behind an abandoned stone building and stopped the car. "We will be met here," he said. "Before they come, we need to put the icon in your backpack. Take anything out of it that you will not need and place it in your suitcase," which Kristen did.

As they were finishing, a very old, very rusty pickup truck arrived with two men in the cab. Alexis quickly placed a burlap cloth over the suitcase he placed in the back and said to Kristen, "This is Stergios and Nikos." Kristen smiled and nodded to them. "*Kali spera,*" she said. Their only reply was to point to a bundle in the truck and point Kristen to the decrepit building. Stergios then said a few words to Alexis in a language that did not sound like Greek to Kristen.

"They want you to change your clothes from what you are wearing to what they have brought. Although this will not fool anyone up close, it will make you look like one of the locals," explained Alexis.

Kristen took the heavy bundle into the house and quickly changed. "How do I look?" she asked Alexis, when she rejoined the group of men. She had been transformed into one of the local women, wearing a costume similar to the ones she had seen the women in Metsovo wearing. "All this wool," Kristen commented. "How do they stand the itching and the heat?"

"They are used to it. The dresses serve them well with the temperature changes in the mountains. It can get very cold at night. Now, go with God," Alexis said and quickly drove away.

After Kristen's modern clothes were put into her suitcase and the backpack safely tucked behind the seat in the truck, Stergios stomped on the gas pedal and they sped away in a cloud of dust, heading for the mountains Kristen could see in the distance.

There was no conversation during the dusty, bumpy trip. After offering Kristen a hand-rolled cigarette, which she refused, Stergios and Nikos chain-smoked. The smoke made her nauseous, but she said nothing and tried to ignore it. The wool of her costume drove her mad, but she also tried not to scratch, knowing it would just make the discomfort worse. *I have got to remember that these people are helping me*, said Kristen to herself, although she felt thoroughly miserable in the foreign environment.

They passed small villages along the way. Most appeared abandoned, with many of the natural stone houses crumbling and the roofs missing. She wondered whether earthquakes or wars had caused the homes to be destroyed. "Whatever it was," she said to herself, "it is sad." They traveled through a few inhabited villages, and Nikos would wave and greet the people as they turned to look at the vehicle speeding past their homes. "*Yia sou,*" he would yell out the window. Nobody seemed to notice Kristen as something unusual, and she was pleased with the disguise.

Their journey was impeded twice when they came upon large herds of goats blocking the road. Stergios brought the truck nearly to a stop, greeted the goat herder, and inched the vehicle carefully through the protesting animals. Kristen found the goat's cries and the numerous notes of the tinkling bells around their necks to be quite musical. "Like a modern symphony," she said to nobody. It was then that she began to enjoy the trip. *I will consider this an anthropological study*, she thought as she relaxed. *Attitude is everything*, she reminded herself.

As the sun was setting, Kristen was relieved to see a populated village when the vehicle slowed to a stop. Kristen followed Stergios and Nikos out of the truck, and stretched out the soreness she had developed over the rough roads. She was hungry, thirsty, and needed to use the bathroom very badly. Nikos seemed to understand and pointed in the direction of a small house. "Go," he said simply, which she did.

As Kristen entered the door, a woman greeted her by smiling and gesturing. She appeared to be in her mid-sixties, was wearing a dress, black stockings, and head scarf like Kristen's, and was stout and sturdy-looking, with coarse facial features and huge hands. Kristen looked around, and was amazed at the beauty of the simple home. It had only two rooms—a bedroom and a room that served as living room and kitchen. The rough stone walls were covered with pictures of family members and favorite politicians. There were two icons over the basic but practical fireplace. Kristen was most impressed by the beautiful and very colorful handwoven cloth that covered every inch of the seating area, the chairs, and the simple wooden table in the center of the room. The kitchen consisted of a brick oven for baking, a stone sink with barrels and spigots placed above, and a "stove" made out of a large, flat stone with raised rod irons to put pots above a wood fire. Kristen was impressed at how clean and orderly everything was.

They exchanged names with gestures and smiles. The woman's name was Maria. She took Kristen's elbow and led her to the back door of the cottage. There, to Kristen's relief, she saw an outhouse. "Thank you," Kristen said in English. Maria smiled and nodded her head encouragingly.

What interesting people, thought Kristen as she walked back to the house. *I had no idea that people still lived like this.*

After returning to the living area, Maria offered Kristen a seat; then she quickly appeared carrying a brass tray with four small glasses, each containing a clear liquid. Maria set two glasses in front of Kristen and two on the table and then sat and raised the glass with a lesser amount in it, as if to make a toast. Kristen followed suit and raised her glass and then sipped the licorice-flavored beverage carefully. It burned as it slid down her throat, but Kristen liked the flavor. *So this is what ouzo tastes like*, she said to herself. *Not bad.* The other glass was filled with water, which Kristen used as a chaser.

Stergios and Nikos entered the house and were greeted by Maria. *Stergios must be her husband and Nikos a relative*, thought Kristen. She heard but did not understand the conversation between the men and Maria.

After a few minutes, Nikos gestured for Kristen to follow him outside. Kristen noticed as they passed by that the suitcase and backpack were missing from the truck. She understood that they would be spending the night here. Stergios and Maria joined them, and the group began strolling into the village, Maria carrying a large loaf of freshly baked bread. The aroma made Kristen's mouth water and her stomach rumble.

Upon arriving at the village square, Kristen was surprised to see what seemed to be a festival in progress. There were at least one hundred people of all ages gathered around a large bonfire. She hesitated, wondering whether or not she should be seen up close, but Stergios assured her with a kindly gesture, as if to say, "Don't worry. They are all friends." She smiled her thanks and proceeded toward the festivities.

There were goats spinning on rotisseries and what she was to learn were the intestines of the goats being roasted. A large table was piled with foods Kristen did not recognize, but that looked delicious, and barrels of wine. A band consisting of a clarinet, a drum, and a violin was playing a very exotic song, while twenty young women, perhaps in their late teens and early twenties, in beautiful costumes, danced to the music hand-in-hand in a circle. Kristen also noticed the young men, most in their twenties and thirties, watching the dancing women carefully.

I understand, thought Kristen. *This is when the men begin the process of choosing a bride.* It was as if she had been transported back one hundred years in time.

Stergios and others beckoned Kristen to follow them to a table that had been set up for them in the crude *taverna*. "Sit," Maria gestured to Kristen. As if by magic, the table was soon covered with food and drink, which everyone consumed with gusto. Although Kristen did not understand a word that was being said, she understood that she was considered an honored guest at this very special event, and she enjoyed every minute of it.

After the meal was finished, Maria grabbed Kristen's elbow and led her to where women of all ages were dancing. "Oh, I don't know how," protested Kristen. "Nonsense," Maria said in facial expressions and gestures. "*Ella*," Kristen heard and decided not to protest.

The women were patient while Kristen learned the simple repetitive steps of the dance. Before long, she felt as if she had been born to dance with these women. Each song was very lengthy, so after three songs Kristen was exhausted and excused herself to go back to the table. *What amazing people*, Kristen thought. *They have so little, yet so much. We could learn a lesson or two from them.*

It was very late before the party ended, and Kristen was exhausted but excited. Never before had she experienced such an outpouring of hospitality and warmth. Upon arriving back at the humble house, Kristen was given a rough cotton nightgown with long sleeves to wear to bed. As Kristen entered the bedroom, she saw the largest bed she had ever seen in her life. It was covered with woven wool blankets. It became obvious that they would all share one bed. *This must be the norm*, she thought, and crawled into the spot at the edge next to Maria. It did not matter that there were three other people in the bed; Kristen fell instantly into a deep, dreamless sleep.

She awoke to the smell of coffee and baking bread. *This has been the most amazing experience of my life*, she said to herself. *No matter what happens in the next few days, I will always remember this with great fondness.*

They ate, packed up the truck, and left within the hour, Kristen still dressed as a peasant. The ride was as bumpy and as uncomfortable as the previous day's, but Kristen did not mind it at all. She was reliving the unforgettable events of the last twenty-four hours.

There were no problems on the journey. Just outside of Igoumenitsa, Stergios stopped the truck and signaled for Kristen to change back into her modern clothes. Kristen did what she was told and sadly bid good-bye to her new friends as she was dropped off two blocks away from the ferry to Corfu. She was once again the typical American tourist on the outside, but on the inside she had been temporarily transformed into a Greek peasant. It had felt good.

Kristen rolled her suitcase while carrying the backpack through the gate and to the office, where she purchased a deck ticket for the short crossing. She noticed a few policemen surveying the ferry's operation, but they did not seem to be watching for anything in particular. She boarded the ferry, stowed the suitcase in an open storage area, carried her backpack onto the deck and found a seat as far away from other people as possible. She had a moment of panic when she opened the backpack and did not see the icon; but then saw that the items she had removed the previous evening had been replaced. *They must have put the icon back in my suitcase,* Kristen rationalized to herself. *Be calm. Everything will be all right.*

As the boat was entering the harbor of Kerkira, Kristen made sure that she stood as close to the entrance of the baggage compartment as possible, wanting to be one of the first to claim her suitcase. She was pushed and shoved when the ferry docked, and the door was opened by a crew member, but she was able to retrieve her suitcase without mishap. "Now, I need to find a place to stay," she said as she planned her next move. "I'll look for a friendly face and see what they have to offer."

Sofia had been correct; the dock was mobbed with locals encouraging travelers to stay at their establishments. Kristen was momentarily overwhelmed until she heard a familiar voice saying, "Can I offer you a place to stay tonight?" Kristen turned to find Demetri standing behind her. She dropped the backpack, flung her arms around his neck, and kissed him enthusiastically.

"I have never been happier to see anyone in my life," she said.

"Me neither," Demetri said with a smile. "Get the suitcase, and I'll take the pack. Remember, we are tourists," he added quietly. Kristen was brought back to reality and realized that their movements could be observed and their words overheard. "How was your trip?" he asked casually, as anyone would ask an arriving loved one.

"Fine," she answered just as casually, "The crossing was very smooth." What she was really thinking was that it had been phenomenal. She would fill him in on all the details later. All that mattered then was that they were once again together, and they seemed safe.

"I arrived only an hour ago. I think it would be good for us to travel to the northern part of the island and dock the boat there for the night," said Demetri.

"Okay by me, Captain!" Kristen said happily as she did her best impression of a salute. Demetri laughed. It was good to have her back.

They walked the short distance to the marina and boarded the boat without an incident.

"Welcome aboard," Demetri said as he stowed her gear below in the cabin, carefully removing the icon and hiding it under the floorboards.

"Thank you. I've never been on a boat like this, so you're going to have to tell me what to do," said Kristen apologetically.

"You can help by pushing the boat away from the pier when I tell you to," Demetri said. "Otherwise, make yourself comfortable, and we can talk as soon as we get out of the harbor."

"Aye aye, skipper," she said happily as they shoved off and got under way.

Chapter 31

"How is your head?" Kristen asked Demetri as they reached open sea.

"*Poli kala*. My headache is gone, and my arm wounds are healing. Look for yourself," he said, bending his head so Kristen could get a good look while keeping a solid hold on the wheel.

"It looks very good, and there is no sign of infection. You should have the stitches removed in a week."

Demetri nodded his agreement.

"And how are you, really?" asked Demetri, searching Kristen's eyes.

"Actually, fantastic," she replied. "If I hadn't been frightened out of my wits in Ioannina, and if there hadn't been any danger of getting caught, I would say I had one of the most interesting days of my life. The people were wonderful to me." She told Demetri the details of her trip, the festival, and the hospitality she had received. "They are incredible, simple people. I hated to say good-bye to them."

"Ah, yes, you have discovered the real Greece. *Bravo*, Kristen," Demetri declared.

They were in no real hurry, so Demetri slowed the boat to medium speed. "It's beautiful, isn't it?"

"Yes, it is very beautiful. How lucky you are to live in a country that has the sea and the mountains so close to each other. The water is so clear and so blue!"

"You have many beautiful places in the States too, don't forget that," Demetri reminded her.

"Absolutely, but there is something here, a feeling I get that I feel at no other place. I don't know if it's the presence of the ancient gods or the Christian God, but I feel something very strongly spiritual," she explained.

"Greece is a very spiritual country," he agreed.

Kristen nodded.

"Why don't you get your swimsuit on?" Demetri suggested, changing the subject.

"Good idea. I need some sun," she replied and headed to the cabin to change.

"Thank you for bringing her back to me safely," Demetri whispered, looking up at the heavens.

Two hours later, as they were arriving at Kassiopi, a small port village of only a thousand inhabitants on the northeast tip of the island, Demetri said, "This should also be the 'real' Greece; I think you will like it. Since it is a port, it will have fuel, at least a couple of good *tavernas*, and enough visitors during the summer so we won't be a novelty."

"It sounds great to me," responded Kristen. She liked quiet places and knew that Kassiopi would suit their needs well."

"It has a twelfth-century Byzantine castle, but I do not think we should try to see it; we need to stay very close to the boat to protect our precious cargo," commented Demetri. "I am sure there will be a *taverna* within sight of the marina; there usually is. We will sleep on the boat."

"Can we go swimming before dinner?" Kristen asked.

"That sounds like a very good plan," Demetri responded.

They docked the boat without a problem and had a drink on the deck before departing. "It is good to relax a bit," Demetri explained. "Everyone else will be having drinks now. We must look as normal as possible."

"Is it okay to talk to some of the other yachtsmen?" asked Kristen, not knowing the proper nautical vernacular.

"Yes, we just need to stick to our story," answered Demetri as he waved to the man tethered to the slip next to theirs. "*Yia sou.*" The man answered his greeting in English.

Thank goodness, Kristen thought. *Someone to speak English to besides Demetri.*

Demetri struck up a pleasant conversation with the man, whose name was Brian. He and his wife were from England, and they loved sailing around the Ionion and Adriatic Islands, including Croatia. It was decided they would have dinner together later in the evening. "He may be able to give us some very valuable information; we just need to be very careful to keep our story believable," he said more to himself than to Kristen.

Feeling better, knowing that there would be someone at least casually watching the boat, Demetri and Kristen wandered out to find the beach for a swim. It wasn't far, and before long they were in the refreshing water, swimming and splashing each other like children. They enjoyed their short swim, which eased their aching muscles and some of the tension they had felt. They did not stay long because it was getting late. As they were returning to the boat in their swimwear, they were startled to see a policeman at the marina. "Be cool," Demetri said under his breath, as he greeted the officer in Greek. The policeman examined Demetri and then Kristen and asked, "Is that your boat?"

"Yes, it is," said Demetri, trying to be very pleasant but secretly wondering what he would do next if the officer gave him trouble.

Kristen tried to act as casual as she could and said nothing.

"May I look inside?" the policeman said, his question more a command than a request.

"Yes, if you wish," Demetri said.

Kristen chimed in, "We just arrived so things are in a mess, I'm afraid," hoping to sound very domestic.

The policeman boarded the boat, looked at the deck and the instrument panel, and then preceded Demetri down the short flight of steps to the cabin area, where he examined it thoroughly.

After returning to the deck and a long pause, the officer nodded to Demetri and said, "It's nice, very nice. Not too big, not too small. There is even enough room for your wife's shopping," he added with a shrug and a smile. "You can get fuel beginning at eight in the morning. Welcome to Kassiopi."

"*Efharisto poli*," Demetri said with a smile, and the policeman walked away slowly.

They boarded the boat and did not say anything until they were safely in the cabin. "I almost wet myself!" exclaimed Kristen. "Please, let's get this over with as quickly as possible; I don't think my nerves can stand much more of this!"

Demetri agreed with her. "We will leave in the morning and with any luck will be at our destination within two days."

They had dinner with Brian and his wife, Felicity, comparing notes on their sailing experiences. Since Demetri had never taken the boat farther north than Corfu, he asked Brian for advice. "There's not much to tell, really," Brian said. "The scenery is beautiful, the islanders are friendly, and things are still relatively inexpensive."

"That's good to know. We are looking forward to it. Have you experienced any problems with customs? Kristen bought some pricey paintings on our way and we have them with us," he added to attempt to justify the somewhat unusual question.

"No, and we have been there many times. They are encouraging tourism and do not want to discourage travelers by making things difficult," Felicity answered. After dinner, coffee, and ouzo, the two couples retired to their respective boats. "It's been very nice meeting you," said Kristen to the Brits. "I hope our paths will cross again soon."

"Well, that was encouraging," said Kristen to Demetri, after they were once again alone in the cabin.

"Yes, it was," he replied. "It has been a long day. We should get some sleep because tomorrow will be just as long. And Kristen, thank you again for everything!"

"No, thank *you*," Kristen said. "I haven't felt this alive in years. It's partially the adrenaline talking, but it's also being with you again—this time as friends and true partners. It means the world to me," as she softly and tenderly kissed him.

"It does me too; until tomorrow then," Demetri whispered, before he turned out the light.

Kristen could feel that Demetri was still awake as she lay quietly, thinking about the days they had spent together. "Isn't it ironic," she said quietly, "that the very thing that broke us up has brought us back together?" There was no reply, but Kristen knew that Demetri had heard and understood the meaning of her words.

Chapter 32

"**G**ood morning," Demetri whispered from his bed.

"Good morning. I dreamed about the autumn of 1987. Do you remember that?" Kristen asked.

"Of course I do. It was the best time of my life; how could I forget?"

"We were such wild and crazy kids then," remarked Kristen. "We could not get enough of each other."

"I don't think things have changed much," murmured Demetri. Kristen smiled. After a moment he added, "Let's have some breakfast and leave as soon as possible. We have a long way to travel, and we can talk about those times today as we go."

"That sounds good," agreed Kristen as she got out of bed and began her day. She wanted to give Demetri a good morning kiss, but resisted, knowing it would lead to other things, dangerous things, especially since they had hours of relative quiet and total privacy ahead of them.

They breakfasted on coffee, bread, and delicious goat cheese. Afterward, while Demetri fueled and readied the boat for departure, Kristen bought water, fruit, cheese, bread, and some wine for their trip. The day was clear and promised smooth sailing. They waved to Brian and Felicity, who were just showing their faces to the new morning, as they slowly left the marina. "Have a great voyage," they heard Felicity yell back in greeting.

As soon as they got out to the open sea, Demetri removed his shirt; Kristen changed into her swimsuit and was sure to cover herself with loads of sunscreen. She offered some to Demetri, who refused. "My skin is used to the sun." It was obvious to Kristen that he was telling the truth; his skin was darkened by the exposure he had already had since school let out.

"Come here, and I will show you how to steer the boat. It is not difficult, as long as you know where you are going," said Demetri.

"Where are we going?" asked Kristen. "Not that I'd know where it is anyway."

"We are going to an island in the southern Dalmatian region called Korcula," he answered.

"Like I said, I have no idea where it is, and I don't really care, as long as we get there and get rid of you-know-what," she added with a shrug.

"I have never been there, so we will have to navigate carefully. You can help. I will teach you along the way," Demetri added.

Kristen liked that she was being included. "You know, Demetri, all I've ever wanted was to be a part of your life," she said with great feeling.

"I am sorry that it did not happen. We both missed out on so much," Demetri responded. "I suppose this is a good time to talk about what happened."

"I dread talking about those terrible moments that eventually came. They were the worst times of my life," said Kristen softly.

"Do not!" said Demetri emphatically. "I told you that things happen for a reason. Why dwell on the terrible instead of the wonderful times? For better or worse, our lives took different paths, and we are who we are today because of the actions we took then. Are you dissatisfied with your life?"

"No, not really," Kristen answered. "I have achieved more than I ever thought I would. I have made a positive contribution to the world, have loved and been loved. I guess that's not too bad."

"I should say not!" said Demetri. "I feel pretty much the same way about my life."

"It's just that we would have been so good together. There were times I rationalized things by saying we probably would have divorced when I tired of your dominating personality, but I know now that we would have found a way to become equal partners. I have two questions," she continued. "One, did you really love me as much as you said you did?" asked Kristen, looking Demetri deeply in the eyes.

"How can you even ask that question? Of course I did! I still do!" replied Demetri looking and sounding hurt.

"Then, in that case, why did you leave me?" cried Kristen with more emphasis than she had intended.

"I did not leave you, not really," said Demetri. "It's just that there were things I could not compromise on; there still are."

"How can you say you did not leave me? You just disappeared!" exclaimed Kristen. "You never even gave me the chance to explain what happened!"

"Why don't you tell me now?" said Demetri quietly.

"I understand that I had promised to keep your secret, and I broke that promise," began Kristen. "I should never have done that, but I did not do it on purpose."

It was clear that Kristen was becoming upset.

"My parents were looking forward to your coming for Christmas that year—almost as much as I was. Dad was rightfully curious about the man who had become so important to his daughter, and he asked me many questions about you. Some of the things I told him did not add up in his mind, and he kept pumping me for information about you. He knew I was withholding something from him, and he kept after me until I told him about your involvement with your cousins and how you were getting away from them. I had never openly lied to him, and when he asked me direct questions I just did not know what else to say," Kristen explained, nearly in tears. "He blew up; there was no reasoning with him. He made it very clear that I had to decide between you or the family. And he did not allow me to decide to go with you. I was stuck in the mountains and could not go anywhere. What could I do? And you did not make things easier, either."

"Don't you see? After that I could not trust you. And I could not be with someone I did not trust, even as much as I loved you. That I could not compromise on," said Demetri, sadly but firmly.

"But how could you just cut me off like that? You would not take my calls or answer the letters I wrote to try to explain! Don't you know how cruel that was? I could have handled anything else; you could have yelled at me or even hit me, but you did not. You just disappeared out of my life. It almost killed me!" Kristen exclaimed. She was crying now, almost as she had those many years before.

"I was angry and hurt. It was the only way I could deal with it. I felt betrayed that you did not trust me enough to allow me to deal with the problems," said Demetri.

"It was unbelievably painful. Had I not been as strong and loved life as much as I did, I would have considered suicide; that's how hurt and alone you left me," she continued. "I was so young, the same age you were when you made your mistakes. Why couldn't you have seen that and found a way to let me back into your life?"

Demetri sat quietly and listened intently. He hadn't realized that he had hurt Kristen so deeply.

"For years, I felt sorry for myself because I knew I had lost the one great love of my life. And now, I feel sorry for both of us, for what we lost. I feel sorry for the years we spent apart that could have been spent together. I feel sorry that you could have spent your life with someone who truly loved you and whom you loved. I feel sorry for the children we never had and for the life we could have built together." The words spilled out of Kristen without thought of how Demetri would react. "And I suddenly realize that I am and have been extremely angry at you all these years. Really, really angry!" She broke down completely, pounding her knees and sobbing uncontrollably.

Demetri was stunned by the outpouring of thoughts and emotions. After a few moments, he said the words that Kristen had wanted to hear for thirty years. "It wasn't your fault," he said with conviction.

In that one moment, all the frustration and anger she had felt for decades drained away; the demons had been exorcized forever.

"Can you forgive me?" he said softly.

"Yes" was all Kristen could manage to say. After a moment she asked the same question of Demetri.

"Yes, I forgive you," he said, holding Kristen tightly as she continued to cry, with her head buried in his chest.

"What do we do now?" asked Demetri sorrowfully.

"What *can* we do?" answered Kristen. "I am not free to love you as I would like. I cannot hurt Richard; that would be unforgivable." She began crying, this time with relief as well as sorrow for what they had lost. She looked into Demetri's eyes, which were streaming with tears, although he did not make a sound.

Kristen knew that she needed to lighten the mood. She pulled herself together and said confidently, "What we do now is get this blankety-blank icon to the right people and finish this mission without getting arrested!"

"Thank you for that—for all of that!" Demetri said and slowly got back to work, as did Kristen.

The effect of their talk was miraculous. All the pent-up misunderstandings and hurt seemed to disappear.

"Can we start over?" asked Demetri.

"No, I don't think that's necessary, or even wise. Like you said, we are who we are because of what happened. We just need to accept it and get on with things. Deal?" asked Kristen.

"Deal," said Demetri as they shook hands solidly.

Chapter 33

They had been traveling all day on the nearly glass-smooth sea as if mesmerized. "I'm getting hungry," Kristen stated. "It's getting late."

"You should be. It's almost eight, and the last meal we ate was breakfast. I guess we forgot about lunch," said Demetri, with a smile.

"Is there anything in the galley," she asked, "besides what I bought this morning, that is?"

"I stocked the refrigerator before I left, so there should be some basics," he called to her as she headed into the cabin.

The galley consisted of a tiny sink, a miniature refrigerator and a two-burner stove without an oven. Kristen searched the fridge and the cupboards and called up to Demetri, "How about an omelet?"

"Perfect," he replied. "If I remember correctly, you're a pretty good cook."

"I used to be, before life became so hectic. But, I think I can whip up an edible dinner. Give me a few minutes, and I'll call you," she added, feeling happier than she had in a long time. The demons had been exorcized, and it felt wonderful.

In no time, dinner was ready. She had found the makings for an omelet with feta cheese, and she had toasted the bread she had brought on board. She made coffee to drink, knowing that they should refrain from alcohol while steering a boat.

"Kristen, you have outdone yourself. The table looks *poli orea*, and dinner smells delicious.

"For a landlubber, I think I'm doing quite well. Of course, it helps that the sea is totally calm," said Kristen. "I did not even have to put on my Scopolamine patch." She hated using it, because it made her extremely sleepy.

"Do you mind if we don't find a port for the night? I don't want to hassle with customs and policemen more than absolutely necessary," Demetri said.

"No, I don't mind. Excuse me for being naive, but how do we anchor here?" she asked.

"We don't. We just let the boat drift. As long as the sea is calm there should be no problem. Unless, that is, you want to take the helm for the next eight hours," he teased.

"No, no, that's okay," she replied, getting into the jovial mood Demetri had set.

"This is very good," he commented as he ate the omelet with gusto. "I remembered correctly, and you have not lost your magic touch in the kitchen," Demetri said with enthusiasm.

"You are too kind, sir."

Suddenly, they were joking and teasing each other as they hadn't been able to do earlier. Feelings of sorrow, anger, and regret had disappeared, replaced by feelings of companionship, levity, and warmth. Kristen felt that she could talk to Demetri about anything without the safety net that e-mail had provided her earlier in their relationship. Demetri felt the same way. They had come to an understanding and a way to let go of the past, and that apparently was very freeing.

Their conversation turned away from the mission to lighter subjects. Demetri said something that struck Kristen as extremely funny. Her unbridled laughter was contagious. "Stop it, Demetri, I can't breathe," Kristen finally was able to say through the laughter.

"*Entaxi*, but you have to stop too!" he exclaimed.

"Oh, that felt good!" said Kristen as she was able to breathe naturally again. "I haven't laughed that hard since the night you and Kari and I were in the restaurant in New York, remember?"

"How could I forget? I don't have enough laughter in my life. Thank you for bringing it back to me," he said.

"*Para kalo*," Kristen said. "We both need more laughter."

"It's getting late, and we have a big day tomorrow. We should sleep," Demetri said.

"Demetri," Kristen said after a moment's hesitation, "could I sleep with you tonight ... nothing sexual ... just to have you close?"

"Of course," he replied. Kristen slipped into the small berth after Demetri and nestled into his warm embrace. "Everything is going to be all right," Demetri whispered, and then he kissed her gently on the forehead and fell into the most comfortable sleep he had experienced in years.

They awoke suddenly to the violent movement of the boat.

"What the hell?" Demetri swore and immediately attempted to get out of the berth. He was thrown back, and he fell and hit his head and shoulder on the cabin wall. Thankfully, his stitches held.

Kristen had crawled out of the berth onto the floor. "What could it be?" she asked, and her question was answered as an excruciatingly loud thunder clap exploded directly above them. "Where did the storm come from?" she asked and then thought of how stupid her question sounded.

"I don't know. All the weather reports were good."

"I think I'm going to be sick," exclaimed Kristen. The closest thing to this she had ever experienced was a carnival ride when she was sixteen. She had avoided them since that time.

"Think about something else. What time is it?" asked Demetri.

Kristen looked at her watch. "It's four AM," she answered.

"I'm going up on deck," said Demetri. "I need to start the engine and head the bow into the waves."

"I'll come too," said Kristen.

"No. It would be safer if you stayed here," Demetri said.

"What about the lightning?" asked Kristen.

"I will be all right. The helm is enclosed. Besides, I have no choice," he added. Demetri quickly put on the raincoat that was stowed below one of the seats and carefully climbed the steps to the deck.

Kristen became very nauseated as she was tossed from one side of the cabin to the other. "If I stay here, I'm going to hurl all over everything. Perhaps if I can get some fresh air it will be better," she said to herself. She donned the second raincoat and a pair of waterproof sandals and climbed the stairs.

She was wrong; being on deck made things worse. She could not see the horizon because it was still very dark due to the storm. She lost her balance on the wet, slippery deck and fell, hurting her right knee.

"How stupid am I? I should have paid attention to Demetri," she chided herself.

Demetri was focusing on getting the engine started and positioning the boat in the correct direction to ride out the storm, so he hadn't noticed Kristen's appearance on deck. He heard her cry out and turned as she fell. He could not go to help her. He needed all his energy to keep the boat in line. To his astonishment, he saw Kristen head for the rail. "Stay away from there," he shouted, but Kristen could not hear him. He knew she was going to be sick but did not want to soil the deck.

As she made her way to the boat's starboard rail, a wave suddenly hurtled the boat to the left. Kristen lost her balance and fell overboard as Demetri watched in horror.

Oh, I've really done it now, thought Kristen as she swam with all her might to stay afloat. *If the sea doesn't kill me, Demetri will. I don't know which will be worse.*

"Hold on," cried Demetri as he gunned the engine and worked to move the boat closer to her. "Swim to the stern and climb up the ladder."

Kristen removed the soggy raincoat and sandals and struggled to reach the boat, which kept moving in the high waves. "I can't," she screamed.

"Yes, you can!" cried Demetri, hoping his words were true. "Just keep trying and don't give up."

Demetri successfully positioned the boat within three meters of Kristen. That gave her enough hope to muster the energy to swim the last five strokes needed to reach the boat and grab onto the ladder, which felt like a bucking bronco. "Now what do I do?" cried Kristen, desperately trying to keep her hold.

"Get a foothold. Use the rhythm of the boat to assist you to climb. Don't let go. You can do it!"

Kristen followed his instructions. With determination, she swung her foot to the lowest ladder rung, steadied herself and pulled herself up. She collapsed onto the deck, unable to move but uninjured. Demetri felt helpless to assist her, as it would be more dangerous if he left the helm.

"Are you all right?" he yelled over the sound of the wind.

"I will be," answered Kristen. "Nothing is broken, I just need to rest for a few minutes before I try to move," she answered.

When he was sure she had recovered, Demetri ordered Kristen to go below. Kristen crawled to the steps and carefully made her way into the cabin.

It was an hour before the storm had subsided sufficiently for Demetri to join Kristen below deck. During that time Kristen had showered and changed into dry clothes.

"What in the world were you trying to do out on deck, after I had told you to stay in the cabin!" demanded Demetri angrily.

"I'm so sorry. I had no idea," Kristen said and began to cry.

Demetri felt terrible about yelling at her. "You could have drowned. If I hadn't seen you go overboard … I just don't want to even think about it. I don't know what I'd do if I lost you!" He held her so tightly that Kristen had trouble breathing. She did not mind.

"Well, I guess we're even now," Kristen said demurely. "I saved you at the monastery, and you saved me here.

"I guess we are even," said Demetri. "Please, let's not have any more excitement or injuries on this trip."

"That's fine with me." Kristen agreed. "I've had more than enough excitement for one trip."

"We should get under way," said Demetri.

"No, not yet. Just hold me like you're never going to let me go," she pleaded.

Demetri complied, not with words but with actions. After removing his rain slicker, he held Kristen to his bare chest, first like a greatly loved child then as a woman being embraced by a man. Kristen felt the change and let herself be enveloped by him. Their bodies became like one without the conscious effort of either of them. They had always fit together perfectly, like pieces of a jigsaw puzzle. Now, thirty years later, it was no different.

Their body temperatures rose as the emotions of fear and then relief swept over them. Kristen raised her face to Demetri's. He understood, and he kissed her, first on the forehead, then on each closed eye, and then gently on her neck, over and over. Excitement surged through Kristen like the bolts of lightning she had witnessed not an hour before. *Kiss me now!* she screamed silently. Demetri seemed to hear, because his full lips moved to hers, gently pressing against hers and then backing away seductively. Kristen pressed forward, making it clear without words what she desired.

Suddenly, Demetri was in no hurry. This would be like their first time in Italy, and he did not want to rush it. He wanted to savor every minute.

His lips played with hers, hesitating, pulling back, and then meeting hers again. Slowly, ever so slowly, he eased his tongue onto her lips, which tasted slightly salty, increasing his excitement. As she responded by parting her teeth ever so slightly, he caressed her lips, her gums, her teeth—slowly, very, very slowly. Their tongues touched, and the electricity that coursed through Demetri was palpable.

Kristen took Demetri's lower lip in hers and sucked on it, ever so gently. She then nipped it, sending Demetri to a new height of arousal. Demetri's tongue probed Kristen's soft and warm mouth, and Kristen responded in kind. Demetri then moved his hands to her breasts and squeezed her nipples firmly. It surprised but pleased her all the way to her loins. "Do you like this?" Demetri whispered. "Yes, oh yes," Kristen sighed.

The response to each other was brought from a depth neither one had quite forgotten, but that had been absent for years. It surprised both of them; neither wished to stop the sensation that had been reawakened, like the activation of a volcano after thousands of years of dormancy.

They moved to the berth, where their kisses continued while they sat on the edge. Hands began exploring each other the way they once had. Although changed by time and circumstance, their bodies felt familiar and inviting to one another.

They lay on the edge of the berth, feeling the passion overtake their resolve. Kristen looked at Demetri's chest; she had always loved his chest—the chest that held the heart that was capable of loving so deeply. His chest was so smooth and responsive to her kisses. To Kristen, it was now unchanged. She lay next to him, stroking the skin on his abdomen, and then she began to lick and suck his nipples.

"Should I stop?" whispered Kristen.

"No," Demetri responded.

The kisses continued. They both felt the heat rise in their bodies as the kisses became deeper and more frantic. His hands searched under her blouse and then under her bra to her bare breasts. "I always loved kissing your breasts," he muttered. With a mastery that surprised Kristen, he unsnapped and removed her bra in one fluid motion and began kissing and caressing her breasts. She moaned softly, never wanting the moment to end.

Kristen could not bear it much longer and arched her back, signaling for Demetri to remove her shorts, which he did. He marveled at her nakedness. "How could this woman still be this beautiful?" he asked himself. Kristen was thinking the same thing about Demetri as he removed his shorts.

No more words were exchanged. They came together with all the longing and pent-up desire they had felt for years. Their kisses were deep and hungry. Clothes were torn off and thrown on the floor in a torrent of emotions. No longer were they restrained. Their bodies joined with an unbridled passion. Their union had been like their kisses—rough, needy and with the desire to totally envelop the other.

The merger of their two bodies was perfect, their enjoyment heightened by the gentle swaying of the boat. After all those years, they had never forgotten how to please each other. Kristen moaned with delight with every thrust. Demetri was thoroughly enraptured by once again feeling the wet and warmth of this amazing woman. They reached their climaxes simultaneously and then lay perfectly still for several minutes without separating, to continue the ecstasy.

"Whew, where did that come from?" said Kristen, but she knew exactly where it had originated. Nothing could bring out the passion in a person like a near-death experience.

"We both know it has been building up ever since we saw each other last autumn," said Demetri.

"Yes, it has, in spite of our best intentions," said Kristen. "What was it that Romeo said? Something like: oh sweet sin, give it to me again."

"Somehow I believe it lost something in your translation, but I'm happy to oblige!" he said, laughing.

They made love once again, relishing the other's closeness, and remembering each other's scents, which had always driven them wild.

Afterward, they lay entwined. Demetri saw a change in Kristen, from deeply happy to outwardly troubled.

"Are you all right?" asked Demetri.

"Yes, of course," she answered, although feelings of guilt were building up inside her after the adrenaline rush began to subside. "It was wonderful," she added. Demetri could see that she was hiding something.

Eventually Kristen asked, "Don't you think we should get under way? People are going to think we're adrift and in serious distress."

Demetri smiled bleakly, knowing that Kristen's feelings were torn. "You have a point," he said as he stood up. "Are you sure you're okay?"

Kristen stood in front of him, looked him squarely in the eyes, and said, "Yes, I am fine; we are fine," she said, although she was having trouble believing it herself.

Demetri nodded his head slightly. "Are you positive?" he whispered.

"Yes," Kristen replied. Nothing was going to spoil the moment for her—not the mission, nothing. She would not even allow herself to think of the other barriers to their being together, they temporarily did not exist. "We'll talk about this later."

"Yes, we should," he replied as he slipped on a pair of shorts and went up on deck to get under way.

After Kristen dressed, she called up to him, "Would you like some coffee? I'll make some and bring it up to you, if you wish."

"You definitely know the way to a man's heart. Yes, thank you."

The storm had cleared as quickly as it had approached; the sea was once again calm, giving them the opportunity to make up some time. Both Kristen and Demetri were lost in their thoughts, saying little as the hours slipped by.

"We are approaching Croatian waters," said Demetri in the early afternoon. "Cross your fingers that all goes well. We need a little luck, and we deserve it, in my humble opinion."

He pulled out his mobile phone and punched in some numbers. "Good, it's working," he said to Kristen right before he began talking. As before, Kristen could not understand the conversation, nor did she wish to know what was being said.

After turning his phone off, Demetri explained the plan to Kristen. "We are to proceed to the southeast part of the island. There we will find a deserted place to anchor and will be met. We hand over the icon, and that will be the end of our responsibilities."

"That sounds simple enough, but how do we find the right cove? Doesn't that island have about a thousand of them?" She had suddenly become the expert after examining the map.

"I have a very good nautical map onboard, so there is no worry. We will find the cove without a problem, one way or another," said Demetri. Then with a smile and a wink, he teased, "I hope you are a better navigator than a deck hand."

"Yes, you'd better hope so," Kristen agreed with a laugh.

Chapter 34

They proceeded toward their destination, passing small islands and many pleasure craft. *The secret is out*, thought Demetri. *It won't be long until the Dalmatian Islands are as popular as the Greek islands are now. I wonder how it will change the area.* He had seen changes in Greece over the last twenty years—most of them good, but some detrimental. Tradition was becoming less and less important, especially to the younger generation in Athens. He philosophized about the future of Greece as he quietly steered the boat northward.

Kristen interrupted his thoughts by bringing him a cold bottle of water. "I thought you'd need this," she said as she pressed it against his bare back. At first he flinched, and then he found the coolness soothing to his overheated body. "Thank you, I needed that," he said gratefully as he downed the entire bottle. "You take good care of me."

"Your wish is my command, captain," she said teasingly. Then, "By the way, where are we?"

"If you look to the right, you will see the island of Mljet."

"Sure, that's easy for you to say," Kristen kidded him.

Demetri laughed and continued by saying, "We have passed Dubrovnik and have about thirty-five more kilometers to our destination. We need to stop for fuel and should be there by five o'clock. Our contacts are to arrive by six, so we are doing well." He turned the boat toward the small island.

They were there just long enough to fill the tanks with fuel, but Kristen was still fascinated with the area. "It sure is beautiful! So many islands and most are so green. The houses look very traditional. It's interesting that they are so different from the ones in the Cyclades of Greece," she commented.

"There are two reasons I can think of immediately," said Demetri in his most professional professor's voice, "One, the climate is different; and two, different cultures built those houses. It's like comparing buildings in New England to ones in Arizona."

"Point taken," said Kristen. "I'll just enjoy the view without asking any more silly questions."

"I was thinking about our arrival. We need to continue to appear like tourists. We will be going to a remote area and need to be prepared," said Demetri.

"We still have the canned food I bought. How about if we have a picnic on the beach or waterfront, or whatever is there? Anyone passing by will think that we are just stopping for a swim and some relaxation."

"That sounds like a good plan," said Demetri. "I'll be hungry by then."

They continued on, and, with Kristen's assistance, were able to find the correct inlet. It had a small pier that accommodated the boat well, and there was no problem tying it up. Nobody was there to meet them.

"We are early. Do not worry," said Demetri.

"I'm not worried. I was just wondering if we should hide the icon on shore until they arrive," suggested Kristen.

"Good idea," replied Demetri, and, after checking to make sure nobody was watching, he took the icon from its hiding place onto the shore and found a place he hoped was safe behind a nearby fallen tree.

There was nothing to do now but wait. Kristen brought the food out, along with a blanket, and they ate on the waterfront. There was no beach, but the surroundings were beautiful, with tall pines for as far as their eyes could see.

"The contrast of the green trees with the blue water is quite spectacular," Kristen commented. Demetri agreed. He was enjoying visiting a new location but wished it was under different circumstances.

They had finished their picnic and waited another hour when a boat approached from the west. It looked official, and Demetri said to Kristen in a concerned voice, "Let me take care of this," as he stood up and greeted the equivalent of an officer of the United States Coast Guard.

"Hello," he called.

"Hello," the officer said in English. "Are you Americans?" he asked.

"Yes," Demetri said simply, not wanting to offer more information than was necessary.

"What is your reason for being here?" the officer asked firmly.

"We are on vacation and decided to have a picnic," answered Demetri.

"May I see your papers, please?" the officer asked sternly.

Demetri immediately complied with the request. The officer examined the papers thoroughly and handed them back.

"Have you had any trouble?" the officer asked.

"No, why do you ask?" asked Demetri.

"There have been reports of pirates in the area. They are targeting sailboats, not powerboats like yours, but I recommend you stay close to the populated areas." Demetri understood that pirates were not just a myth but a real danger in certain waters.

"Thank you for the information. We will finish here and be on our way," he responded. The officer barked out an order, and the boat turned away and was out of sight within a minute.

"What are we, police magnets?" said Kristen. "I don't know how much more my nerves can take!"

As she said those words, a small, middle-aged man emerged from the forest and startled Kristen, who unintentionally let out a short scream. Demetri turned and smiled.

"Do not be alarmed. This is George. He is expected," Demetri explained. He proceeded to talk with George for a few seconds and led him in the direction of the hidden icon. Within two minutes, Demetri was back, alone and without the icon. He was carrying a large envelope instead.

"The deed is done," he said with relief. "Now, let us go and begin to enjoy our time together."

Kristen quickly picked up the blanket and the picnic trash, and took them back on board. "So that's it, is it?" she asked. Kristen knew not to ask questions about George, or what would happen to the icon from there.

"Yes," said Demetri quietly.

"What a relief!" sighed Kristen. "What next? Are we completely out of danger?"

"The only things we have to be concerned about are the pirates in the area. I suddenly became a relatively wealthy man; or should I say, we just became relatively wealthy?" he corrected himself.

"No, Demetri, you keep it. You need it more than I do. I don't need or want any of it. I did not do this for the money; I did this to free you from your cousins," she said firmly.

"Are you sure?" he asked. "You have earned half."

"Absolutely!" she insisted. "And I won't take no for an answer. You know how I am about that!"

"Yes, I do. You are nearly as stubborn as I am," he said.

"I would not go as far as to say that. When it comes to stubborn, you are an expert; I am only an amateur," she said, laughing.

"I admit you are probably right. Well then, we better get it stashed away where it will be safe," replied Demetri gratefully. "Thank you for everything you have done."

"*Tipota*, as I said before, it is nothing. Besides, it's been a very exciting adventure. Now that it's completed, I can say that overall it was an excellent time," Kristen said, attempting to underplay the effect of the last week. "That is, except for almost drowning, you falling off a cliff, almost being bitten by a venomous snake, and escaping arrest numerous times." They both laughed and agreed that maybe it was a bit more excitement than they would normally desire.

"I do not want to stay here. Let's go to the island of Lastovo; it is near and quite beautiful, I hear. We can spend the night in a hotel, have a proper shower and a meal, fuel up and head out tomorrow morning. How does that sound to you?" he asked.

"It sounds perfect," she replied. "I can use a shower and need to wash my hair."

They shoved off and were on their way within minutes. It was time to celebrate; their mission was completed, and both were alive and well.

They docked at the town of Lastovo, named for the island, and found a room instead of a luxury hotel, as there were none. Their room was tiny and a bit of a disappointment, but both were exhausted and did not have the energy to look for better accommodations. They were feeling the letdown that comes after an adrenaline rush, but neither wanted to admit it.

"Give me a few minutes, and I'll be ready to paint the town red," said Kristen jovially, trying to improve the mood.

"Given that we are in the former Communist Yugoslavia, it might be better to say that you're going to enjoy the evening," Demetri advised with a smile on his face.

"I'd say so," she laughed, appreciating his effort at levity. "Will the boat be safe?" she added, concerned about the large sum of cash hidden away in it.

"There is an all-night watchman, and very little ever happens in a small town like this. I think we will be safe as long as we do not start throwing too much money around. Somehow, I do not think we would do that," Demetri answered.

They found a nice seaside restaurant and splurged just a little on lobster but kept the rest conservative and ordered the house wine. They had earned a little luxury and wanted to celebrate the end of the mission and the beginning of Demetri's freedom.

"To you, Demetri," Kristen said as she raised her glass.

"No, to you," Demetri responded.

"Okay, to us then," said Kristen cheerfully.

"That I will gladly drink to," said Demetri, who raised his glass, clinked Kristen's glass, and then took a deep swallow of the wine. Kristen noticed a wave of sadness or concern come over his face—she could not tell which—but she chose to ignore it.

"Delicious!" exclaimed Kristen as she finished her dinner.

"But not as delicious as those lips of yours," Demetri said sadly. "We need to talk about what happened this morning."

"Yes, but not tonight," agreed Kristen. "We have all day tomorrow to do that. Tonight, I just want us to be together, celebrating your freedom and our accomplishment."

Later, Kristen lay in Demetri's warm embrace and fell asleep instantly from emotional and physical exhaustion. Sleep did not come as easily to Demetri, however; he could not still his overactive mind. *What are we going to do?* he asked himself over and over. *We cannot continue like this; it is not right.* Eventually, his exhaustion overwhelmed him and he too fell into a deep, dreamless slumber.

Chapter 35

K risten awoke feeling rested and happy. Her lips were slightly
swollen, and there were some small bruises on her right
breast—telltale signs of the previous day's passion. She did
not mind. On the contrary, they were reminders of the union of body
and soul that she and Demetri had experienced.

Although she felt a little guilt, there was no regret. Theirs was a
private world that was separate from any other part of their lives. Kristen
held on to the belief that Demetri was the only person she was destined
truly to love, and that love overshadowed everything else in her life.
Nothing about the love between Demetri and her could be wrong,
although most people would have disagreed. And she must never allow
it to diminish her sense of responsibility to Richard. Never; that she
promised herself. *Am I being fair to Demetri?* she wondered to herself. *I
don't want to hurt him, but this relationship can go no further.*

Demetri was feeling similar emotions. He had found Kristen, had
loved her, and knew that it was not right, not under the circumstances.
He needed to talk to Kristen, to make her understand the torment he
was experiencing; but he wanted to do it at the proper time. That time
was not now; it would have to wait.

"I have an idea," said Demetri, enjoying the thought that they did
not have to rush anywhere. "We have nothing we have to do. The island
of Kefalonia is on the way back to Patras, and it has always been my
favorite. Would you like to stop over there for a few days?"

"Yes, please," said Kristen, without thinking. "Tell me a little about it."

"It is the largest of the Ionian islands," Demetri recited in his
teacher's voice, "and it is tree-covered and has some of the prettiest
beaches in the world."

"It sounds wonderful. Go on," she urged.

"We can stop in Fiscardo, which is at the northernmost part of the island. Some people call it the Saint Tropez of Greece, with its beautiful, quaint harbor that is perfect for yachts and sailboats. We could stay on the boat for one night and then go to Sami, a port village halfway down the east coast of the island, and stay in one of the friendliest hotels in the world."

"Who could resist a pitch like that? Count me in," she replied.

"Then I guess we should get going. Would you like to explore the town before we leave?" Demetri asked.

"Actually, I'd like to get back into Greece as soon as possible. I know it doesn't make sense, but for some reason I'd feel safer there," replied Kristen.

"Then, let's go," said Demetri, "but not before this," as he rolled over and kissed her tenderly but not passionately.

"Goodness, I've had more loving in the last few days than I have had in the last five years," Kristen let slip before she realized what she had said. Her statement brought back the reality of their situation, which they had both conveniently and temporarily forgotten.

"That is sad," said Demetri. "A beautiful woman like you should be loved in all ways."

"Yes, well, I guess we'd better get up," suggested Kristen, who wanted to dispel the guilt that was creeping into her conscience.

They left Lastovo within the hour, after some coffee and a quick trip to the market for the day's provisions. "Good-bye, Croatia, perhaps we'll see you again sometime," Kristen said as she watched the island diminish in size, knowing they had a long day of traveling ahead of them. Kristen did not mind. She loved being on the sea and the movement of the boat, especially knowing that Demetri was there with her.

After another short lesson, Demetri let Kristen take the wheel to relieve him for a time. "This is great," said Kristen. "I could definitely get used to this." She did not even mind when Demetri went to the cabin to take a nap. As long as they were out in the open sea, away from the islands, Kristen felt she could handle the helm. They continued to trade places and made excellent time, but were only to Corfu by sunset.

"We should stay here for the night," Demetri advised. "It is not worth the risk of traveling after dark if it is not necessary."

"Whatever you say is fine with me," agreed Kristen. "I'm just here for the ride."

"Do you mind sleeping on the boat tonight?" asked Demetri. "I would feel better not leaving it alone in the bigger port."

"Of course not! We do very well on the boat," she said with a sly smile, and then she frowned slightly as if to say, "Stop that, Kristen, it isn't right."

Demetri, as if he understood the meanings of both her expressions, smiled and quietly said, "We will talk tomorrow." Then he steered the boat into Kerkira harbor.

They stayed close to the boat, eating at a *taverna* next to the marina. They were both very tired from the day's trip, so they returned after a short walk. "Good night, *agapimou*," whispered Demetri. "Good night to you too," replied Kristen. Although they slept in each other's arms, they both refrained from instigating anything sexual. They instinctively understood the other's concerns and respected them. Tomorrow would come soon enough.

The next day's journey to Kefalonia was short. They decided to go ahead and sail directly into Sami, where they could check into the hotel and have a good shower. Demetri explained that they would be able to visit Fiscardo by road, and both were anxious to get settled into one place.

As the boat approached Sami, Kristen saw the contour of two islands, Kefalonia on her right and Ithaka on her left. They looked similar in nature, mountainous and green, although Ithaka was much smaller.

"Do you remember your mythology?" asked Demetri as he looked at Ithaka. "Ithaka was Odysseus's birthplace and home."

"And what is Kefalonia famous for?" asked Kristen.

"There was a devastating earthquake in 1953 that destroyed or damaged almost every building on the island. Fiscardo was the only village spared from the destruction. If you ask the older people here, they will be able to tell you exactly where they were when the earthquake struck," said Demetri, again in his teacher's voice.

"It must be similar to the September 11th attack in New York, or the assassination of John F. Kennedy. Every American remembers exactly where they were when it happened," said Kristen.

"You are probably right," said Demetri. "Have you noticed that the buildings here all look new? That is because they are, by Greek standards, anyway," Demetri added as he pointed to Sami's harbor.

"They look Italian, with the beige stucco and the red tile roofs," observed Kristen.

"You are right. The Ionian islands were under Venetian control until the 1800s. The influence is still very strong," Demetri continued to lecture, but Kristen was fascinated. "Do I bore you with my lessons?"

"Absolutely not!" replied Kristen emphatically. "I love listening to them! You know, I have always envied your students because they have had the benefit of your vast knowledge and your passion for teaching."

Demetri was flattered and simply said, "Thank you. From the first day I stepped in the classroom, I knew that was what I needed to do."

"And you do it so well," said Kristen.

"Now, help me get the boat docked," he said, changing the subject, "and we can get settled into the hotel."

"Aye, aye, skipper."

Demetri locked the boat carefully and wheeled Kristen's bag as well as carrying his own onto the jetty.

"I'd be happy to take my own bag," offered Kristen.

"No, thank you," Demetri said. "There is a cab about thirty meters from here. Although the hotel is not far by foot, I think with the luggage we should ride. I called ahead, and they are expecting us."

Demetri was right. By road, the hotel seemed a long distance from the town, but when they looked from the beach to the harbor, it was very close. "The roads do not follow the coast," Demetri explained, "but there is a nice walk that we can take into town anytime we want. *Pame.*"

"Oh, Demetri, this is so nice!" exclaimed Kristen when she took her first look at the hotel grounds. "What is its name?"

"It's called the Sami Beach Hotel. Clever name, huh!" he smiled brightly at his attempt at a joke.

"Well, it's the perfect marketing name. It tells everyone exactly what and where they are," replied Kristen.

Before Demetri could take the bags from the taxi's trunk, they heard *"Kali spera"* from the entrance. "Welcome, dear friend; it has been too long since you were here. Don't worry about the bags; we will take care of them. Come inside and have some ouzo." The voice came from Yiannis Doriza, one of five brothers who owned the medium-sized hotel. Demetri and Kristen followed him into the lobby, bypassing the front desk. "Don't worry, we will take care of the paperwork later; first, a drink," as he disappeared behind the bar for a minute, returning with two glasses of ouzo mixed with a little cold water.

"*Yassas,*" he said as Kristen and Demetri sipped the cool, anise drink, which was surprisingly refreshing. "Now, Demetri, *ti kaneis?*" he asked, and he added in Greek, "I can see you are doing well. She is very pretty and looks very nice."

"*Efharisto poli,*" she heard Demetri respond. He immediately switched to English to make Kristen feel like she was part of the conversation, and he introduced her.

"Now, let me tell you about the island," said Yannis as he pulled out a large map and continued to recite the many sights not to miss during their stay.

Demetri turned to Kristen and said, "We can rent a car, but I prefer to rent a motorcycle to see the island." Yannis shook his head, "Many people are hurt on the scooters. Be careful if you choose to do that. Go slowly, and wear a helmet," he said in a fatherly tone. Demetri assured Yannis that he was very experienced, and that he would be careful, especially with such precious cargo aboard, meaning Kristen. Yannis nodded his head in agreement.

They were shown to adjoining rooms. "Oh," Kristen said in surprise. She did not argue but gave Demetri a questioning look.

"It is for the best. We haven't had a chance, but there is much to talk about," said Demetri quietly, but with a sense of urgency.

Kristen understood, was actually mildly relieved, and began unpacking. It was nearly the first time she had been alone the entire time she had been in Greece, and it felt strange.

Before long, Demetri was at the door. "Should I knock now?" he asked, half-kidding and half-seriously.

"I'm not sure. Do you want to?" replied Kristen, not quite understanding whether what she said was what she meant to say.

"No, but I think it is for the best," said Demetri firmly. "*Pame,* we'll walk into town and rent a bike; then we can begin to explore the island. Or, would you like to swim first?"

"The water looks beautiful, but we can swim later," she said as she flung her purse over her shoulder. "I'm all ready. Lead on, McDuff." Demetri did not understand the reference but let it slide.

They walked the kilometer into the village in under fifteen minutes, enjoying the scenery and the serenity that midday brings to most of Greece. "I wonder if the rental agency will be open. This is siesta time," Demetri said, chiding himself for forgetting.

"Don't worry," Kristen said quickly to diminish Demetri's concern. "If it's not open, we'll walk around for a while until it is. It's not a problem!"

Demetri needn't have worried. Sami depended on tourism for its livelihood and had adjusted store hours to fit the mainly British tourists' schedules.

"What can I help you with?" the man smoking behind the desk asked in Greek. Demetri explained their needs, and within ten minutes he and Kristen were shown to a scratched and dented but seemingly well-running motorcycle.

"I wish you'd wear a helmet," said Kristen. "I see the results of motorcycle accidents in the emergency room all the time. We don't call them morgue cycles or donor cycles for nothing."

"I can't see properly with a helmet" was Demetri's explanation. Kristen dropped the subject because she knew it was a losing battle.

"Where to?" asked Demetri.

"Can we get acquainted with the village before getting on the cycle?" Kristen asked. Demetri nodded, and Kristen hung her helmet on the handlebars. "Nobody will bother it," she said as they walked across the street.

"Sami is a typical island village," Demetri commented, noting the long row of *tavernas* strung along the sea, with the kitchens and shops on the opposite side of the street.

"Isn't it dangerous for the waiters to be crossing the street with all the traffic?" asked Kristen.

"I think they are used to it," Demetri replied with a smile. "Is there anything you would like to buy?"

"Yes," Kristen replied after stopping at a jewelry shop. "I'd like to buy necklaces for myself and Kari."

"Why didn't you say so earlier?" smiled Demetri. "Let's go in." He seemed pleased that Kristen was finally doing something for herself.

They found the perfect necklaces and matching earrings with a Greek key design. They were identical except that Kari's was silver and Kristen's was gold. "Kari is going to love this!" exclaimed Kristen. "Thank you, Demetri," she said, after he insisted on paying.

"It is my turn to say *tipota*," he said. "It is my way of showing you my thanks for everything you have done. Keep it and remember me."

Kristen was touched by the gesture. She would treasure the necklace almost as much as the plastic worry beads she still carried with her.

"The afternoon is passing quickly. Let's stop at the hotel, put on our swimsuits, and drive to Myrtos Beach," he suggested.

"That sounds perfect," Kristen agreed.

Kristen loved riding behind Demetri on the motorcycle. It gave her a chance to hold on to him tightly, without having to be self-conscious. In less than an hour, they were at the turnoff to the beach. As they hesitated, Kristen looked below and saw what was without a doubt the most beautiful beach she had ever seen. The water was startlingly blue; the bleached white beach was nestled into a cove of vertical cliffs, and no houses or hotels were visible. "Unbelievable!" was all Kristen could say as she produced her camera and took a number of pictures, with and without Demetri. They had a stranger snap a picture of the two of them together, and then made the steep, slippery, winding descent down the dirt road to the beach.

"Now I understand why there aren't thousands of people on this beach. That last half a mile is pretty challenging, but worth the trip!" Kristen said somewhat breathlessly as she swung her leg over the seat. Demetri quickly parked the bike and unloaded their gear.

"Last one in the water is a rotten egg," called Kristen loudly as she flung the blouse covering her swimsuit onto the beach and ran toward the water. Her run quickly degenerated into a careful tiptoe. "Ouch!" Demetri heard her yell as she picked her way through to the water. "This isn't sand; these are little egg-shaped rocks!"

Demetri laughed at Kristen, enjoying her childlike joy and exuberance, and he followed her into the water.

"It's heavenly!" Kristen exclaimed, and began swimming in the warm, crystal-clear water. "I'll race you to the raft," she challenged Demetri, who began swimming swiftly toward the destination. In spite of her head start, Demetri quickly passed her and won the challenge.

The physical exercise released a lot of the tension both had felt. They climbed up the steps of the small raft that was anchored one hundred yards off shore and lay down to catch the sun's rays and their breath. It was the perfect time to talk.

"We need to talk about what has happened between us," Demetri said as bluntly as ever. "It was a natural thing for us. Although we are older, little has changed. We are very attracted to each other in many ways. It is a private thing, just between you and me. However, some things are taboo and must be respected. You are married, and we must remember that. We have no right to continue as if we are married to each other; it would be wrong. As much as I enjoyed our physical intimacy, it must not happen again. Can you understand?"

"Of course I understand, and agree with you," said Kristen quietly and with relief. Her love for him only deepened along with the respect she had for his uncompromising values, especially since she had been so weak. "So what do we do now?" she asked.

"Can we go back to our original plan of spending time together as friends?" Demetri asked, hoping for a positive response.

"We can try, although it will be difficult."

Chapter 36

Demetri and Kristen spent the next two days happily exploring the many natural sites of the island. They had come to an understanding and stuck to it. They enjoyed each other's company without the stress of feeling guilty.

Demetri especially liked Fiscardo. He loved boating and appreciated a beautiful craft when he saw one, and there were many gorgeous yachts in the marina. Kristen enjoyed the atmosphere of the village, which was quietly wealthy.

They also explored Assos, a beautiful village hidden away on a peninsula with a ruined castle high above it, and they visited nearby caves. They swam in the hotel pool, which was pleasant when the winds picked up and the sea became too rough in the late afternoons, drank at the outdoor bar, and thoroughly enjoyed a relaxing holiday. They both felt they had earned it after their adventure-filled mission.

"Your time is getting short," said Demetri to Kristen. "Your plane leaves in three days. I need to take the boat back to Corinth. What would you like to do?" His question came out of the blue and caught Kristen off guard. After thinking a minute, she asked, "Would it be all right with you if I stayed here?" She felt that Demetri had asked his question in such a way that would allow her options. "I think it would be good for me to spend a day or two alone to decompress before I go home."

"I think that is wise. I would be happy to have you along on the voyage home, but I think that we both need some time. You will have a four-hour layover from the time you arrive in Athens from Kefalonia until your flight leaves for the States. Could I meet you then?" It was clear to Kristen that Demetri had given this a lot of thought.

"Of course!" she said excitedly. "It would be wonderful to see you one last time before I fly home," she said, adding in her own mind, *to my life there, with all the responsibilities and stresses.*

"Then I will leave tomorrow morning and see you in Athens, much like the summer we met. Do you remember going to Delphi for two days before I met you in Athens?" he added. Demetri saw tears forming in Kristen's eyes. "Don't be sad," was all he could say.

"Just the thought of saying good-bye to you brings tears to my eyes. It always happens!" she explained. "I just can't help it." He held his arms out to her and Kristen dissolved into his chest. *How can I have the courage to let him go?* she asked herself, feeling him close to her again.

They tried to keep the rest of their time together pleasant and easygoing, not wishing to upset each other. They had their last dinner of roasted lamb at their favorite *taverna* up the road from the hotel, instead of in the touristy part of the village, holding hands and trying to be brave.

There was no big good-bye the next morning. Kristen walked Demetri to the marina, saw him safely onto the boat, kissed him, and waved as he left the harbor. She smiled on the outside, but was dying on the inside. She suddenly felt very alone. She tried unsuccessfully to keep the tears from streaming down her face as she took the short walk back to the hotel.

Demetri was feeling equally alone. This was worse than the time he had said good-bye to Kristen and Kari at the ferry in Brindisi. There was hope for a future then; there was none now. The one saving grace was that he had to concentrate on making his way safely, which would busy his mind so he would not have to think, to feel, and to miss Kristen so badly.

Kristen returned to the hotel, where Maryann, the innkeeper's wife, was sympathetic, without knowing the details. "Is there anything I can do to help?" she asked. Kristen just shook her head, offered her thanks and wished Kari were there to help her through the next two days. Although the island was still as beautiful as ever, it had lost some of its magic with Demetri's departure.

I need to focus on the days and weeks ahead, she told herself as she changed and headed for the pool. She wasn't alone long. A friendly British couple started chatting with her almost immediately when she arrived at the poolside. Something they all had in common was the love of Kefalonia and a deep loyalty to the Sami Beach Hotel. "We've been coming here every summer for the last fifteen years," said the British woman. "We traveled just about everywhere and haven't found any place we like better than this. So tell us what you do for a living." Before long, Kristen had temporarily forgotten her sadness and her self-pity as she engaged in a conversation with these gracious new acquaintants.

Kristen dreaded eating alone the most. A single woman in Greece stands out like a sore thumb, although nobody ever says anything. Dinner, at least for tonight, would not be a problem. The British couple asked her whether she would like to join them for dinner, and Kristen accepted gratefully.

She knew she could not put things off forever, and she called Kari. She heard a bit of hesitation in Kari's voice as she told her of her plans. "Just get home as soon as you can, Kristen," she said.

That was strange. "Is everything all right?" Kristen asked in a concerned voice.

"Uh, yes, fine, just get home soon. I really miss you," Kari said.

"I'll be home day after tomorrow at the originally scheduled time. Please be sure to check with the airlines before anyone heads out to the airport. The flight from Atlanta is notoriously late," Kristen told her. *That was weird*, she thought as she replaced the receiver. *Maybe Kari needs a vacation too.*

Kristen did not leave the hotel the next day. She wanted to get packed and get a thorough rest for the long and emotional flight home. She was able to spend some quiet time thinking but did not want to obsess about her thoughts. Eventually she just refused to think about things at all. She concentrated on the sun, the sea, the lovely environment, and figured she would have time on the plane to get her mind straightened out.

Chapter 37

rue to his word, Demetri was at the Athens airport as Kristen disembarked the plane from Kefalonia.

"Has it only been three days? How wonderful and tan you look!" said Demetri. "Let's go have a coffee and talk."

"I had some time to relax around the hotel pool," Kristen replied, not knowing what else to say. She wanted Demetri to take the lead.

"Did you have time to think? Are you okay?" Demetri asked bluntly, without preamble.

"Actually, I tried not to think too much. I do know that I absolutely do not regret the last two weeks, no matter what happens in the future. You are so important to me. If it is wrong to say that I love you as much now as I did thirty years ago, then I will have to be wrong.

"I know that the next months, and possibly years, are going to be very difficult with Richard's illness. It is optimistic foolishness to hope for a cure; we can only hope for time and a good quality of life until the end," she said sadly. "I only wish there was something I could do to make it better. I'm a doctor, for God's sake, and I am completely helpless when it comes to my own husband. Do you have any idea how frustrating that is?" she blurted out. "I feel like a complete failure."

"One thing I do know," she continued, "is that I don't want to lose touch again. Your friendship and love have become something I desperately need."

"You have it, in whatever capacity you need. I will be out of touch by e-mail for a couple of weeks because I will be at the village, but you can call me whenever you'd like. And please call me to say that you arrived home safely. I don't care what time, just call me."

"Thank you, Demetri. I truly don't know what I'd do without you!" cried Kristen, unsuccessfully trying to hold back the tears. "See what you made me do!" she said, trying to lighten the mood with a joke.

"I have something for you," said Demetri, reaching into his pocket and drawing out a small box.

Kristen opened the box slowly. Inside was a set of beautifully crafted silver and crystal worry beads. "I still have the worry beads you gave me thirty-three years ago," she said.

Demetri said, "They were plastic and inexpensive, but they were given as a token of my love and affection for you. I now give you these as a symbol of my continuing love and devotion."

Kristen was speechless. "Oh, Demetri, they're beautiful," she said gratefully, "but more important is the thought behind them! How am I going to have enough courage to get on that plane?" cried Kristen.

Demetri said firmly, "They are boarding your flight. You must go and do what needs to be done. This is not good-bye. Distance will not part us, I promise you that. How could six thousand miles separate us, when thirty years hasn't? Now, go," he insisted. Kristen was openly crying, and Demetri's eyes were filling with tears. They gave each other a final good-bye kiss, and Kristen turned to go through security. As Demetri watched her disappear through the door, he silently wished her a safe journey and whispered, "*Sagapo*, Kristen."

Chapter 38

The moment Kristen settled into her seat and fastened her seatbelt for takeoff, she felt as if she were being ripped apart. Part of her wanted to stay in Greece; the other part knew she had to return to her real life, a life that had its pleasures and successes as well as its frustrations and tribulations.

She held the worry beads in her hands close to her chest, closed her eyes, and prayed silently one last time, *Bless Demetri, and keep him healthy. Please help me to make the right decisions, not only for myself but for others as well. If we are worthy, please bless the love we share. Keep it safe from all intruders, even if we are separated. I also ask that this love make Demetri happy. He deserves to be happy, above all else.*

Kristen felt better after her silent prayer and a strong gin and tonic as the plane took off. She waved good-bye to Athens, a place that had been dear to her heart for three decades, and to Demetri, who had stolen her heart all those years ago and still owned it.

It was now time to look forward, not backward. Resolutely, she put her thoughts of Greece aside and began planning the next week. It would be busy with catching up at the office and domestic chores. She knew Richard would be waiting for her to return and would be happy to have her home. She looked forward to telling Kari about everything; she would be the only person on earth who would completely understand. With those thoughts in her head and the two glasses of wine she had with dinner, she slept peacefully for the rest of the long flight to Atlanta.

It was nearly nine p.m. when she finally arrived in Tucson. Kristen was surprised to be greeted by Kari instead of Richard.

"Hi. Where's Richard?" she asked.

"He would not allow me to say anything while you were away," Kari began, "but he's very ill and is in the hospital."

"Why didn't you call me?" exclaimed Kristen, "I would have come home!"

"That's exactly why Richard made me promise not to. He absolutely refused to let anybody inform you of his turn for the worse."

"Will you take me to see him now?"

"Of course. And Kristen, welcome home!" The two sisters hugged tightly. Kari knew what Kristen must be going through at this moment, and sympathized with her.

"Thanks," Kristen said as they separated from the prolonged hug. "I'll tell you all about my trip later. I feel terrible now, knowing that Richard has been so sick; but it was wonderful."

Kari could imagine. She had been in Greece with Demetri. She remembered and understood.

They drove straight to the hospital, where Kristen went directly to Richard's room. He was sleeping as she entered.

Kristen was shocked by the change in him over the last two weeks. When she had left, he was strong and healthy-looking. His color had been good and he'd been eating like a horse. Now he was extremely pale, his skin looked like gray tissue paper, and his face was gaunt, as was his body. If she hadn't known this was Richard's room, she would not have recognized the man lying there so quietly.

Although she was used to seeing patients with similar outcomes in her practice, she broke down. This wasn't just a patient, this was the man she had shared the majority of the last years with; this was her husband. She knew deep in her heart that this was the end; he would not leave the hospital alive.

Kari heard Kristen's sobs from the hallway where she had been waiting and went to console her.

"Somebody should have told me," Kristen cried.

"I tried, but Richard insisted. There was nothing you or anybody could do. Richard's family has been here constantly, so he has not been alone."

"What they must think of me!" exclaimed Kristen.

"What they think of you is that you have been the best thing that ever happened to Richard. They love you and know how hard it has been. They agreed that your vacation should not be interrupted, especially since there was nothing you could have done," Kari said sternly.

"But," Kristen began.

"But, nothing," Kari interrupted. "You have gone above and beyond the call of duty for a very long time. You must not feel guilty for being away. Nobody, especially Richard, would want that!

"I will stay with you as long as you want," Kari added gently.

"Thanks. Yes, I need you here," said Kristen appreciatively.

Kristen stayed by Richard's bedside for hours, watching him sleep. He was heavily sedated from the high doses of morphine given him to control the pain and keep him comfortable. He finally stirred a bit and opened his eyes when he felt Kristen's hands squeezing his.

"Hi," he said weakly.

"Why didn't you tell me?" Kristen managed to squeak out through the constriction in her throat and the tears filling her eyes.

"I could not spoil your trip. I have been responsible for spoiling so much of your last few years. I could not take this one bit of happiness away from you, no matter what," he said. "Thank you for all you have done for me—not only for being there when I was sick all these years, but for giving my life meaning, happiness, and love. I would not have had those without you." Richard was visibly weakening from the effort of talking.

Kristen noticed and said, "You mustn't tire yourself." Then she added, "You haven't been a burden; you've been my husband, and I love you."

Richard relaxed and sleep overtook him instantaneously. The nurse came into the room and said, "He'll sleep for a number of hours, Dr. Davies. Why don't you go home and get some rest? I'll call you if there is any change in his condition."

With Kari's encouragement, Kristen reluctantly agreed. She had been traveling for over twenty-four hours and was in need of a shower and some sleep. On the short drive home, Kristen and Kari were quiet. Kari was anxious to hear everything about Kristen's trip but knew this was not the time to ask. There would be plenty of time later.

"I called your partners in the practice and told them about Richard's condition. They told me to tell you that everything is under control and that they don't expect to hear from you until the worst is over. They were totally understanding and sympathetic," said Kari.

"I told Demetri that I would call him when I arrived home. I just can't right now—not in the condition I am in," Kristen said to Kari. "Will you call him? He knows about Richard, so go ahead and tell him everything."

"No problem. I'll call him and let him know that you arrived safely, and what's going on. I'll also tell you will call him as soon as you feel able to. I'll be happy to have an excuse to talk to him again! It's been way too long."

"What would I do without you?" asked Kristen. "By the way, there is a nine-hour time difference between Arizona and Athens."

"Ouch," was all Kari said.

"Thanks for the ride—and for everything," Kristen said as Kari pulled into Kristen's driveway. "I'll see you later."

"Do you want me to come in and keep you company?" asked Kari.

"No thanks," Kristen replied. "I'd rather be alone for a while. I'm just going to take a shower and try to sleep, anyway. I would not be very good company, I'm afraid."

"Good company or not, it doesn't matter. What matters is that you're all right," said Kari.

"I'll be okay, and I'll call you in a few hours. Thanks for everything, Kari. You're the best sister anyone could ever ask for," she said as they hugged tightly. Kristen gave Kari a prolonged kiss on her left cheek. "By the way, the kiss is from Demetri." A weak smile crossed Kristen's face as she thought of Demetri giving her the kiss to pass on to "Little One." "We'll talk later," she said.

Kari was concerned, but she knew that Kristen liked to be alone in times of crisis. She would give her the privacy she needed but would check up on her in a few hours.

Kristen entered the empty house, put her bags on the bedroom floor, flung herself on the bed, and had a complete meltdown. Her sobs were from the depths of her body and soul. She had feelings of guilt for not being there for Richard when he needed her most; great sorrow; and pity—pity for a life that was soon to be cut short.

She thought of Demetri, surprisingly, without guilt. She had an overwhelming urge to call him but knew she shouldn't; it would bring him too close to the situation. What was happening here needed to stay here. Demetri would want to help. This was something she needed to deal with privately, and she knew he would understand.

Kristen did not bother unpacking. She showered, put her favorite sleeping shirt on, and fell into a deep, exhausted sleep.

The urgent ringing of the phone startled Kristen into consciousness. Disoriented as to place and time, she scrambled to answer the phone before the message machine picked up the call. A moment of panic swept through her until she heard Kari's cheerful voice.

"Rise and shine," chimed Kari quietly.

"What time is it?" asked Kristen.

"It's ten in the morning. I figured you had slept enough to get over some of your jet lag. Has there been any word on Richard?" Kari asked.

"No news is good news. I was planning on going over to the hospital as soon as I get ready and talk to his doctor to get a full report. I'll call you from there and let you know what's going on," Kristen said.

"Do you need anything?" inquired Kari. "I stocked your fridge with the essentials, so you would not have to go shopping."

"You're a doll. That was so thoughtful of you," sighed Kristen.

"Hey, that's what sisters are for. By the way, I called Demetri, and he knows what's going on. He says he is very sorry, and you were right, he wanted to know what he could do to help. I told him to just hang in there for a few days and be patient about hearing from you. He seemed to understand," said Kari. "And I had forgotten how thick his accent is, but he sounded really good!"

"He is," added Kristen. "But now I have to think of Richard. I'm going to need you to help me through all of this."

"You have helped me through a number of crises in my life," replied Kari. "It's the least I can do. I'll be at work, and you can always get me on my cell phone. And Kristen, I'm sorry you had to come home to this. And I'm sorry that Richard is sick."

"Thanks for everything. You're a godsend," said Kristen. "Now, I've got to get going."

They signed off, and Kristen immediately went to the kitchen. Kari had made sure there was fresh-ground coffee and milk. *She's a peach*, Kristen thought to herself. It wasn't long before Kristen was showered and dressed, and she arrived at the hospital by eleven.

She conferred with Richard's doctor, who gave her very bad news. She was told that Richard's chances of surviving another week were slim. Although Kristen had known that deep in her soul when she had seen him, it was a shock to hear it from someone else. Vocalizing it made it real.

"If there is anything I can do to make Richard's last days more comfortable, just let me know," said Dr. Russell.

"Thank you, John. I appreciate it," Kristen said. "I guess we doctors learn a lot about compassion when our loved ones are the patients. I just want his pain to be sufficiently controlled. Will you make sure that happens?"

"Of course, and Kristen, I'm very sorry," said the doctor sincerely.

"Thank you. If there's anything Richard needs, I'll be sure to contact you," replied Kristen.

Kristen then went directly to Richard's room, where his sister was sitting quietly. She looked up and saw Kristen enter the room. She immediately got up out of the chair and embraced Kristen. "I'm so glad you're here," she said.

"Why didn't you call me, Becky?" asked Kristen.

"Richard absolutely forbade anyone to," Becky explained. "Otherwise I would have. We knew you would want to know."

"Of course I did!" exclaimed Kristen. "How long have you been here?"

"Since about six this morning," responded Becky. "The whole family has been taking turns staying with him."

"You're an amazing family. I've been proud to be a part of it," said Kristen.

"You are using the past tense. No matter what happens with Richard, you will always be a member of our family," said Becky.

"I know that," Kristen said as they embraced. Both women had tears in their eyes as they separated.

"So what's next?" asked Becky.

"There's nothing to be done except keep him comfortable. We all need to prepare for the worst."

"I was hoping for some good news, but deep down I knew that this was what you were going to say," cried Becky.

"We all need to be there to help him through this transition. I don't want him dying by himself," said Kristen quietly. "Although, in the end, we all have to make that journey alone," she added philosophically.

The next few days were torture for everyone involved. Kristen was at Richard's side most of the day and night, taking time only to grab a quick bite to eat and shower. The hospital had arranged for a daybed to be brought into the room so family members could sleep nearby.

Richard intermittently regained consciousness. During those brief periods of lucidity, he and Kristen would talk of their life together.

"Is there anything I can do for you?" Kristen asked Richard.

"Promise me that you will be happy," he said. "You deserve it. You've been through a lot in the last few years."

"I promise I will try," she said softly.

Richard died one week after Kristen's return. Kristen felt many emotions on his passing, grief for him and herself, sorrow for his family, guilt because she had not been able to cure him, and a little relief, knowing that his suffering was finished. Although it was extremely difficult, she was glad that she had had the opportunity to be with him, holding his hand, as he breathed his last breath.

The ordeal had taken its toll on Kristen. She had not had a moment of privacy or peace since her arrival home. After the funeral, she was emotionally and physically exhausted. She took another week to gain her strength before going back to work.

During that week, she felt strong enough to call Demetri. Having lost two close friends in the previous year, he knew the agony she had been through. He was supportive and comforting, and only slightly disappointed when he heard Kristen say that she needed some time to recover before she could continue their relationship.

"Be patient, Demetri," she said. "I need to go through the grieving process before I will be any good for you."

It was difficult for Demetri; he had always been the problem solver for his friends and family. This was one situation he could not make better. But patience, at least involving Kristen, had become an art form for him. He knew that if he was patient, Kristen would be able to open her heart to him once again.

Chapter 39

*K*risten knew she had to get back to work, not only because the practice needed her, but because work was a way of turning off her thoughts of the events of the last month. The depth of her grief at Richard's death surprised her. She had thought her feelings of indifference for him in their marriage would continue. She was wrong. His death had brought out memories of good times they had spent together, and she realized that it was probably stress that had made her feel so empty.

She began e-mailing Demetri on a daily basis, although he was not close to a computer and would not be able to receive her messages on a regular basis. He had gone to stay with his mother in their village for the summer, and he had decided to take an extended trip in his boat to get away from civilization. He liked to get back to nature and a rhythm of life that was not dictated by the clock. *What will be, will be* was the way he liked to spend one month a year. No watches, no telephones, no newspapers or TV. He would eat the fish he caught and would share his time with anyone who wished to follow. Often he found himself alone, which suited him fine. It was a way for him to restore his energy for the challenges of being a university professor and administrator.

Kristen envied him for being willing and able to go out on his own like that. She would have joined him in a heartbeat if the situation had been different. She had spent too much time away from the practice and did not want to disappoint her partners further.

Her letters to Demetri were an extension of the letters they had begun writing the year before. She expressed herself openly to him, talking of her feelings of grief, frustration, and her determination to get through her ordeal, as well as her longing for him. Her grief for Richard did not in any way dissipate the love she felt for Demetri, and she let him know that in many ways.

My dear Demetri,

Thoughts of you are constantly in my mind. I hope you are well and strong and healthy. I wonder what you are doing at any one moment in time. Are you on your boat? Are you sitting with your friends drinking ouzo and talking about nothing for hours at a time? These are the things I see you doing in my mind.

I wish I could be there to share those times with you, but the timing is not yet right. I am still going through the grieving process. It would not be fair to you to have to share me. Only when I have completed the process and my heart is free can I be good for you.

Be patient, my love. It should not be much longer. I adore you and always have. You captured my heart all those years ago and nothing has changed.

I hope that soon there will be no barriers to our love. I want with all my heart to share my world with you, and want to know your world better.

Soon. Sagapo. Kristen.

Kristen received occasional e-mails from Demetri, whenever he was able to find access to a computer. His letters were just as heartfelt as Kristen's, talking of his devotion to her, and his adventures during the summer break.

Chapter 40

Demetri returned to work in September, healthy, very tan, and physically and mentally prepared for the new semester. His only disappointment was that he and Kristen had not been able to be together before he had to go back to work. His work schedule made it practically impossible for him to get away for any extended period of time.

Demetri had confided in his mother about his rekindled relationship with Kristen. She had known about her son's feelings for his American love thirty years before and had seen the devastation their breakup had caused Demetri. He had never told his mother the real reason they had broken up, because she never knew about his relationship with the cousins in New York.

"Do you love her with all your heart?" Demetri's mother asked.

"Yes," he answered.

"Does she love you?" she asked searchingly.

"Yes." he answered sincerely.

"I don't know what happened before. Could that happen again?" she inquired simply.

"No," Demetri replied.

"Then you have no choice; you must do everything you can to be together," she stated with conviction.

Demetri's mother rose with great effort from her chair and carefully walked into her bedroom. She was there for a few minutes and then stiffly shuffled back to where Demetri was sitting. She held out a gnarled hand to Demetri. When she opened it, Demetri saw a small gold ring with a pearl. He recognized it immediately, despite the fact that he had not thought about it in many years.

"You gave me this ring for safekeeping all those years ago. It is time to return it to its rightful owner," his mother said wisely. It was a way for her to give her blessing and to give him permission to let another woman into his life.

"Thank you, mama," said Demetri softly. "No matter what happens, I will take care of you."

"I love you more than words can say. I want you to be happy. It is your time. I know you will take care of me; it is now time also to take care of yourself."

Demetri was determined to do just that.

Chapter 41

*I*n the meantime, Kristen had fallen into a routine of working in the practice during the day and spending time with family most evenings. She needed to be closer to family now than she had before; it gave her the strength to continue.

Every day, Kristen felt a bit stronger, physically and emotionally. She had gone through the worst of the grieving process and seemed to be getting back to herself again. Her strong work ethic helped her to keep focused and on track, and to keep her mind off other things.

As she became stronger, she was able to face her relationship with Demetri. She knew that she loved him and wanted to be with him. She had broached the idea of Demetri coming to Arizona for Christmas. He told her that the school schedule did not leave him much time for such a long trip, and it would be better to wait until summer. She would have been happy for a couple of days with him but could see his point. It was a very long journey for such a short amount of time. She had thought of flying to Athens, but she had taken so much time off during the late summer and fall that she did not feel it would be right to ask.

The holidays were upon her before she knew it. Although Kari and her friends had been there to support her through the tough months after Richard's death, Kristen knew Christmas was going to be very difficult. She stayed especially busy during the weeks following Thanksgiving, volunteering for extra work, so her partners with young families could spend more quality time together.

She tried with all her might to stay positive. If she and Demetri could get together only once a year, how would it ever work? How could they possibly make a long-distance relationship last over time? Demetri had his career, she had hers. She knew she must keep the faith. She needed to be patient; Demetri had been patient with her. Her frustration grew as the weeks passed.

Her mood worsened as the holidays drew near. Something needed to be done, but what? She had not been able to come up with a solution.

Kristen's frustration had grown to anger in the two weeks before Christmas; she felt so alone and isolated. She had known that the holidays were going to be difficult, but she had not expected them to be so miserable. Everyone but her seemed to have vast numbers of social engagements and family activities that kept them busy. She only had work.

She did not like herself when she felt this way. She felt she should be thankful for all the things she had—a man who loved her deeply, although he was half a world away, a family nearby who had supported her through the bad times, and a very fulfilling and challenging career that made a positive difference to other people. *You should be happy*, Kristen, she told herself. *You have so much.* But deep down she was very lonely and was in danger of becoming bitter.

Kari had seen the change in Kristen and made a point of including her in the family activities. Kari's children were grown and living away from home, so the Christmas plans were different from those of a family with small children. She decided to have a Greek night for Kristen, like they had so many times before. They would prepare many different Greek dishes and invite friends over for as authentic an evening as possible, including wine and music. They would sometimes rent a movie that had a Greek theme or had been filmed in Greece to add to the festivities.

It was a week before Christmas. Kari had told Kristen that she would be preparing all the food, and that Kristen should pick up three or four bottles of wine and then come on over to the house about seven that evening. Kristen had to work until five, so she appreciated Kari taking care of the cooking. She bought the wine two days prior to the dinner so the white would be nice and cold.

Kristen decided to go Greek-style and changed into a flowing dress, although she knew it would probably be too cold to sit outside in it for long. She also put on her Greek key earrings and the necklace Demetri had purchased for her in Kefalonia, and the leather sandals she had purchased in Monastaraki. If she was going to go to a Greek night, then she was going to look the part, even if she froze!

Kristen arrived at Kari's, where she was a little surprised not to see cars parked on the street near the house. Kari normally invited between ten and fifteen people to her parties. "Perhaps I had the wrong time and am early," she said to herself. No matter, it would give her a chance to have a glass of wine and a chat with Kari before the other guests arrived.

She parked her car in the driveway and went to open the front door. *That's strange*, she thought. *Kari knows I'm coming. Why is the door locked? Maybe I have the wrong day.* She rang the doorbell, and Kari answered it.

"Why was the door locked?" Kristen asked as she went to go to the kitchen to put the wine in the refrigerator. Kari took the bottles from her. "Am I early? Why aren't there cars out front? When are the guests arriving?"

"All the guests are here," Kari said smoothly. "Go ahead into the living room and see."

"All right, but is there anything I can do?"

"Yes, go into the living room!" said Kari emphatically.

"Okay, okay, but, may I have a glass of wine first?"

"No," insisted Kari.

"Geez, what a grouch!" said Kristen. "I'm going!"

Kristen walked into the living room ready to be pleasant but was a little miffed. Then she saw who was waiting for her, and every bad emotion she had felt dissolved away in an instant.

"Oh my God!" was all she could say as she saw Demetri standing there as handsome as ever. She started crying.

"I knew I would have an effect on you, but I did not think tears would be it," said Demetri with humor.

Kristen ran over to Demetri and threw herself into him. She felt the kisses that she had missed so much. She felt his strong arms around her again, a feeling she had desperately longed for.

"Do you remember how you surprised me that Thanksgiving? It was my turn," Demetri said into her ear. "You look beautiful, and so Greek!"

"I can't believe it! How long have you been planning this?"

"About a month. It was not easy, but with Kari's help we managed it," Demetri said.

"Of course! Kari had to be in on this, that little rascal!" said Kristen, and after a pause, "I love her."

"And I love you!" said Demetri. "I could not stay away any longer."

"What about work?" Kristen asked.

"I was able to extend the vacation."

"For how long?"

"Indefinitely. I retired," said Demetri calmly.

"You what?" screamed Kristen.

"I retired. Although I hated to leave in the middle of the school year and disappoint the students, I was able to retire with full benefits. I thought it was important to be with you now, not in six months."

"This is incredible!" exclaimed Kristen. "So you're staying?"

"If you will have me," said Demetri tenderly.

"Of course I will!"

"I was hoping you would say that."

"I want to share my world with you in every way possible," said Kristen. "You know that."

"Now that we have that established, I have another question for you," he said as he pulled the pearl ring out of his pocket. "Do you remember this?"

"That's the ring I gave you in Brindisi in 1987!" exclaimed Kristen incredulously.

"Yes it is. It belongs back with you. With us," he corrected himself. "Many years ago I promised to love you always, no matter what. As you know so well now, my promise is sacred. The promise to love you forever was the easiest one I have ever had to keep. I couldn't stop loving you. Never. This pearl ring is a symbol of the eternity of our love for each other. Will you wear it again? And will you marry me?"

Kristen could hardly breathe. This was the last thing she expected to be hearing and experiencing this evening. In a matter of five minutes, her life had changed completely. "Yes I will, and yes I will!" She threw her arms around Demetri's neck and kissed him with all the love she felt.

Suddenly, the past was no longer important. They had their future together, and that was all that mattered.

CPSIA information can be obtained
at www.ICGtesting.com
Printed in the USA
JSHW050424220922
30840JS00001B/4